UNEXPECTED *Weather*

FOX KELLY

©2026 Fox Kelly

E-book ISBN- 979-8-9989904-3-4

Paperback ISBN-979-8-9989904-4-1

Library of Congress Control Number: 2026905923

This novel is entirely a work of fiction. The names, characters, and incidents portrayed in it are the work of the author's imagination. Any resemblances to actual persons, living or dead, events, or localities are entirely coincidental.

Editing by Mallory Day Editing

Cover by Author

 Formatted with Vellum

Playlist

You may have noticed some of the chapter titles sound familiar. That is because they are all songs, some of them just evoke the feelings of the chapter and others make an appearance in the story but together they weave a beautiful narrative created by music and feeling.

Below you will find a Spotify code to listen to the music I curated for this story. This is not at all necessary to follow along. This can also be found by searching Unexpected Weather on Spotify.

EDWARD AND JACOB

DOM AND SEAN

CALEB AND DARIUS

IF YOU EVER READ A BOOK AND WISHED SHE GOT TO KEEP THEM BOTH…

THIS BOOK IS FOR YOU.

Author's note and Content Warning

Reader,

Thank you for taking a chance on my book, it truly means the world to me and I wish I could thank you myself for even giving me a try.

This book is a passion project, something I wrote because a man on the back of bull and the sexy bartender at the local watering hole will distract you every time. Just ask Caroline.

This book is sweet, adorable, and has the most swoon worthy of men but I need to warn you about a few things first because your mental health matters.

Content warning:

-Miscarriage (occurs off page but is discussed.)

-Domestic Violence (occurs on page, not between the main characters.)

If you have any additional questions, or concerns related to the content, please contact the author at LK@foxkelly.com.

One Way or Another

Prologue

Swiping up on the tablet screen, I enter the passcode and hear the click of it unlocking. Roger uses the same passcode for all his devices, 0921, September twenty first, the day we met. Staring down at the icons, I click on the messages app with its seventeen unread messages. Clicking on the highlighted text thread between Roger and 'Steve-Work,' I scroll to the most recent messages.

STEVE-WORK

Dinner tonight?

Yeah, I have a project I can pin it on.

STEVE-WORK

We can go to the sushi place you like. We can get that private table in the corner, again.

Only if you'll let me feel how wet you are sitting at the table.

STEVE-WORK

> You make me so wet, especially when you slide your fingers inside me at dinner. I'm wet right now thinking about it.

I want to throw up reading through the message thread. My husband of a decade, discussing fingering a strange woman at a restaurant. Dropping my hand to the small swell of my belly, I cradle my little baby. *My baby, our baby.* I just wanted a family, and now, I'm not sure what's going to happen.

My phone pings with an incoming text message. Opening the text thread with Roger, I read the predictable message.

ROGER

> I have to take a client to dinner. I'll be late, don't wait up.

> Are you sure? I was already cooking.

ROGER

> Callie, I have to take a client to dinner. I'll be late, don't wait up.

> Do I need to repeat it again?

> No, I got it. Goodnight, I guess. I love you.

ROGER

> I love you too.

Returning his tablet to the drawer beside the bed, I settle in for another night by myself. There have been a lot of lonely evenings recently, and it seems this has become a pattern for Roger.

In the morning, I clean the house from top to bottom before printing out the text transcripts between Roger and his mistress.

When he gets home after work, I wait calmly in the dining room, my evidence laid out on the table.

"Hey Callie," he says as he walks into the house, dropping his keys on the front table and his backpack to the floor. "Where are—what are you doing?" he asks as he walks into the dining room and finds me sitting here with all the papers surrounding me.

My hands shake as I prepare to confront him. "Hi, Roger. Would you like to sit down?"

He looks at me warily before looking at the papers spread on the table, the text messages, the dating website profile, the pictures I found deleted, months' worth of evidence from the tablet that mirrors his phone.

"What the fuck is all this, Caroline?"

"You tell me what it is; you know." My voice is even, emotionless. I feel my belly, heavy under my shirt, and my sweet, innocent baby that I'm keeping safe.

Throwing his hands out, Roger swipes all the papers onto the floor, his face turning red.

"You went through my stuff?" he says accusingly, as though *I'm* the problem. I don't respond, I just watch him. Reaching out, he grabs me roughly by the arm and hauls me to my feet.

Bringing his face close to mine, he calmly whispers, "Don't touch my fucking shit." The level of malice in his eyes terrifies me and my heart races in my chest. Pushing me to the floor, he stalks out of the room. Pulling myself up, I grab my keys and cell phone, sliding them in my pockets before I rush upstairs to grab my bag.

Loud stomping follows me as he all but chases me up the stairs."

"Get back here, Callie!" he calls to me.

"I'm done, Roger, enough is enough. I'm pregnant. You're never going to change." I rush into our bedroom, closing the door, and clicking the lock.

Roger pounds on it relentlessly while screaming about

kicking the door down. I clutch my stomach and cry. Our little family.

"I'm so sorry, baby. I tried. I really did."

I ignore him and look around, throwing anything I see remaining into the bag before opening the door to an enraged Roger.

"You're not going anywhere!" he screams in my face, spittle flying from between his lips, his whole body shaking with barely restrained rage. He snatches the bag from me and throws it to the end of the hall.

I push past him and exit the room. I don't need my things; I can get new stuff.

"I *am* leaving. I can't keep living like this." I try to keep my voice level; I try not to antagonize him. This needs to be the last time. When I reach the stairs, he wraps his fingers around my arm again, this time so tightly I can already feel the bruises blooming under the skin and the bones grating together.

"Get the fuck back here, Callie. You're not going anywhere." He spins me to face him. "You're my wife, and as my wife, you will stay here. And I will do what I want, when I want, with whomever I want. YOU'RE MY WIFE AND THAT'S MY BABY!"

I yank my arm free and turn back toward the stairs. As my foot lands on the first step, both of his hands slam into the space between my shoulder blades, and I go flying. My feet leave the ground, and I watch in slow motion as the tile of the first-floor entry way hurtles toward my face. I throw my arms out to try and catch myself and scream as I freefall.

Slamming into the ground, my wrist crunches beneath my weight and the front of my body collides with the floor. Lying flat on my front, the bump of my baby pressing into me, pain ricochets from my injured wrist to my cheek, where it presses into the floor, to my abdomen and pelvis. Tears well in my eyes.

Roger's thundering footsteps approach as he half-runs half-tumbles down the stairs calling my name.

"Callie? Callie, baby, I'm sorry." He kneels next to my head, eyes wide.

"Roger, please call 911."

Chapter 1
Heads Carolina, Tails California

Callie

One year later
April 26th 11:46 PM

"Fuck!" I scream, slamming my hand into the steering wheel. "Ow," I whisper into the quiet; quiet being created by the blanket of snow covering my car, which sits in a ditch, in the middle of nowhere Montana.

Tap. Tap.

A light tapping distracts me from my self-pity.

Lowering the window, I see my very first, honest-to-God, Montana cowboy. He's tall, lean, and wearing a worn-in flannel under a heavy canvas jacket, snow filling the brim of his black cowboy hat. Tears fill my eyes before spilling over. I try to explain but I can't.

"Hey, you okay? I saw you go down into the ditch," he tells me, his dark eyes narrowed as he studies me.

"I–I–I'm not sure." I try to talk around the lump in my throat. "What—" My voice catches in my throat, and I make a very unappealing gasping sound. "Happened." More tears run down my cheeks as I stare up at him.

"You spun out. You can't park here. Your tires suck, your car isn't made for this weather, and you don't seem to know how to drive in it."

But, it turns out, my cowboy savior is a world-class dick.

"Wow, you're an asshole," I tell him matter-of-factly, choking out a laugh-sob.

"I do what I can. Look, I brought you a blanket. Emergency services will be along soon. Turn your hazards on. They'll take you home, or," he gestures vaguely in the direction of town, "wherever you need to go tonight." I watch him climb back up the hill toward the road and wave to a tow truck that pulls up behind his partially snow-covered truck.

Dropping my head against my steering wheel, I take a deep breath. This has officially been the worst week ever. The worst month ever. The worst *year* ever. The kind that begins with a hospital bed and ends in a ditch.

"Callie? Callie, baby, I'm sorry." Roger tells me over and over, as he runs his hands across me, trying to figure out if I'm hurt.

"Roger, please call 911."

It's the last thing I remember before waking up in a hospital bed. The constant fighting had gotten worse, more aggressive and physical over the years. I thought when I got pregnant, we could finally relax and be the family we were supposed to be.

The night I lost the baby was the worst night of my life. The blanket of snow suffocates me as the past roars to the forefront of my mind.

I feel his hands shove into my spine an instant before I'm freefalling, face first down the stairs before landing on my stomach on the tile floor.

"Callie? Callie, baby, I'm sorry."

I didn't stick around. As soon as the hospital cleared me, I disappeared. I took as much as I could, jumped in my car, and started driving.

I've been on the road nonstop for a year with no destination in mind, no plan, just driving from place to place. Only staying a few days, or weeks, before moving on. No reason to stay anywhere longer. Just me and myself. And now, I ride in the passenger seat of some man named Tommy's truck heading toward the only hotel in this tiny town.

Eventually, I will need to stop, settle in, and get a job. But I have enough savings from the money my parents left me, plus money I have squirreled away from Roger, to start over. But for now? I want to find somewhere that feels right.

Checking in with the older man with kind eyes behind the counter, I'm led to the only available room—a sweet, charming, single room with an attached bath in the corner of the old house-turned-hotel. The scent of laundry detergent clings to the room. The bed is made with flowered, pink linens and matching pillows cover half of it. A small writing desk and chair sit in the corner by the windows that offer a view of the whole downtown. Inspiration, Montana, a quaint rural town time has forgotten.

A small settee sits in front of the gas fireplace, which already bathes the room in warmth when I enter. In the bathroom, I find a stall shower, simple, but full of soaps and lotions with a woodsy, comforting smell. Sitting on the small sofa, I drop my head in my hands and exhale a long, exhausted breath.

I prepaid for a week, and I feel like I might just enjoy my time here, relaxing in this little room, taking a break from traveling.

Chapter 2
Hooked on an 8 Second Ride

Cash

April 26th 7:45 pm

"In Chute two, we have Ashley Colter, Inspiration, Montana! Bring some noise for the winner of..." I stop listening once the announcer gets to my accolades and awards. The stands are jam-packed tonight, despite the late spring cold snap we're having. The weatherman is forecasting snow again later in the week.

I focus on the heaving one-ton beast beneath me, watching the breath steam from his nostrils. The barely restrained anger fueled by testosterone, the flank strap around his waist, and his indignation that I've dared to climb on his back, is palpable. The air smells musky, and dirt clogs my lungs.

Checking my bull rope for the third time, I give it a yank before wrapping the tail more securely around my fist. Using my left hand, I push my hat securely over my brow as my introduction ends.

Breathe in, breathe out.

Nod.

Breathe in, breathe out.

The gate swings wide, and the bull takes off out of the chute, bucking wildly. I ignore the distraction of the crowd and the barrel men.

One second.

Breathe. I tighten my thighs, trying to hold my seat.

Two seconds.

The wild bull beneath me kicks his legs out behind us, propelling me forward, between his shoulders.

Three seconds.

Kicking up and into the air, I'm nearly unseated by the change in direction.

Four seconds.

I dig my heels into his side, fighting to keep my balance as his frenzied bucking grows wilder and more unpredictable.

Five seconds.

My labored breathing comes in rapid pants. I lean into his movements as he tries to throw me from his back.

Six seconds.

The bullfighters run around us, keeping the bull's attention divided between me on his back and them.

Seven seconds.

His sides heave under me but his relentless twisting, jumping, and bucking doesn't slow.

Eight seconds.

Bwooooom! The horn blares, my time is up. Releasing the rope, I slide from his back. I'm immediately grabbed around the shoulders by my barrel men as the bullfighters drive the bull in the opposite direction. Scrambling, I run to the gates, jumping over in a smooth movement.

I'm pleased to find that my hat stayed on my head.

"Fantastic ride, Cash!" Sleepy tells me as he pats my back.

Thomas 'Sleepy' Jenkins has been my coach since I started riding in high school and has kept my head in the game through two national championship runs and a hundred buckles in between.

"Thanks, Sleepy. He was an angry shit, but we got there."

"Come on. The scores are coming up." Following behind him, toward the scoring area, many hands reach down from the stands, hoping to catch a glimpse—or a handful—of Ashley Colter, rodeo champion.

I keep my head down. I don't celebrate a ride until the scores are in. I know what the ride feels like to me, but I have no idea what it looks like to them.

Living my life for nearly twenty years in the space between eight-second rides has been amazing, but it's the rides that keep me moving forward. At thirty-four though, I'm expected to stop riding in the next few years. There just isn't any further career growth for an aging rider.

"Spectacular ride for Ashley Colter! Ashley was riding Goliath, from Kingston Ranch. Their scores are as follows— Goliath has a total score of forty-one and Ashley scored in at forty-seven for a combined score of eighty-eight." The crowd instantly goes wild. Eighty-eight is a good showing, and something I should be proud of, but last season I consistently scored in the nineties.

"Proud of you son. Eighty-eight is a great score for the first bout of the season," Sleepy tells me, dropping his arm lightly over my shoulder.

Shame colors my cheeks that I even consider a solid score like this to be less than amazing. Some riders never break the nineties their entire career.

"Thanks, Sleepy. I'm going to the tent for a drink before the calves come out."

Leaning back in the lounge chair in the rider's tent, I close my eyes and lay my dusty hat in my lap, trying to relax a bit before my next event. I'm ahead on the leaderboard against the other riders but Miles Wilkes is coming up and we're always neck and neck, every season.

"There he is—Ash." I hear whispers from my left, and crack one eye open just enough to see who's speaking.

Two women, decked out from head to toe in 'cowgirl' outfits, are staring and whispering. They aren't whispering quite low enough that I can ignore them and not quite loud enough to make out their words. Calling me 'Ash' grates on my nerves.

A woman, thin as a reed, with long tan legs in very short shorts, a flannel tied up at her waist, and white boots with some sort of jewels on them, giggles loudly as her friend whispers something in her ear. The second woman, in equally short shorts watches me with fixed intent. I attempt to keep my eyes closed, ignoring them. Her belt, with its large buckle, highlights her slightly curvier waist which, if I'm being honest, I appreciate a lot more than the tiny woman next to her. Her brown boots look like they've at least been in dirt before, though neither of them seems like they've ever seen a real ranch.

Also, they look a little young to be sneaking into the rider's tent trying to get my attention.

Popping my head up, I look at them and they startle, surprised at my movement. "Y'all can't be in here, riders only," I tell them, flashing my best smile and keeping the annoyance out of my voice.

They look around and notice, seemingly for the first time, they are the only women present. Blushing, they turn and flee from the tent, laughter trailing in their wake. Shaking my head, I watch new scores populate on the leaderboard. I'm first but Miles is riding now.

Ten seconds, twenty, pass as I wait for his scores. Ninety-one. Flopping my head back against the chair, I sigh heavily. At twenty-four, he's a quickly rising star and at ten years his senior, my star is heading down. Second place in the first show of the season and I'm already tired.

"Riders, if you're showing in roping, head into the arena," a cracking voice announces over the speakers. I know I will do well in roping. My experience on the ranch makes me damn near an expert.

In my truck that evening, I head back toward Inspiration. On my passenger seat rests a new buckle for my collection, for winning the roping portion, but coming in second riding today won only prize money.

Pulling off the road and onto the dirt track leading toward the farmhouse, I bump along under the huge arch reading, "Colter Ranch," the gates already swung open. It's lonely here since Daddy and Mama left for Bozeman a few years back. Just me and the dogs, the ranch hands, and the horses.

"Hey Tank, Snapper." I rub each of their fuzzy heads as I pass them on the porch, hearing them pad in through the door behind me. Tank's closing in on his retirement of cattle wrangling too, at ten years old. Snapper runs in circles, his puppy energy too much to contain in his compact body, his oversized paws making him clumsy.

"Settle down," I order with a snap, heading over to the pantry to fill their bowls before grabbing a beer from the fridge and sitting down on the couch. Exhausted, I fall asleep to the sounds of the dogs snoring at my feet before I even finish my beer.

Chapter 3
I Love this Bar

Duke

April 26th 10:27 pm

I toss a cardboard coaster onto the beat-up, dull wooden counter and set the open beer on it. Turning, I flip the TV off now that the rodeo is over. Cash put on a decent show tonight, but Miles edged him out again.

"Hey, Duke. Let me get a vodka-cran." At her voice, my head whips around and a smile breaks out across her face. "Aw, come on, Duke, don't frown at me like that." She leans across the bar slightly, giving me a look down the front of her shirt, which I take full advantage of.

I raise a brow and ask, "Indie, what are you doing here? The bar is mine. You got everything else in the divorce. Why can't I even have the bar?"

Her smile falls. My heart lurches at the face she makes; I've always hated when she was sad.

Seeing the tears running down her face the day she walked out broke my heart, just as surely as anything else that had happened up to that point. I was a bad husband, I know. I worked too much; I smiled too little. I never took her on the trip to Cancun she'd been asking for since we got married. We were never able to fill the house with the laughter and footsteps of children. All she wanted was to be a mother, and I couldn't even give her that.

After a decade of fighting, fighting each other, and the inevitable, she left. It was the hardest day of my life. Not hard because she left, but the look on her face, the way her brow furrowed, and the tears welled up in her eyes. I wanted to hold her and make it better, fix it somehow. But I couldn't; it was too late. It only took a few months for the divorce to go through. I gave her everything she wanted, and half of what she didn't. I owed her too much for putting up with me for all those years.

All I asked for was the bar. Waylon's is mine. I opened it at twenty-three, still wet behind the ears, with the little bit of money left after my father died. I've worked behind this counter ever since. I have no idea why she walked in here tonight. Small towns are rough for breakups, and in a town as small as Inspiration, I see Indie a few times a week. At the grocery store, at the church bake sale, and at the hardware store. But the bar is mine.

"Duke, don't be like this. We were happy sometimes, right?"

"Indie, you know the answer. And it's the reason you're on your side of the bar and I'm on mine. What's up?"

"Alright, alright." She holds her hands up placatingly, an envelope clutched in one of them. "I'm getting married. I know things didn't work with us, but I loved you. I didn't want you to hear it from around town." Extending her hand, she holds out the envelope with *Duke Williams* scrawled in familiar handwriting across the front.

I look at her surprised. Everything about this surprises me. I didn't even know she was seeing anyone. "You don't...expect—"

"No." She shakes her head. "I don't expect you to come. You can, if you want, the invitation is here, but I don't have any expectations of you, Duke. Not now." Leaving the envelope on the counter, she walks out.

Swiping it right into the garbage, I grab the rag off my shoulder and start wiping everything down.

A while later, I lean down and pull it back out, shoving it in my pocket.

"Duke, man, how's life treating you?" I hear the familiar voice as the old man with the dusty hat perched on his balding head claims a seat at the bar.

"What's up, Sleepy? Not too bad, not too good. Saw your boy on the show tonight. Pulled a pretty decent score." I've seen better from our hometown rodeo hero, but it wasn't bad.

"Yeah, I was pretty happy with the score myself, but I wasn't the one ridin'. Cash seemed pretty down about it even if he won roping." He rolls his eyes. "Miles just had a better bull tonight. Goliath only pulled a forty-one. Torpedo scored a forty-six. Five extra points would have won Cash the buckle. Oh well. Let me get a beer." He's right, even though I know Cash will let it get to him. A forty-seven is a damn good score for a rider, but Goliath didn't show well.

Twisting the top off his lager, I set it on the coaster. "He'll get 'em next time."

"Damn right," he responds, lifting his beer in salute.

Walking around my bar, I grab empty glasses and bottles from high top tables, the edges of the pool tables, and sitting on the half wall partially ringing the tiny scuffed-up dance floor. All the music at Waylon's comes from an old jukebox that only plays old country and rock-n-roll and hasn't been updated since 1998. It came with the place.

We're mostly empty, with a few regulars sitting at the bar, and Sleepy. On a Tuesday night in a small town, I manage my expectations. Waylon's is, for sure, the local dive. We don't even have any food, just liquor and beer. I stock what the regulars order, nothing more, nothing less. The atmosphere sucks; it's dark and smoky, with a few neon lights over the pool tables and lining the walls. No honky tonk line dances or whatever passes for a good time in the larger cities. I love Waylon's like it's my child, and they may have to bury me out back.

A loud tone shrills from my cell behind the counter, the emergency alert going off. Heading over, I pick it up to see a weather alert. Turning the TV back on, I click to the weather channel.

"Breaking News out of the Bozeman Weather Center. A sudden late spring snowstorm has developed over the mountains and is moving rapidly across western and central Montana. This storm has caught residents and travelers alike unaware, and we will likely see damages in the coming days.

"An urgent Winter Storm Warning has been issued from Belt to Inspiration and down to Billings until twelve pm Wednesday. Please be advised: road travel will be treacherous and to proceed with caution. We are expecting a period of power loss. Snow accumulation totals near twenty inches. Seasonal weather is expected to return on Friday." The broadcast concludes before starting over again, replaying the same message.

Walking toward the front door, I call out to my patrons, "Last call, guys, let's get home before this turns ugly." I can hear the wind gusting through the closed door. Pushing it open, I see the trees bending under the strain and snowflakes already starting to coat the grass.

Dropping their bills on the counter, the men start filing out.

"See ya, Duke," Jim says.

"You going to be open tomorrow?"

"Not sure, Sam. Give me a call if it looks bad. If I answer, I'm here." He chuckles at my response.

"Night, Duke." Sleepy gives me a wave as he heads out. Slamming the door shut behind them, I lock it and flip the exterior sign off. Grabbing my cash and stuffing it in the register, I rinse the barware quickly, shut everything down, and head out the back door.

My old truck is already half covered, and the snow is coming down so fast, I can barely see. Sudden storm is right. I can't remember the last time we had a storm this late into April.

Heading toward my house in town, I find cars with their hazards on stranded everywhere along my drive. Emergency responders, and trucks, make their way down the streets, helping drivers, and taking them to safety to wait out the storm. Straight ahead of me, I see a small two-door sedan spin-out from the traffic signal, turning in a full circle before landing themselves in a ditch.

Pulling onto the shoulder, I climb out of the cab, grab my jacket off the seat and flip the bench forward to grab my old flannel blanket, before making my way down into the ditch. The little red BMW 3-series sits sideways in the grass, mud and snow covering everything. I tap on the fogged-up window. It slowly descends, and inside, I find a stunning woman with bright green teary eyes and blonde hair seated behind the wheel. The look of surprise, and horror, on her face is almost comical.

"Hey, you okay? I saw you go down into the ditch."

Tears immediately begin running down her cheeks, and great, hitching sobs come out of her. "I–I–I'm not sure." Sob. "What." Hiccough. "Happened." More sobbing.

"You spun out." Leaning back, I see her tires have had better days. "You can't park here. Your tires suck, your car isn't made for this weather, and you don't seem to know how to drive in it."

Her mouth drops open, and her sobs cease momentarily. "Wow, you're an asshole." A half-choked laugh-sob erupts from her.

"I do what I can. Look, I brought you a blanket. Emergency services will be along soon. Turn your hazards on. They'll take you home, or," I wave my hand generally toward town, "wherever you need to go tonight."

Who are you?

Climbing back up the hill, I get in my cab just as Tommy in his truck, yellow spinning light on top, pulls up behind me. Throwing him a wave, I pull away.

She called me an asshole. I am. But she took the blanket, so I win.

Chapter 4
To Build a Home

Callie

The next morning, sitting in the comfiest bed I've ever laid in, I peer out the windows. It looks like the entire town has been covered in a giant white blanket. No tire tracks indicate where the road is, and the whole place is silent and restful. The snow falls in wispy flakes, blowing peacefully around. For the first time in an incredibly long time, I feel a sense of calm in my chest. A sense of rightness.

Is this what I've been looking for?

Throwing on an oversized t-shirt, a pair of leggings, and mismatched socks, I get ready to head downstairs where I was promised breakfast. Sweeping my hair up into a messy bun on top of my head, I walk into the hallway.

I follow the scent of coffee and bread down the stairs and find a kind-looking older woman setting out a breakfast spread consisting of fresh bread, jams and jellies, fruit, yogurt, and delicious, rich-smelling coffee. Orange juice and milk round out the options.

"Good morning, dear, I'm Mrs. Cox. I believe you met my husband last night." She smiles openly, and something about her makes me want to tell her everything about myself. "I heard you had a bit of an accident. That happens when the snow comes on like this. You're from North Carolina? I've never been myself, but I hear it's lovely." She speaks animatedly, her short, rotund body moving easily around the space, a floral-patterned apron tied around her middle. Her gray hair is pulled into a plait at the nape of her neck and her blue eyes are bright behind the giant glasses covering half her face.

She finally takes a breath and leaves an opening for me to speak. Laughing a little awkwardly, I reply, "Ah yeah, I got caught up, I guess. Apparently, my tires aren't great, or at least, that's what the very gruff man who gave me a blanket told me."

"Oh, who was that, then?"

"I'm not sure. He was just sort of rude and gave me a blanket, then Tommy drove me over here."

"I'll find out who it was. What's your name? My old memory fails me." She laughs.

"Caroline, or Callie, Pearce. Either one works." She seems to know every bit of information I passed along to her husband or reached her by way of gossip before I even made it down this morning, but my name was apparently too much for her.

"What a lovely name. Have some breakfast; I'll be just in the kitchen. Let me know if you need anything," she tells me before bustling off to the kitchen, her flowery apron billowing slightly as she goes.

Sipping the best cup of coffee of my life, I moan—out loud. I hear a chuckle behind me and slowly turn to see a tall man standing in the doorway to the dining room. My eyes widen at the sight of him, which elicits another deep chuckle causing my cheeks to warm.

I scan him from a well-worn, brown cowboy hat with dark

blond peeking out around the back to dirty, old, brown boots. He wears a navy blue, long-sleeve henley tight across his biceps and abdomen, outlining his abs, and form-fitting jeans, sporting a rather large silver belt buckle with a man on a bull on it. Realizing I've been appraising him longer than is strictly polite, I clear my throat and focus back on his face.

"Good morning, darlin'. Have you seen Mrs. Cox around here?" he asks with an accent that's a little bit country and a little bit mid-western, a flirty smirk slightly lifting the side of his mouth.

"She's, uh, she's in the kitchen." I try to regain my self-respect after just ogling him like he's on the cover of a magazine.

"Aunt Lizzie!" he yells out unexpectedly, shattering the silence in the room, making me jump.

She comes rushing out of the kitchen, a beaming smile on her face and pulls his large frame into her arms, hugging him tight around his middle. Seeing him smile and wrap his arms around her too feels comfortable and loving but also like I'm interrupting. I move to stand.

"Oh no you don't, you're not done. Don't let us interrupt," she scolds me and I sit back down. "Callie, this is my nephew, Cash. He's my sister's boy. Of course, she's down there in Bozeman for her treatments, and has left my sweet boy all alone." She gently pats his cheek, eliciting an eyeroll from him.

"You don't have to tell every stranger who passes through town all our business. And I'm thirty-four, Aunt Lizzie, I don't need my mama to take care of me." He lovingly teases her.

"Now look here, Cash Colter—" His laughter-scrunched bright blue eyes swing to me with a knowing look before he rolls them, again. "—until you have a woman of your own to lead you around, we have to take care of you."

"Alright, into the kitchen with you, woman." He herds her

toward the kitchen door, shooting me a wink over his shoulder. I stifle a laugh in response.

In the afternoon, having spent most of the day in the library curled up reading a cowboy romance, I wander into the reception area in search of Mrs. Cox. I can't quite identify why I'm all restless today, but I suspect it might have to do with the cowboy bursting into my breakfast this morning.

"Good afternoon, Mrs. Cox. I was hoping you could point me in the direction of somewhere I can buy sundries, like a pharmacy or something. And a place to have a meal."

"Well, the snow has stopped so most stuff should be opening but Ralph's, the pharmacy, you know, won't open until tomorrow. I think the diner—oh wait. I talked to Tommy's mom who told me that he told her about the accident last night. And I know who left the blanket." She looks at me with excitement shining in her eyes.

"Oh, do you?" Small towns, news travels fast.

"Yes, it was the Williams boy. Duke's his name. He owns the bar, right at the end of Pike Street. Waylon's it's called. He opens around four. Head out the door, down the street two blocks and you'll see it. Not much else up that way. That was real sweet of him, worrying about you."

"Yes, so nice. You were saying about the diner?" I need to end her speculating about the 'sweetness' of his gesture. I don't want to talk about the grumpy cowboy. Are there any *not* attractive men in this town?

"Right, right. Just down Mainstreet a-ways, green awning. Mable's Diner. She has delicious tuna salad sandwiches."

"Thank you, Mrs. Cox. I'm going to head out. I'll be back later."

Turning, I push through the door, in search of anything but tuna salad sandwiches. I find Mable's a few blocks down and swing the door open, kicking the snow off my boots as the bell jingles over my head. Every face in the place turns in my direction, and blood floods my face under the scrutiny of the tiny diner's customers.

"Hey, you want a table? How many?" a young woman in black pants and a white polo, wearing a red apron with Mable's written across the front, asks me from behind the long counter.

It's a small restaurant, exactly what I would expect from this miniscule town. There are only six small tables, a few booths, and a long bar. The floor is pale blue and white checkered, and the tables are dark wood. It's warm and comfortable.

"Oh, it's just me."

"Want to sit at the bar or a table?" She holds up a menu.

"The bar is fine."

"Sit anywhere, then," she tells me, handing me a menu. Nothing crazy to be found in the selections, just expected diner food.

"What can I get for you?" She comes over, pen and pad in hand. "Wait, are you the girl Tommy helped in the ditch during the storm last night?" Good Lord, small towns. Can I have no anonymity here?

"Yep, that's me. Can I get a turkey sandwich and a coke, please?"

She scribbles on her pad. "You're staying with the Coxes, right? Up at the B&B?"

"Sure am." I keep my answers curt, dissuading further conversation. She wanders away and I drop my head in my hand.

"No, you can't disappear into the floor but I'm willing to

sacrifice my stunning reputation to sit with you, if you'd like?" Lifting my head, I see Cash has occupied the stool next to me, offering me a friendly smile.

I hesitantly smile back. "Hey. No sacrificing necessary, I'm okay alone. They'll stop staring—eventually."

"Not likely. Less likely with me sitting here. At least you'll have a friend, though."

My waitress comes back, setting a Coke in front of me. She looks at Cash and flashes him a truly blinding smile. "Hey, Cash. What can I get 'ya?" She leans slightly over the bar, as though food isn't the only thing on offer.

I side-eye him, trying to sort this out. "Hey Dani, can I get the tuna salad sandwich please and a Coke?"

"Sure, honey."

I snort out a laugh as she walks away. I can hardly contain my giggles. The flirting. The sandwich. It's too much. I'm coming undone at the seams. Clutching my abdomen, I choke a little on my laughter. Cash lands a warm hand on my back, patting slightly.

"You good, darlin'?" He looks equally amused and concerned, like perhaps I'm having some sort of mental episode. I laugh harder. "Callie, you've gotta tell me what's so funny, I'm dying here." Leaning in to stage whisper, he says, "People are staring."

Sucking in a few lungfuls of air, I take a huge gulp of my drink, and it's so cold I can't breathe momentarily, which spurs on more laughter, and the whole while Cash casually rubs circles between my shoulder blades, his hand large and warm.

Finally getting myself under control, I manage to squeak out, "The last thing your aunt said, as I walked out, was *Mable's has really good tuna salad sandwiches.*" I start laughing again, holding up a hand. "I'm sorry, I know it's not that funny. It's been a really long week."

Cash joins in my laughter, and I enjoy the deep, throaty quality of it.

I may look slightly like a lunatic, but it feels so good to laugh with someone. No pressure, just laughter over sandwiches.

I have to say, though, the look on Dani's face makes me a little uneasy.

Chapter 5
Rock You Like a Hurricane

Cash

Walking through the doors of Aunt Lizzie's bed & breakfast on Thursday, I get a little thrill in my stomach at the thought of seeing Callie again. Seeing her seated at the counter of Mable's was a welcome surprise and watching her absolutely fall apart in giggles was easily the highlight of my week. She looked as though she needed that laugh too. Parting ways made me a little sad. It's time to admit, I'm lonely.

If I see her today, I'm going to ask for her number.

Don't be a coward, Cash, she's just a pretty girl. Except I can't even lie to myself that she is *just* anything.

Walking through the house, I find her in the same place as yesterday. Her beautiful, round ass seated in a dining chair, her back to me. Her blonde locks are piled on top of her head in some elaborate twist, little wild curls falling around her.

She must feel me standing behind her as she slowly turns her spring green eyes to me leaning against the doorframe with a smile on my face. Again, she blushes as she gives me a once-over, taking in the details of me from hat-covered head to beat-up boots. I can't stay today, I have to move some calves around on the ranch, but I needed to see her face again.

"Good morning, darlin'." I give her my flirtiest country greeting, tipping my hat to her for good measure.

She huffs out a laugh. "Good morning, Cowboy Cash. What are you doing here?"

I hear the southern drawl in her words and find it absolutely adorable. Her grabbable hips, the ass I kind of want to sink my teeth into, and her cute chipmunk cheeks with dimples all serve to distract me from the matter at hand.

"Where ya from, Callie?"

"North Carolina, near the beach."

"Is it pretty there?"

"The Crystal Coast is the prettiest place to call home I can imagine." A wistful look colors her features.

I want to know how she finds herself here, but it seems a heavy question for first thing in the morning. Taking the seat at the table next to her, I sit facing her way.

"I'd like to show you some pretty places here too, if you'll let me," I tell her shyly. I'm used to women who come on to me so starting this conversation from scratch is rough.

"Oh, Cash! Two visits in one week? What brings you—oh. I think I've got the good of it." Aunt Lizzie looks at us, appraising the situation. "I'll leave you to it."

"Wait, Aunt Lizzie, you don't have to rush out."

At the exact same time, Callie says, "Mrs. Cox, come back. I wouldn't want to monopolize your visit with Cash."

"You two are awfully cute together. Bye!" she sings as she glides back through the kitchen door and Callie and I both laugh.

"Subtle," she whispers.

"Back to what I was saying, can I? At least, can I have your number?"

She looks at me suspiciously, like she doesn't believe I'm real. Like maybe I'm another man entitled to something I haven't earned. I can't be sure though.

"Okay, how about I give you *my* number, and if you want to talk, you can reach out?" I switch my tactic. Maybe she has trust issues.

"Um, sure." She hands over her phone and I program my number in for her under **Cowboy Cash**.

"Text me if you want to talk. We are moving cattle this week, lots of babies and mamas, so I'll be busy through the weekend, but I'll answer when I can."

She studies my face, and I hope I look earnest and not predatory. There's something about her. Something I can't get out of my head.

On the ranch, watching the sunset over the snow-covered pastures, I sit on Daisy's back, where I've been since I got back at a little after eight. We moved 500 new calves and their mamas across the ranch today, taking them toward better feeding areas. There's nothing more beautiful in the world than watching the sky turn pink, blue, and orange over the ten-thousand acres of Colter Ranch. It's a heady feeling knowing this is mine, and I'm responsible for five-thousand odd cattle, and everyone who works this land with me.

We will move 1000 head a day until all the cattle have been rotated. I've checked my phone probably a dozen times today and haven't heard from Callie. Maybe she isn't interested. I won't push, if she wants, she will come to me. Turning Daisy's head, I tell her to head home. I let her take the lead—she knows the way, with Tank and Snapper at our heels the whole way.

It's full dark by the time I have her bedded down in her stall, fresh hay and water available.

"Sweet dreams, pretty Daisy. We have another long day tomorrow." I rub her long nose and place a kiss on it. My animals keep me company these days. It's so hard to meet people when people only see me as Ashley, rodeo champion, instead of Cash, lonely rancher. I was hoping the east coast hurricane that blew into town might be it, but maybe I read it wrong.

I grab my guitar and head to the porch to play a little in the moonlight before I go in for the night. Settling into my chair on the wide porch overlooking the ranch, I strum a couple chords before raising my voice to sing the words of an old Garth Brooks song.

I belt out the rest of the lyrics in a clear voice as my dogs start howling in response. One day, there'll be a girl sitting beside me. Singing along. Laughing at the dogs.

Mine.

After a few more 90's greatest songs for the lovesick, I take my guitar in and rest it on its stand.

I stand my boots up by the door, reach over my head and pull my shirt off, unbuckle my belt, and drop my pants to the floor. I go upstairs and right into the bathroom attached to my bedroom and straight to the shower. I can smell myself, but I wish it was her vanilla and strawberry scent around me instead.

Toweling off after my shower, I pick up my phone to turn on some music and see a missed text that I immediately open.

UNKNOWN

How were the baby cows?

A huge, mile-wide smile spreads across my face. I stare at myself in the mirror; this is my chance. I save her number, grateful she's taking a leap.

Dirty? Dusty? Noisy? Just as cute as they could be.

CALLIE

Sounds tiring. And adorable.

Just showered off the dirt. We get to do it again tomorrow.

CALLIE

Then you better get to bed, Cowboy.

Out in the fields, before sunshine, we nearly freeze trying to get these calves and their mamas where they need to go. They are further away from their destination than the crew we moved yesterday. The cows are noisy this morning, voicing their displeasure of us dragging them from their rest before the sun breaks over the rocky terrain in the distance.

As the fireball crests the rocks, throwing bright rays across the snow-covered ground, I take out my phone and snap a picture.

Almost as beautiful as the blush of a girl getting caught moaning at her coffee.

Her reply is almost instantaneous.

CALLIE

It was really good coffee!

It was a really loud moan.

I laugh to myself, picturing the blush I know is creeping up her neck. Putting my phone back in my pocket, I get back to work. The cows won't herd themselves.

Chapter 6
Neon Moon

Callie

Cuddled up in bed, I grin at my phone, blushing at the memory of being caught moaning. Cash is turning out to be a very sweet cowboy casanova. He's a little too good at saying the right thing. It's been such an incredibly long time since I was desired—someone interested in me, for me, not as a possession or something to control.

I don't know yet if it's genuine or some sort of ploy, so for now, I have to play it safe. I can't let myself get in the same position I was in before.

I reach for the red checkered blanket folded up at the end of the bed and pull it toward me. It smells like a grumpy cowboy—a little spicy, but warm like sandalwood. I inhale deeply before folding it back up and putting it back. Today, I'm returning it. I don't have the right to get comfort from the blanket of an asshole who just happened to be driving by. He didn't even introduce himself.

He clearly has no desire to know me. Everyone in town has

made it clear they know who I am and where to find me, so he could have if he wanted to.

After another day of lounging in the library and snacking on pastries from Mrs. Cox's kitchen, it's after four so I can take the trek down to Waylon's. It's warmer today and the snow is melting. I should be able to pull my car out of the ditch this weekend, and I could leave Monday; just in time for my prepaid week to be up.

My phone buzzes in my pocket and I pull it out, see an unknown number flash across the screen, and block it. I don't answer unknown numbers anymore. Roger has called me from all kinds of numbers over the last year and I've made the mistake of answering a few times.

Not today, Satan.

I see the text notification light up.

> UNKNOWN
>
> Please Callie, answer the phone. I miss you.
> Please.

Delete.

> COWBOY CASH
>
> The cows were all over the place today but
> luckily, my trusty sidekicks got it under
> control.

Attached is a photo of two cattle dogs, sitting side by side in front of a gorgeous brown horse, saddled and looking content. Is this his little family?

> Let me guess. Curly, Larry, and Moe?

> COWBOY CASH
>
> hahaha. No—Daisy, Tank, and Snapper. My
> best friends.

Almost melting into the ground at the adorableness of this man, I slip my phone back into my pocket, grab the blanket, and head out the door.

The weather outside is glorious; it's a bright, clear day over Montana, and the sky goes on for miles. I have trouble tearing my eyes away from the fluffy clouds. The snow is starting to melt, and the bright green spring grass starts peeking through. Even the dirty snow-ice in the gutters is disappearing. I can see the rooftops of the houses and buildings, and the little town I've been absorbed in the last couple of days transforms into something out of a movie.

I think I might be in love with this place. Something about it just feels right, like I have been searching and searching for something that has been waiting here for me.

Waylon's is at the end of the block, right where Mrs. Cox said it would be. It's a black building with large windows I can't see through, though the neon signs in them are clearly visible. There is just a large wooden sign affixed to the building. No hours of operation, no little sticker to indicate they take Visa or Mastercard.

Yanking the heavy door open, I step inside the dimly lit, smokey room. There is that smell—the warm grumpy cowboy smell, a little spicy, a little musky, and sandalwood. An old country song croons through the speakers; I listen carefully and hum the tune to *Neon Moon*.

Approaching the long bar against the wall, I find it empty. I look around; there isn't anyone in here at all. The door was open, and it's after four, when I was told he would be here. Clutching his blanket to my chest, I get another hit of his smell, and it warms me down to my toes. I'll just leave it here.

"I'm coming!" comes a yell, from somewhere behind the bar, his breathing sounding a little labored. I snort at his phrasing—and the way he's clearly out of breath.

I settle down on one of the barstools, pulling out my wallet to check my cash reserves since this definitely seems like a cash-only sort of place. I figure I can get a beer, or something, introduce myself, say thank you. The polite thing, the right thing. I hold his blanket tightly to my chest, unsure about laying it on the bartop, though it does appear clean.

I look around and take in the comfortable, but definitely divey, atmosphere. It's dark, cozy almost. Though, if it was crowded, I might feel differently. The floors and bartop are well worn hardwoods. The high-top tables with their stools look well-loved and the pool tables are a little too large and a little tilted. It's beautiful in the same way this town is. It fits perfectly.

"I can just pour my own drink," I call out, growing some confidence, since I'm the only person here.

A head, covered in shaggy, sweaty, brown hair, immediately pops through the door to the right of the bar, dark eyes finding me and going round like saucers. I laugh at the face he's making; he clearly wasn't expecting to see me. I hold up his blanket and his eyes narrow.

The head disappears and reappears a moment later, with the same black hat jammed on it, except now, he's standing there in just a tank top, in the process of putting his flannel back on. He has colorful landscapes and wildlife tattooed up and down both of his arms. His stomach is flat and his body well defined, like he works hard but not at the gym. I stare, baldly, at him before he covers himself.

Buttoning just enough buttons to hide the art from me completely, he cocks a hip against the bar. "Hey, bad driver. What can I do for you?"

"Hey, grumpy cowboy, I brought your blanket."

"If you want a cowboy, you're in the wrong place. There isn't one here." He inclines his head toward the door, uninviting me to his bar. This man is such a jerk. Why am I kind of attracted to him?

"I just wanted to return your blanket and say thank you. I appreciate you stopping to make sure I'm okay. It was—*nice.*" I over pronounce nice, since he's clearly unfamiliar with it. I hold the blanket out, but he stares at it like it's a snake.

"You can keep it. That all?"

"I was hoping for a drink."

"Well, just like there ain't no cowboys, there also ain't no juices and umbrellas. Beer and," he trails off, gesturing vaguely to the wall of bottles behind him, "cash."

"Perfect, Grumpy, I'll take a Walton's and ginger. Can you handle that?" I sass back, sick of his attitude.

"Yep. Name's Duke, by the way." He gives me a knowing look. "Though I figure you know that, since you're here."

I shrug at him. "Small towns, Duke. Where everybody's business is everybody's. I'm Caroline."

When he turns his back to me to grab my whiskey, I take the opportunity to ogle him a little more. He has a nice ass in his jeans; cowboy or no, he fits what my brain thinks one looks like. His shirt is stretched across his shoulder blades, and I wonder what it would feel like to run my nails over them. How would it feel to have his smell on my skin and his hands on me?

Callie, what the hell, girl?

Chapter 7
Bartender

Duke

I'm not at all surprised she was able to find me, I'm surprised she wanted to.

Bottle in hand, I turn away from the shelves behind the bar to make her drink, and catch her, very obviously, staring at my ass. Pouring her whiskey and ginger ale into a glass, I slide it across the bar to her, daring her to make eye contact with me, one eyebrow raised in question.

She looks me right in my face, staring me down, like she's daring me to say something in return. But I can see the blush, the crimson spreading across her cheeks. It's entirely too cute.

I turn away, gathering my wits.

Cute? Honestly.

Walking out of the backroom, covered in sweat and half-dressed, I wasn't expecting her. Her sweet voice calling out to me, its light southern drawl infiltrating my brain, threw me off balance. Seeing the blanket I gave her held possessively against her chest, I wanted her to keep it. I wanted her to have the comfort it was so obviously offering her.

Her blonde hair is braided in a single thick braid thrown over one shoulder, her t-shirt a bit too big for her but I can make out the soft curves of her hips, the fullness of her. She looks soft, huggable.

"So, Duke, Mrs. Cox said Waylon's is your bar." It's not a question, just a statement.

"It is. And Lizzie gossips too much for her own good." My comment draws a snort of laughter from her. A real, live, I've never actually heard anyone do before, snort. I crinkle my nose, entertained by this laughing version of the sobbing woman I saw in the ditch. "Tommy got you all set up then?"

"Yep, only hotel in town. I'm hoping to get my car out of that ditch tomorrow, so I can leave next week." She smiles at me, and it softens my rough edges for a minute. "Know where I can get some tires? Some grumpy ass told me they're bald."

I tap my chin, as though in concentration. "Yeah, I might know a guy. I'll send him your way."

"Do you want to give me his number, or I can give you mine, and he can just text me?"

"Sure, write it down here." I pass her a bar napkin and the pen I keep tucked in my pocket. She writes her name and number, the letters all loopy.

"Listen...It's Friday night. Gets loud. Handsy. Not exactly a place for someone like you. I'm not trying to run you off, I just —" I rub the back of my neck, unsure of how to continue. I'm not trying to kick her out, but she's a distraction and I don't know if I can handle watching the animals that will be in here tonight trying to paw her.

"Ah, got it. I don't need to be where I'm not wanted." Swallowing back the remainder of her drink, she drops ten dollars on the counter. "Thanks again, Duke."

"Caroline, I didn't—" I start, but she has already walked out. Maybe she will get her car out and disappear the same way she appeared. Then, I don't have to deal with the fact I've hurt another woman, one who was looking at me so earnest and open.

Cash walking in through the door a few hours later is exactly what I need to get my mind off the blonde hair and curvy, soft body of Caroline. If I have to keep picturing her every time I close my eyes, it's going to be the longest night of my life.

"What's going on, Duke?" He sits on the same stool she vacated earlier this evening, laying his hat on the bar. "Just a beer. Fuck, I'm beat. Moving cattle sucks. Been up since before the cocks rose."

Laughing, I twist the top off his beer. "Get your sweaty ass hat off my bar, Dick," I scold him before sliding his beer over.

He grabs the offending hat, settling it on his head. I wipe the spot clean. "Boo hoo, I'm a rodeo champion and I have to move thousands of head of cattle on my little ranch." I mime crying.

"Wow, you're an ass tonight," he responds, laughing.

"That's what everyone keeps telling me," I say, picturing a smiling blonde with curves and grass-colored eyes full of laughter sitting in the same spot. "Congrats on the roping buckle. We watched it up here, cheering you on."

"Did you see that shit showing from Goliath? Cost me my riding win. I'll get 'em next time." He chugs his beer like a man who should be drinking water instead. I fill a glass for him and slide it next to his beer. "Thanks, Dad," he snarks, rolling his eyes.

"Oh, please, I just don't want you to collapse in my bar. Drink your damn water."

"Phhft, you were a lot more fun when we were younger."

"Yeah, because you were eighteen and I was twenty-one, so I could buy the beer. I was always older and wiser."

"Yeah, you're an old ass man." He tips his beer to me before picking up his water and draining the glass. "Happy?"

"Yep. What else is going on?" I ask him, by way of distraction.

"Same stuff as always. I think maybe I met someone. God, she's sweet as pie. She's not from around here and doesn't know who I am so I can be myself, you know? I don't have to put on a show. And she's absolutely stunning. I just want to take her in my arms. Wow, I sound like such a sap." His words strike true in my chest as I glance over at the bar napkin with her swooping letters, feeling like I understand Cash in this moment.

Caroline doesn't know me or my history in this town, where everyone knows everything. Like it might be possible to be someone better. If I even can.

"Oh yeah, good for you man. I know you're all alone up there at the ranch, it would sure be nice if someone was up there with you. You're almost too old for the show anyway." I throw the barbed insult, but only because he knows I don't mean it.

"Shut up. Miles is killing me out there. It's not a joke." He rolls his eyes, and his shoulders as if trying to shake it off. "What's going on with you, man? You look like someone kicked your puppy tonight."

I look at him, trying to decide if I'm ready to bear the truth to him. I decide now, it's too soon. "Indie came in on Tuesday," I tell him instead.

"Why? She knows the bar is firmly in Duke territory."

"She's getting married." I watch his jaw drop. "I don't know to whom. She left me an invite, but I haven't opened it. I don't really care."

"Well, I do. Get it. I'll open it. Find out who it is and tell you if it matters."

Walking toward the register, I hesitate before grabbing it. It's not about the man—never was. It's about the part of me she took when she walked out, the part I still can't name. "I seriously don't care, Cash. This isn't necessary." Pulling the gold envelope from beneath the drawer, I hand it to him.

"Yeah, yeah." He rips the envelope open, and gasps, theatrically, at the card inside. "That dirty rascal."

Dammit, now my curiosity gets the best of me. "Alright, who is it?"

Laughing loudly, he shoves it back into the envelope, holding it out to me. "I don't fucking know. Some loser. He's not from town."

I blow out a loud sigh. "Jerk-off." I throw my bar towel at him and his laughter chases me as I walk into the office in the back, dropping the envelope on the desk.

At my desk later that night, I save Caroline's number into my phone. I don't know what to say or how to even open the door. I don't know if I even should. She didn't say I could use her number to reach out, just to help with the tires. Sadie's running the bar, so I just sit in the quiet for a few minutes.

You're welcome.

CAROLINE

Hey, Grumpy.

Her instant response feels important, and her response makes me smile.

I'm not grumpy.

I'm stoic.

CAROLINE

Whatever you say, Grumpy. Good night.

I read the text a few more times, leaning back in my chair. Hovering over the keyboard, I try to decide how and if I should respond. Shaking my head, I put the phone away in the desk drawer.

"Hey, Boss?" Sadie calls from the door to the backroom. "Can you man the bar? I need to restock and can't leave these heathens alone." I move toward the door, hearing muffled laughter followed by, "Yes, John, you are a heathen!"

Chapter 8
Fat-Bottomed Girls

Callie

Seeing Duke last night confused whatever feelings I had about my flirtation with Cash. Before I walked into the bar, I knew his blanket was giving me something, comforting me somehow, but Duke was just kind of a jerk. My feelings and the contentment I got from his warm, man-smelling blanket is more of a coincidence than anything. Last night, even though he was undoubtedly still a jerk, there was an attraction, beyond my ability to explain.

He's straight-forward; he says what he means. There is no sugar coating or love bombing, just genuinely himself. Even when he told me to leave last night—which hurt my feelings—it was also pragmatic, he saw the practicality of the situation. Mentioning it being "handsy" felt almost...jealous? Like he didn't like the idea someone might hit on me. The way he speaks and lives, unapologetically, disarms me but also brings out someone fierce and confident.

The way his eyes feel on my body, the way he pauses at my

collar bone, my breasts, my hips, is appreciative, not judgmental. I've been judged a lot in my life for being heavier, thicker, larger than the prettier, skinnier girls. Roger liked to poke that wound over and over.

"Jesus, Caroline, how about you worry less about when you're going to eat next and go for a run or something?" Roger yells at me from behind the wheel of the car.

"I was just asking if you had thought about what you wanted for dinner so we could stop if we need to," I respond, fearfully, under his attack.

"Yeah, well, you might get rid of your fat ass if you stopped asking."

Frowning at the memory, I try to ignore the feeling in my stomach that Cash and Duke might be toying with me, seeing me as easy prey. But it doesn't feel that way.

Duke barely wants to look at me, let alone play games. And Cash? He hides behind his flirty grin, but something in his eyes tells a different story

Completely opposite Duke's stoic reserve is Cash, who is open and friendly. He has definite golden retriever energy, something that is contagious and makes me want to dance and relax. Chase laughter in the sunrise, spin in the rain, and truly understand what it's like to be loved honestly and selfishly. Cash feels like that guy, someone I could sit beside and contentedly watch the sunset, a dog's head resting in my lap.

I suppose I will just wait and see what happens. In the meanwhile, I think Inspiration, Montana might be a nice place to settle, for now.

"Hey, is this Mick?"

"Yeah?" comes a gruff, questioning reply.

"My name is Caroline. Duke gave me your number." When my phone dinged with a message this morning, I was anxious to see which of the men I've met this week was on the other side. It was just a phone number, a name, and 'Mechanic/tow truck. Tell him I sent you.'

"Yeah, he told me you would be calling. You need me to pull your car out the ditch? He also mentioned you have bald tires." I roll my eyes at not only the words, but the fact Duke already spoke on my behalf.

"That's what Duke tells me. So, yes, that's the gist of it."

"Can you meet me over there around noon? I'll get you sorted."

Peace settles in my chest. Duke didn't have to do this, even just providing me with the number would have been enough. He removed any awkwardness or uncertainty from explaining, negotiating, even if I didn't need him too. It's comforting, like he's a problem solver by nature even if he's standoffish and hard to read.

After asking Mrs. Cox exactly how to find my car and waving to Mr. Cox as he worked diligently on the flowers he's trying to coax into blooming, I set off on foot. According to my directions, it's only a fifteen-minute walk and it's another beautiful spring day. I enjoy the warmth of the bright sun, tying my sweatshirt around my waist about halfway there as I start to overheat.

I thought North Carolina was beautiful, and it is, but Montana feels like I walked onto a movie set where bad things never happen, and everyone gets a happy ending. I mean, obviously that's unrealistic but it just—*feels*—that way. The quiet peacefulness of my walk holds me tightly as I become more resolute in, I think, sticking around here for a while. Maybe through the summer, to see if Montana soothes the ache in my chest and heals the wounds in my soul.

Approaching my poor, beautiful car in the ditch brings such heavy sadness to my heart. She looks okay, and I hope Mick doesn't discover anything horrible. This little coupe was the only thing I purchased with my parent's money after I lost them. She crossed all over the country after I left Roger. This car is the only comfort I had at the end, knowing despite everything, I had a way out.

At the rumble of an approaching truck, I look over my shoulder from my position next to my half-sunken car and see a large, tan tow truck with 'Mick's Recovery' painted in bold black letters on the side. The man who climbs out of the cab is a mountain—easily six and a half feet tall, broad in both shoulder and hip. He dwarfs Duke and Cash by a long shot. A thick beard covers most of his neck and jaw, and a backwards ball cap is perched on his head. His blue work shirt—*Mick* stitched across the breast—strains slightly at the seams. Heavy boots crunch the gravel as he walks toward me.

An easy smile graces his face, so different from the man I spoke to on the phone.

"Caroline? Hey, I'm Mick." He extends his large, calloused hand in greeting which I eagerly shake and it wraps around mine, covering it completely, warm and firm. He whistles, lowly. "Look at this. Poor girl. We'll get her out then assess the damages." Walking back up to his truck, he proceeds with Operation Rescue, dragging my car up onto the street.

Walking around the car in appraisal, he tells me, "She looks sound, no underbody damage but Duke's right, those tires are bald as hell." He gestures to his truck. "Hop up in the cab, we can head over to the shop."

Riding beside Mick for the ten-minute drive to his shop is fun. He has his radio on and his window down, enjoying the spring air as much as I was. It's comfortable, and speaking isn't necessary.

Hopping down when he parks, I take in his small two-bay garage, with large tires in stacks of four scattered around. A woman walks out from around an old black Camaro parked in one of the bays, wiping her hand on a shop rag. She's wearing blue coveralls with 'Kayla' on the pocket. Her dark hair is cut in a neat pixie cut and her dark eyes are bright and happy as she approaches me.

"Hey, Dad, just drop it there. I can take a look." She smiles at me with the same easy smile her dad gave me back at the ditch. "Caroline, right? I'm Kayla. New in town or passing through?" She gets right down to the small-town business of interrogating as she watches Mick offload my car.

"Oh, uh, still deciding, I think. Maybe sticking around. Hard to say." I stutter through the non-explanation.

She laughs as she approaches my tough little car. "No worries, Inspiration, and its people, find a way to burrow inside you. Damn, these tires are bad. I'm surprised you made it this far." As she reaches the rear, she reads my Carolina plates and raises an eyebrow at me. "Far from home."

"Yeah, it's been a journey. I wasn't paying attention."

"Need an oil change too? I'll check it. I want to get her on the lift, but everything looks okay. Start her up." She inclines her head toward the car as she leans down to look underneath and I spring into action.

After a thorough check by Kayla, I've committed to four new tires and an oil change. She gives me, what she calls, the friends and family discount, which she tells me with a wink, "On account of Duke calling in a favor." So my brand-new tires put a much smaller dent in my wallet than I expected.

While she works, Kayla's friendly questioning continues, and I squirm a little.

"So...Duke, huh?" She looks at me knowingly. She's my age, maybe a year or so younger but definitely old enough to find Duke attractive. I briefly consider that I may be encroaching on someone else's territory, though I'm not sure whose. She must see it on my face, and laughs. "I've known Duke a long time; he went to school with my older brother. He's real good people. Looks out for those that matter to him. Which is why..." She trails off, not asking the question but hoping for the answer anyway.

I decide to put her out of her curious misery, at least a little. "He saw me go into the ditch on Tuesday night. He was the first one who stopped. Gave me a blanket while I waited. I went over to Waylon's," I add, trying not to picture him sweaty, shirtless, and annoyed, "and asked him if anyone could help with the car and the tires. I guess that's when he called Mick," I say, almost more to myself than to Kayla.

It feels...strange, having someone quietly take care of things for me. No fanfare, no strings. Just a favor, just because.

She looks at me like she knows there might be more, but she doesn't press.

"Well, like I said, he's a good one. In case you were wondering." Her smile is a little bit smug. Grabbing a business card off the counter, she flips it over, writing in tiny, cramped numbers on the back. "If you need a friend, let me know. It's hard starting somewhere new, even if for a little while. And me and Sadie are always looking for friends to have over for dinner or whatever."

Taking the card, I slide it in my pocket. I may need a friend or two, after all.

Promising a return Monday, I take off down Main Street toward Mable's to grab dinner. What else is there to do in this town?

The view out my window Sunday morning is grey and cold-looking. I'm so anxious to have my car back, so I can, at least, range a little further than my legs will carry me. I haven't spoken to Cash in a few days, but I know he's busy with the ranch. I decide to send him a text anyway, just to say hi.

> I hope it's not too cold wherever the ranch is.
> It's awfully grey in town.

I include a selfie of me sitting up in bed, hair in messy waves in a giant sleepshirt with a band logo on it. Climbing out of bed to get ready for another day of boredom, I pull on a comfy sweater in bright pink with 'Crystal Coast' written on it. I got it a few years ago, before things with Roger got bad. It makes me think of my carefree self, when I thought bad things only happened to bad people. Sliding on black leggings, pink crew socks bunched at my ankles, and tennis shoes, I feel ready for the day. I guess the pink theory is real. For the first time in years, I want to wear pink again.

My phone dings in my room while I brush my teeth.

GRUMPY NOT-COWBOY

> Hey, I have to run down to Roundup to pick
> up some supplies. I figure you might be going
> stir crazy by now. Wanna ride along?

Surprised it's Duke and not Cash, but over-the-moon excited to go anywhere and do anything outside the four-block radius I'm stuck in, I answer immediately.

> Yes, please.

GRUMPY NOT-COWBOY:

I'll be there in 15.

One thing I can count on with Duke—succinctness. My phone vibrates in my hand again. This time I see Cowboy Cash flash across the screen.

COWBOY CASH:

Wow. And I thought the view out here was a good way to wake up.

His attached selfie is him, cowboy hat pulled low, long sleeve work shirt tight across his chest, sitting on the back of Daisy. One hand holding the reins and his strong thighs gripping the saddle. I think I lose my train of thought momentarily.

I tap my chin, formulating the perfect response.

Funny how one picture can make a girl want to go for a ride.

I grab my bag and head into the hallway to meet Duke. It takes Cash a few minutes to respond.

COWBOY CASH

You're going to be the reason I fall off this horse, woman.

Be careful, we need you in one piece, Cowboy.

COWBOY CASH

I'll take you riding darlin', just gotta figure out which kind you mean.

I send him a smiley face; I have to keep the mystery. I rush down the stairs and out the front door just in time to see a big black old square body Chevy pull up to the curb. Beautifully restored, it looks brand new.

"Good morning, Grumpy Not-Cowboy. That's what I saved you in my phone as. In case you were wondering." I see just the slightest twitch of his cheek and a thrill of victory thrums through me. Drumming his fingers along to the radio, his posture is relaxed.

"Good morning, Caroline. I put you in as Caroline."

I burst out laughing at his response as he shifts into first gear, pulling into the street.

Bad Moon Rising flows from the speakers, and Duke keeps time with the drum beat as he shifts gears. We ride with the radio for company for a while until we are cruising through back roads with nothing around. Duke is settled comfortably in his seat, arm resting on the open window, lightly holding the wheel, the other resting on the shifter. There's something so incredibly sexy about a man and a manual transmission.

The song on the radio changes to *Fat Bottomed Girls*, which reignites the finger drumming and a cute half-smile shows on Duke's face.

He looks over at me like he just remembered I'm there and sees me staring back. He gives me a long, lazy once-over.

"You know, when I invited you to come along, I didn't realize I was bringing a bubblegum ball," he says, lifting his eyebrow.

Smiling, showing as many teeth as I can manage, I tell him, "I'm just a girl, Grumpy."

I can see his shoulders shaking with a restrained laugh, his mouth tight like he's trying not to enjoy himself and it makes me crack up.

"Mmhmm. Bored in my small town yet?" he asks me inquisitively.

"A little. I'll have my car back on Monday. Thanks for calling Mick, by the way." I'm genuinely grateful and hope he can hear it in my voice. "He was really great, and Kayla took care of me with the tires and an oil change."

"Good. I've known Kayla since she was a kid. Her wife works as a part-time bartender at the bar."

"Sadie? She mentioned her."

"That's her." We lapse back into quiet, the wind and the radio noisy enough for both of us.

We spend the remaining drive enjoying the fields and animals we pass. I point out every single one I see in a chorus of 'cows,' 'sheep,' 'ooh a donkey,' 'horsies!' and anything else I see, much to Duke's chagrin. He tells me random facts, things like "that's the wildlife preserve, they have wolves" and "this is where I wrecked my first car, an old Chevy Nova."

For a man who doesn't say much, he makes the time together easy, safe.

I consider, not for the first time, not only the obvious differences between the two men I have discovered this last week, but I think I may have a crush on them both. I'm unsure what to do with this information.

Chapter 9
Have You Ever Seen the Rain

Duke

I think I have sunshine in my passenger seat.

Glancing over at her for what feels like the thousandth time in the last hour, I'm struck speechless by how relaxed and beautiful she is. I picked on her pink sweatshirt and socks but it's so completely her, I can't imagine her any other way.

Her excited exclamations at any sort of farm animals makes me chuckle. I've been looking at these smelly beasts my entire life, but something about seeing them through her eyes makes them seem charming and interesting.

Pulling up to the warehouse, I lean over a little. "You can wait in the truck or come with me. We have to pick up some supplies for the bar." Before I even finish what I'm saying, she's jumped out of the truck and slammed the door. "Okay, with it is."

Climbing out myself, I meet her at the front. Walking toward the warehouse, Smith comes out to meet me. I notice

Caroline trailing me a few steps and look over my shoulder at her curiously. She's cautious but I don't think that's why she's trailing me. It's almost like it was an automatic response.

Reaching back, I grab her hand and pull her up to stand next to me. I release hers and reach out to shake Smith's.

"Duke, good to see you, man. I got your order ready to go." He looks between us with open curiosity.

"Thanks, Smith. This is Caroline. We had some other stops to make so I brought her along." I see her side eye me, but I don't look at her.

"Nice to meet you, Caroline." He shakes her hand, lingering a little in her space. I close the gap between her and I, possessively. I have no idea why I felt the need to do it. Smith is a good man, but I can't help myself. "Come on, I'll get your stuff."

We follow him into the warehouse, my hand wrapped around Caroline's to keep her next to me. I don't know why she's trying to walk behind me, but I would rather be in her wake than the other way around. She deserves to lead me. She smiles shyly at me, her smaller hand feeling right in my palm. Smith pushes a cart full of boxes my way before handing me a clipboard.

"Just sign off and it's all yours."

I scribble my name at the bottom, hand the clipboard back, and push the cart out.

Seeing her fall back, I stop walking once we're outside and alone. "Caroline, why are you walking behind me?"

"What?" She seems startled. "I was just...walking." She almost flinches and my gut tightens. I recognize that look. The look of a woman who is expecting an explosion. My mother used to wear the same face.

"When you walk with me, you walk beside me or in front of me. If anyone should be following anybody, I will follow you.

It's a far better view, I promise." She hangs her head just slightly, but I can see her blush.

Resuming my walk to the truck, she walks beside me. Satisfied, I load the boxes in the bed and secure the tarp over them.

Climbing back in the cab, I shift into reverse, not looking at her. "Lunch?"

"That would be nice." I study her momentarily, noting the way her hands are knotted in her lap. I drive for a few miles until I reach a turnoff and park, killing the engine.

She looks over at me with that look on her face again. Fear. I am so furious—furious someone, probably some man, made her feel afraid this way, and furious that she's now looking at me fearfully.

I take a few calming breaths. "Caroline, you don't—*won't*—ever have to be afraid of me. Ever."

"I-I'm not." She watches me, wide eyed.

"Someone made you afraid. You don't have to tell me who or what happened, but I need you to know, sitting beside me, you are safe. Safe from me and anyone else."

Tears well up in her eyes, and I almost fall apart on the spot. I can see the hurt, the pain, she's trying so hard not to let come to the surface. Sliding across the seat, I pull her into my arms, pressing her head against my chest. Her tears turn to sobs, wetting the front of my shirt. I just hold her against me tightly, keeping her safe like I promised until her sobs turn to sniffles.

She presses her face harder against my chest, wrapping her arms around my middle, breathing hard, inhaling against me. She begins to calm down, little-by-little. When she tries to pull back, I let her go.

I move back to my seat, and she reaches out and grabs my hand, squeezing my fingers. She whispers almost inaudibly, "Thank you."

I start the truck, put it in gear, and continue driving toward town to take this sad little bit of sunshine to lunch.

I turn into a spot behind Comfort Cravings and see her studying it, trying to figure out where we are.

"Come on, sweetheart. All they sell is mac and cheese." I catch another of her bright smiles. I took a chance that this would please her. I'm beginning to worry I have a new goal in life, and it revolves around the smile on her face.

Grabbing her hand once we are out of the truck, I drag her inside, seeing her face light up as she takes in the silly, macaroni and cheese themed restaurant. It has bright yellow tables and orange walls with giant elbow noodles suspended from the ceiling and painted cheese splashes on the floor.

"Two please," I tell the host, not releasing her hand. It feels natural to hold it; it fits perfectly in mine.

Seated across from her, I watch her eyes dart from place to place on the menu. I chuckle a little. She snaps her eyes to mine, surprised, I think, and smiles at me.

"How did you know this is my favorite?"

"Lucky guess."

After eating as much macaroni and cheese as we can, we get in the truck to head back to Inspiration. I hope I gave her something she needed. A day away to get some space, and a little bit of fun.

I watch the sky quickly darken from light grey to black, a plains storm blowing in fast. An emergency alert over the radio warns of a severe thunderstorm warning right along the path we're taking home. I try to drive as quickly, but safely, as I can, trying to get us home in one piece.

When the tarp comes loose from my boxes, I pull over.

"Be right back," I tell her before jumping out in the rain that begins pounding against the truck. Holding onto the rope, I try and wrangle it back into place. I hear the door slam and find her beside me, grabbing the tarp, wrestling it with me. I pull my hat off and set it on her head, shielding her face from the raindrops. We get it back in place and jump back in the truck, both of us soaked to our skin.

Our eyes meet and she bursts out laughing which makes me laugh. I begin unbuttoning my shirt, trying to get the wet fabric off me. She stops laughing and watches me carefully as I peel it from my arms. I watch her watching me, my hat perched on her head, her breathing picking up. I don't put a lot of stock in 'hat rules,' especially at my age. But something about my hat sitting low on her brow feels like I actually propositioned her.

Blood starts to flow toward my lap and I'm minutes away from embarrassing myself with a boner sitting in my truck. If she keeps looking at me like that, I won't be able to stay on my side of the seat.

She takes my hat off and sits it on the bench between us, then pulls her bright pink sweatshirt off, leaving her sitting there in just a small tank top that leaves almost none of her glorious body to the imagination. And now that I've seen it, I won't be able to stop imagining it. Her nipples are peaked under her shirt; she isn't wearing a bra.

She's audibly breathing now, her breaths coming rapidly. The tension between us is so palpable, I could touch it. I'm sporting a full erection now, and as she moves her eyes across the falcon tattooed across my pecs, down my abs and to my lap, her eyes widen before rising back to mine. I don't do or say anything. I don't want to scare her or make her think I expect anything, but I want to taste her lips more than anything I have ever wanted.

A few more breaths later, still staring into my eyes, she launches herself at me, wrapping her body around mine, landing herself in my lap, right on my straining dick. I groan at the contact just before she presses her lips to mine. The rain bangs into the truck and lightning flashes all around us.

Grabbing the back of her neck, I pull her completely against me, thrusting my hips up so I can rub against the heat of her body. I move my tongue into her mouth, kissing her deep. I use my tongue like a weapon, tasting her, and imagining my mouth other places. I memorize the taste of her, the feel of her tongue moving against mine. My dick is so hard, I can barely think.

Moving down her jaw, I nip, lick, and suck the delicate skin. She grinds against me, the heat of her skin imprinting her onto my flesh. My hands roam, slipping under the hem of her shirt to rub the soft skin of her back. As we push against each other, the sky lightens and the rain slows until just a few drips remain here and there.

Her movements start to slow, and her kisses become lazier, sweeter. I put a few gentle kisses on her lips, her neck, her collar bone. She unwraps herself and moves back to her side of the truck. I'm in such a worked-up state, my skin hurts. Her lips are swollen from our kisses. She puts her seatbelt back on, all while still watching me.

I pick up my hat, settling it back on her head, this time truly wishing she knew what it means to put a man's hat on her head. I clip my seatbelt on and put the truck in gear. She holds my hand over my shifter the rest of the drive.

Stopping at the curb in front of Lizzie's, she removes the hat from her head, putting it gently on the seat between us. Grabbing her sweatshirt, she opens the door, sliding out. She looks at me, standing with the door open.

"Bye, Grumpy. Today was...fun," she whispers, a faint, but happy smile on her face. She closes the door and disappears into the hotel.

I throw my head back against the headrest and groan.

Just as quickly as she came in, her storm blew back out. The perfect bubble we had on the side of the road was more than I could have imagined.

What the hell do I do now?

Chapter 10
Pickup Man

Callie

Flopping down on the bed, I breathe out a sigh.

Holy shit.

That was the hottest thing I've ever experienced. I would never have guessed going to first base in the front seat of a bartender's truck, during a thunderstorm, would be the highlight of my sexual history. I've never been so turned on in my life.

Pulling my phone out, intending to text Duke, I see I have a couple already.

UNKNOWN

Callie, seriously. Please answer me.

Delete.

COWBOY CASH

Today has been so long but thoughts of a pretty blonde kept me going.

Want to get lunch tomorrow?

Three unanswered texts is probably too
many. I can't unsend them.

The text from Roger sours my mood a little but Cash's make me smile. He's so sweetly kind and cute. So different from Duke.

Were you thinking about yourself? You're a
pretty blond.

Who knew you were so obsessed with me?

I add a cheeky smiley face to the next text before opening my text thread with Duke.

I needed so many things out of today and you
delivered. Best not-cowboy ever.

A ding and a text from Cash scrolls across the screen.

COWBOY CASH

So obsessed. It's kind of becoming a
problem, actually. So...lunch?

As I smile down at my phone, another text comes in, this one from Duke.

GRUMPY NOT-COWBOY

Happy to be of service, Sunshine.

My heart melts in the best way. At the same time, it cracks down the middle. How do I choose what to do here? Cash, on paper, seems like the perfect man. A roughneck cowboy with a sunny personality and an open heart. Duke is a dark, moody bartender who is hard to read but seems to genuinely want to cherish and protect me.

I think the only way to navigate this is to not decide anything about them, for now.

Lunch tomorrow sounds great.

COWBOY CASH

Perfect. I love to eat.

I'm already overheated and overstimulated and his words make me tingle all the way to my toes. I can barely formulate a coherent thought in response.

Careful, Cash. Keep talking like that and I'll start to think you're interested in more than lunch.

COWBOY CASH

Darlin', you have no idea.

Let me know when you're ready for that ride we talked about.

Shameless flirt.

COWBOY CASH

Damn right, baby.

Throwing my phone down and pounding my head back in frustration, I make a plan. If I can't decide what to do about the men who have consumed my brain, maybe I can figure out what to do with myself, in this town.

Changing into dry clothes and throwing my hair up, I make my way downstairs. Searching around for Mrs. Cox, I almost run right into a woman walking through the front door.

"Oh, sorry!" I say to her, stepping back.

"No problem. You know where I can find Lizzie?" she asks, tilting her head to study me. She's tall, maybe five-ten, a good four inches taller than me. Thin with a very narrow waist, small perky breasts that, thanks to her height, are right at my face, or at least feel like it. She stands in her tank top, braless, and low-slung skinny jeans, boots on her feet. She's beautiful, in an *America's Next Top Model* sort of way.

"I was just looking for her myself. Maybe the kitchen?" I spin, heading toward the back of the house. "Mrs. Cox?" I call out once I'm in the dining room.

"Callie? Coming, hun!" she yells through the kitchen door. Swinging the door open, the smile on her face immediately fades when she takes in the waifish model standing beside me.

"Indie, what are you doing here?"

I back out of the room, not liking the tension.

"Lizzie, why are you still so mad at me? It didn't work out with him. It happens."

Oh, God. Is she talking about Cash? Is this supermodel running the streets of Inspiration also an ex-girlfriend? I feel short, and a little dumpy, next to her. Not only am I shorter than her, but I have large breasts, my belly is more squeezable than fit for low-rise jeans, and a round ass. Roger used to use my insecurities against me, but I'm finally trying to accept myself.

But next to 'Indie'? I feel woefully inadequate.

"It happens? Indie, you were married for a decade and you just got up and walked out one day." A decade? Married? That's a lot of history.

"Lizzie, what happened between Duke and me has nothing to do with you or this town. Never mind, coming here was a mistake." She sweeps by me where I'm pressed against the wall outside the dining room. My stomach drops into my feet. Duke? Duke was married to her. For ten years. They had a whole life.

Stepping away from the wall, I move to flee up the stairs.

"Oh, Callie. Did you need something or were you just

looking for me for Indie?" she asks, her matronly smile back on her face. Her protectiveness of Duke has disappeared now with Indie.

"I wanted to talk about something with you and ran into her. So, Indie and Duke?" I ask, distractedly. I shouldn't be prying into his business. In fact, I should just walk away. If I want to know something about Duke's past, he deserves to tell me. "I shouldn't have asked. It's none of my business."

"It's fine, dear. Everyone in town already knows, you may as well too. About a year ago, Indie just packed her stuff up, after ten years married, and a few more before that dating. I mean, you never know what's happening in someone's marriage, but no one saw it coming." She sits in one of the dining chairs, ready to tell her story. I sit opposite her. "I think, least of all, Duke. He was blindsided. It was rough seeing how broken up he was. Gave her damn near everything in the divorce. Except that old bar."

She seems upset about all of this, but I didn't get the impression before that she and Duke were close.

"No one has seen a single woman catch Duke's eye since. He was perfectly faithful during their marriage and now I'm so worried he will just be alone. Indie is getting remarried, of course, only seven months after the divorce. I suspect she was here to ask about booking my rooms for the wedding party."

I sit, stunned. Only seven months. Remarried. Duke all alone. But Duke isn't alone. His lack of aloneness was quite apparent earlier when I was grinding on his lap, something large and commanding between us. I blush and hide my face.

I seem to be the opposite of Indie the same way Duke and Cash are opposites. I don't want to be some rebound tour, a new girl in town. Like a fun new plaything not privy to all their dirty deeds.

"Mrs. Cox, first, I want to extend my room another week, if it's available?" I tell her, regaining control of the conversation.

"Of course, Callie. As far as I'm concerned, the little corner room is yours, as long as you want it."

"Second, I'm thinking of hanging around for a bit. I need to find some work, at least something part-time. And I'll need to find an apartment. You seem to be up to date on all the news around town, so I was hoping you might have heard something," I tell her candidly. It's lovely here but if I'm staying, I need something of my own.

"I think I know of a few places hiring. I know Pete at the feed store is looking for a cashier, if that's something you might be interested in. Or Mable's?" Dani's face flashes behind my eyes, the dirty look she gave me over my lunch with Cash.

"I don't think waitressing is a good option for me. Pete's it is."

"I'll just call over to his wife and let her know. She will take care of it." She reaches over and pats my hand. "I can see you're a good person, Callie. And Cash really seems smitten with you. I think Inspiration will be good for you."

"Thank you, Mrs. Cox." I clutch her fingers.

"Call me Lizzie, dear, everyone does."

Monday morning is another warm, sunny day. I will admit, the weather in Montana in the spring is proving to be rather unpredictable. May is right on the horizon and it's warm enough for a t-shirt but I still need long pants, and I decide to break out my boots today. I can't pass for a cowgirl, or even pretend to be one, but I did have boots packed amongst my stuff in my car.

I squeal with pleasure; I get my car back today. Finally, I get to feel freedom again. Being trapped is one of my biggest fears, especially after Roger. I need the independence of coming and going.

> Hey, Cowboy. I have to pick up my car today from Mick's. Afterwards, I'll meet you for lunch. Where to?

COWBOY CASH

> How are you getting to Mick's?

> Walking?

COWBOY CASH

> Nope, not when you can have a cowboy in a pickup truck at your beck and call. I'll be there in 20.

> Okay, bossy pants.

I guess I'm getting a ride. Swiping a little lip gloss across my full bottom lip, I smooth down my hair. I've put a bit of effort into my look today since after lunch I was planning to head over to Pete's Farm Supply to see about a job.

I thump down the stairs and find Lizzie behind the desk.

"Hey, I'm going to pick up my car. I'm going to head over to Pete's after lunch."

"Great, I spoke to Vickie, and she let Pete know to expect you. I suspect it will all work out." She gives me a wink.

Cash throws the door open with a flourish before I can head outside to meet him. Today he has a crisp white hat on his head, a white t-shirt I can see his undershirt through, his standard tight jeans, a shiny belt buckle, again with a bull rider but a different one than last time, and his old, scuffed boots. His arms look strong, shown off by his t-shirt, and I sort of want to bite one.

"Good morning, Aunt Lizzie!" he singsongs as he blows

into the room like a tornado. Wrapping an arm around my shoulder and pulling me close, he smells the top of my head, sighs, and says, "Good morning, darlin'. You ready?"

I think the smile on Lizzie's face will blind us; she looks ready to explode at Cash's appearance. "Yeah, I was just saying goodbye to Lizzie."

"Then let's go get your car. Love you!" he throws to Lizzie before ushering me out the door.

Outside, I stand frozen on the spot. I don't know what I was expecting, but it wasn't this. Based on what I know about Cash though, this fits perfectly.

In front of Lizzie's hotel is the biggest truck I've ever seen. A white Ram 2500 with heavy duty tires and black rims. It has four doors and is at least four or five inches taller than I would expect. I don't know how to even get in it. It's the perfect mix of show-off and cowboy.

"Uh, Cash, how in the hell do I get in this thing?"

"Don't worry, darlin'. Getting in's the easy part. What happens once you're there though...that's the interesting part." I don't miss the meaning in his words. I can't help but think a wet, shirtless, grumpy man makes the inside of a truck really interesting. I shake my head to clear the thoughts of Duke.

He gives me a little boost onto the rail running the length of the truck before running to the other side and jumping in, like an expert. These men are so comfortable in their world. They exist in the same place, the same time, but they are so different in it.

We pull up in front of Mick's in the giant truck, and I look over at him helplessly.

"I'm up here, now how do I get down?" I ask him, eyes wide.

He chuckles. "Down is what I'm best at." He winks and I just shake my head.

"I don't think I've ever met anyone who makes every single thing sound dirty, like you."

"It's a talent, darlin'. You haven't even seen dirty yet." He jumps out and walks around the truck to help me. He reaches up to let me slide down his body, his strong arms holding me tightly against him. He stops my progress when our faces are aligned. "The question is," he leans in close, until we are sharing air, our lips almost touching, "do you like it?"

The sound I make in response to the butterflies filling my chest at his words—at his closeness—borders on pornographic, somewhere between a sound of affirmation and a moan. Heat low in my belly begs for release.

Leaning in, his mouth, right next to my ear, so close, his breath tickles me. "I'll take that as a yes." He slides me the rest of the way down before setting me on unsteady feet.

I walk away, a little wobbly, like a newborn deer. He chuckles where he leans against his truck, waiting for me.

The bell over the shop door jingles when I walk through, and Kayla pops her head up from behind the counter. "Oh, hey Caroline. The little lady is all ready for you. Let me know if you have any issues, alright?" I see her look over my shoulder, so I glance back and see a very sexy cowboy leaning against his tailgate. She looks at me but doesn't voice her opinion if she has one. "I went to school with Cash. You should see him in the arena."

"The arena?" I ask.

"Ask him about it. He didn't get that shiny belt buckle with his good looks. Though the way the girls act, you would think so."

"Thanks, Kayla. Hey, you sure it's okay if I text you? I might need some friends; I'm planning to stick around for a bit."

She gives me a genuine smile. "Definitely."

I take my keys and my receipt and walk back out to my cowboy.

He follows me back to Lizzie's where I park in the lot, stroking the roof lovingly before barely succeeding in getting into Cash's truck on my own.

He squeezes my hand across the center console before he heads out of town. "Where are we off too?" I ask.

"Just a little surprise. I know you've been here for a week but since you've been trapped in town, I figured you might want to try something that isn't Mable's." He turns into the parking lot of a little building next to a river, with an outdoor seating area featuring swings, picnic tables, and railings where you can sit and look at the water. Following him inside, I discover it's a counter service restaurant with hot dogs and grilled cheeses.

I order a grilled cheese and tomato sandwich with chips and Cash gets three hotdogs. We both get large lemonades, which are the largest I have ever seen.

"You weren't joking when you said you like to eat," I say, laughing, as we sit at one of the railings, side by side, our shoulders touching.

He gives me a side-eye followed by the most obviously sexual smirk I believe I have ever seen. I gasp. "Cash!" I scold and he breaks out in laughter.

I am so red I can feel it from the top of my head to the tips of my feet. He doesn't miss it, and it makes him laugh harder.

"Scandalized, darlin'?" he says.

I stutter, unable to reply.

"You've got the prettiest blush I've ever seen." He runs two fingers down my cheek, looking at me like I mean more to him than just a hotdog date by the river. "Seeing you let go and laugh, it makes me so happy."

Chapter 11
There was This Girl

Cash

Callie's blush was the most adorably sexy thing I've seen in a long time. I didn't even need to say anything, and she broke out in goosebumps, her nose and cheeks pinking. I can feel my cock twitching in response.

She's definitely interested and intrigued. I want to get on my knees, right here next to the river, and worship her like she deserves, taste her on my tongue. Feel her quiver beneath my hands.

Too soon, Cash.

Slow down. She isn't ready just yet.

Hearing talking behind me, I look over my shoulder and see a couple standing there. Now that they have my attention, the man steps forward.

"Hey, Ashley, big fan, man. World Championships last year, a ninety-four? So unbelievable. I can't wait to see what you do this season." He holds out his hand for me to shake. I look over at Callie and see confusion written on her face. Doesn't seem like anyone has told her yet.

"Hey, nice to meet you. Always nice to see people out and about. Yeah, it was a good show. It was Colossus as much as me." I see his girlfriend standing awkwardly behind him. I hold out my hand. "Ashley Colter, ma'am, nice to meet y'all." She smiles and sensing my dismissal, she drags him away. He looks a little starry eyed.

"Ashley?" is the first thing Callie says to me when she has closed her mouth.

I chuckle. Of anything she could have pulled out of the conversation, it was Ashley?

"That's me, darlin'."

"But every single person I've met calls you Cash," she tells me a little stilted.

"Well, for the past week you've been around people who have known me since I was practically in diapers. Those people," I point to the retreating couple, "they don't know Cash. They only know Ashley." I try to explain it in a way she will understand.

"But who is Ashley? What was all that?" I honestly can't believe no one has mentioned it to her. Maybe I'm not as big a deal as I think.

"Well, Cash Colter is a small-town rancher. I run Colter Ranch, a 5,000 head cattle operation out of Inspiration, Montana." I duck my head, a little embarrassed to have to even say this part. "*Ashley* Colter is a rodeo champion. I'm a bull rider, darlin'." I lean back and grab my buckle and tilt it toward her. "I won this last year at the Bull Riders World Finals."

Her jaw drops open again, before realization dawns across her face.

"That's what Kayla meant."

"What?"

"She told me to ask you about the buckle since you didn't get it from your good looks, though she found that part debatable." She huffs out a laugh.

"Yes, that's what she meant. When I'm home, I just want to be a rancher. I don't want to deal with all this stuff."

She nods her head sagely. "I get it. It makes sense. I bet you're hot shit on a bull."

The laugh bursts out of me without me even realizing it. "I'm alright."

This time, she laughs. She pulls out her phone. "I'm totally going to find some videos." She starts typing furiously.

"Oh Lord," is all I can say before she starts playing the first video—it's my ride from the finals two years ago. The ride that got me second place in the world. Watching it over her shoulder, I try to picture what she's seeing.

"It's so...scary. Scary is what it is. Oh my God." When it's over, she looks at me. Awe in her eyes, like she just discovered something amazing.

"It's a little scary. I'm just Cash to you," I tell her, pointing my finger at her. "The season just started Tuesday. I had my first ride right before the snowstorm. I came in second, behind Miles Wilkes," I say resentfully. "I won calf roping though, so there's that."

"Calf roping?" She looks at me horrified. "What are you doing to calves? You can't hurt babies, Cash."

I try not to laugh since she seems sincerely concerned about the calves. "I promise no calves are hurt during roping. It's the same thing we do on the ranch. Look up a video, everyone is fine."

She does and soon she's laughing at the little calves running around.

Her phone beeps with an incoming text as we are watching. We both watch the text flash across the top of the screen.

GRUMPY NOT-COWBOY

No thunderstorms today. And your car is back. It was good to see you.

Her eyes raise to mine, a little fearful but mostly defiant. She thinks I'm going to have an opinion on who she's talking to.

"It's okay, Callie. You don't have to look at me like that." Relief floods her face. "I would like to think this is our first date and if it is, I'm hardly allowed to have feelings or opinions on who you're friends or more than friends with," I tell her, holding her hands in mine.

"Are you sure?" She looks a little like she's holding her breath, her lower lip between her teeth.

"Callie, I want to earn the right to be possessive of you because you choose me, not because I bullied you into it. So, I am asking you, right now—are you giving me the chance?"

She nods her head yes and I reach up, pulling her lips from between her teeth, before leaning forward and pressing my mouth against hers.

She inhales sharply, and I take the opportunity to slip my tongue through her parted lips. She opens more to me, tilting her body my way, angling herself until she is between my spread thighs. Looping my hand in her hair, I gently tug, eliciting more gasps from her. Sucking her lip into my mouth, I bite it gently, before plunging my tongue back in, tasting her the way I have been dreaming of. Well, one of the ways I have been dreaming of.

My hand finds her waist and I hold her tightly, pulling her against my body, as close as our positions at the railing will allow.

We break apart, both of us breathing heavily, stunned

expressions on our faces. We fit perfectly together. Her mouth against mine felt so right, so perfect, and I want to claim her now, make her mine. But I want her to be ready, and she isn't yet. I need to take it slow with her. I want her to choose me.

I didn't know until now I had competition but now that I know? I will make her mine. Inhaling through my nose, I get another shot of her vanilla and strawberry scent and my cock is instantly hard, as if the kiss wasn't enough. She leans in, pressing the tip of her nose to mine.

"Yes, Cash, you have a chance."

I smile before sticking my tongue out and licking her lip, making her giggle. As she leans back, she looks down at our bodies and sees my straining erection pressed against the zipper of my jeans. She looks back at my face and I cock a brow at her.

Got something to say, Hurricane?

Placing her hand on my thigh, she runs it slowly up my leg, getting closer and closer until right before she touches me. Then she lifts her hand and slides it under my shirt, rubbing her soft palms across my stomach muscles, tracing the ridges with her fingers. Leaning my head back, I groan, equal parts pleasure and frustration.

This causes more giggles.

"Very nice, Cowboy," she sasses with a wink.

I drop her back at Lizzie's so she can go to her job interview and drive over to the park. Sitting down on a picnic table and staring out over the land, I find myself excited for the future for the first time in a while.

I want to be worthy of her, I want to hold her in my arms, knowing I earned every minute I get to spend there. She is, by far, the most interesting woman I've ever encountered. I've brought dozens of women to my bed over the years, and no one has ever fascinated me the way Callie does. Maybe because she isn't throwing herself at my feet, begging to worship me but I don't think so. I respect no matter what they choose to do with their own bodies, and I have never judged a woman for jumping into bed with me or anyone else, so I don't think it's the chase—the fact that I have to work for it.

I want to be seen by her. I want her to see the public version of me and the private version and love us both. More than anything, I want her to stay, and to choose me. I want her in my bed, yeah. But what's more? I want her in my life. I want to wake up to her laugh and fall asleep to her voice. That's the part that scares the hell out of me.

Standing, I walk to the truck, pulling my phone out of my pocket.

> Hey, you home? Figured we could hang for a bit before I head back to the ranch.

DW

> Yeah, come on over. I'm throwing some steak on the grill. I have enough for two.

Pulling up in front of the small craftsman house on the edge of town, I'm proud that my best friend, the man I've known for most of my life, bounced back from his divorce and is making a new life for himself.

It would be nice if he met someone, but we both struggle with it. He's so aloof and hard to get close to that women tend to not stick around to sort him out. I don't think he has even been on a date since Indie left.

Bounding up the steps, I knock on the door, once, twice. I hear the dogs lose it inside, excited for a visitor. He pulls the door open half a second before two giant dogs come running out, nearly knocking me over.

"Hank, Dolly, leave it." They immediately stop and pad their way back inside. "What's going on, Cash?"

"Not much. I was just in town and figured I would stop by, catch up. You know."

"Come on in then, brother."

Chapter 12
Small Town USA

Callie

Floating on air after my interview, I get back to Lizzie's in time for her to offer me dinner of the best meatloaf I've ever had. Actually, I don't think I've ever had meatloaf, but it was the best either way.

"I'm going to head up and change then go over to Waylon's," I tell Lizzie and Mr. Cox as I carry my plate into the kitchen and rinse it in the sink.

"Leave it, I will take care of it. You can't go to Waylon's tonight."

"Why not?" I ask as I walk back into the room.

"Closed on Mondays, Sundays too." Well, there goes my plans.

"Nevermind then, I'll just read. Thanks for talking to Vickie. Pete was so incredibly nice, and I can start next week."

"That's amazing. I'm working on finding out anything about apartments," she tells me, pride in her face at my, very small, accomplishment.

"Pete has an apartment above the feed store, remember Lizzie? That Tara girl lived there?" Mr. Cox adds to the conversation. He's a man of few words but his words always bring value.

"That's right! Callie, it would be perfect." She looks so happy with this development. Score one for Mr. Cox. "I'll ask Vickie about that, too."

"Thank you, Lizzie, Mr. Cox. You guys have been so wonderful."

"You can call me Bud."

"Thank you, Bud." He just inclines his head. He reminds me of Duke.

Upstairs, I decide to text Duke and Cash to tell them both I got the job.

> I got the job *dancing* I can start next week!

COWBOY CASH

> Congratulations darlin'. Can't say I'm not as pleased as possible you're staying. I want more days like today.

He is always the sweetest. He isn't making it easy to decide what to do. Now that I've punched a few things off my list, my mind drifts back to my dilemma with Cash and Duke.

> I had a job interview today. I got the job. I start next week. I guess I decided to stay.

GRUMPY NOT-COWBOY

> They would have been stupid not to hire you. Congratulations, Sunshine.

> If I don't respond, my friend Cash is over, so I don't want to be rude.

I don't respond to him. My mood immediately deflates.

Oh shit, I think this just got a lot more complicated.

Bzzzzzz

My phone buzzing on my nightstand wakes me up. Glancing at the clock, I see it's three in the morning.

COWBOY CASH

You're so pretty.

> Are you drunk? It's the middle of the night.

COWBOY CASH

Oh fuck. I actually sent that?

> Yes

COWBOY CASH

Can I unsend it?

> No

COWBOY CASH

May as well go all in then. I can't stop thinking about you, baby. Your mouth pressed against mine. All I've been thinking about since lunch is pressing my lips against your skin. All your skin. Tasting you and feeling you on my tongue.

I visited my best friend tonight, and while he droned on about his bar and his dogs, and some girl he likes, all I could think about was your mouth. And how it would feel.

And you smell so good.

> Go to sleep, Cash.

COWBOY CASH

Goodnight, Hurricane.

Rolling my eyes at his middle of the night confessions, I roll back over, cuddling under the blankets. Duke is his best friend? It seems fate isn't done toying with me yet.

And am I 'Hurricane'? Why?

Too many unanswered questions tonight. I fall back to sleep smiling at his texts.

The sun the next morning is warm, streaming through my window. After getting dressed in an old Reba concert tee, skinny jeans, and hiking boots, I wrap my hair on top of my head, spray on some perfume, and hop down the stairs to breakfast.

Yesterday, Cash mentioned he had a slow day today since moving the cattle is done, and most of the mamas are being left to hang out with the calves and do their own thing. His ranch hands handle the heavy work and he's practicing for the rodeo season. So, I have a plan.

"Good morning, Lizzie!" I greet the older woman warmly as I sweep into the dining room. I've just been here a week and already have strong maternal feelings toward the kindly woman.

"Hi, Callie! Don't you look cute today. What are you up to?" She smiles, setting a coffee cup in front of me, filling it to the brim before sliding the cream pot toward me. The last few days, it's been almost entirely just me and her in the little bed and breakfast. We have gotten into a somewhat comfortable routine.

"So, I was thinking. I saw Cash yesterday and he mentioned things being a little slow up at the ranch." At the mention of her nephew, her eyes fill with love. "I was hoping to drop by, sort of a surprise, you know? Except I have no idea where the ranch is."

"Oh, that's easy." She carries on with far, albeit easy, directions up to Colter Ranch. It's about a twenty-minute drive but relatively straight forward.

"Thanks, Lizzie. Don't warn him!" I tell her as I gulp down my coffee and head out the door. I have a to-go coffee for him and a bag of pastries from Lizzie's kitchen she insisted I bring.

"You shouldn't show up empty handed, especially not first thing in the morning."

Carefully putting my treats on the empty passenger seat, I set off on my adventure. It's early, eight thirty, so I should be there by nine. Considering the night he had, I'm hoping he's not hungover but also not already out and about for the day.

Pulling into the open gates, under the huge wooden arch reading Colter Ranch with its bucking horses, I am, again, reminded of being on a movie set except this movie is less small-town-romance and more dude-ranch. I rumble over metal grates; I assume to keep the cows from escaping.

I follow the dirt track, taking the left fork as instructed by Lizzie, and pull up outside a large white farmhouse nestled amongst some trees. Cash's giant truck sits parked alongside a few other pickups in the dirt lot. I can just see a stable off in the distance, about a football field away, and a barn out back. It's the most perfect setting to live a life.

Are you lonely up here?

Walking up the front steps, bag and coffee in hand, I ring the doorbell.

I hear it ring through the house and I wait. I don't hear any noise or dogs from the other side of the door. I give a light tap. Still nothing.

I'm about to give up, sad my plan failed, when I hear a noise around the side of the house. Walking around the back, I see a man, short and stocky, in an outfit that matches what I generally see Cash wearing, hat, boots, tight jeans. He's carrying some sort of mechanical implements.

Seeing me standing there, my food in hand, he startles, dropping one or two things through his loaded hands.

"Shit," he mumbles.

I put my things down, carefully, and jog over. "I'm so sorry, I didn't mean to scare you," I tell him, kneeling to pick things up and try to find a place to put them so they won't fall again.

"S'kay. You didn't scare me. I just wasn't expecting to see a woman standing there. You got a delivery or something?"

"I was just looking for Cash. I rang the bell..." I trail off as he watches me.

Nodding once, he eyes me suspiciously. "Cash?" He thinks for a second before deciding on something. "He's up at the stables." He inclines his head in the direction of the building I saw earlier.

"Great, thanks!" I give him a giant smile which seems to relax his face a little before he goes back about his business.

Trudging across the land toward his barn, I realize it's further than I thought. I'm huffing a little before I reach the doorway, but I can hear voices, or at least, a voice, inside as I approach.

"Daisy, I tell ya what, I'm the biggest idiot God put in Montana." Silence.

"Don't look at me like that. I barely even remember texting her in the middle of the night, but my confessions are right there—in black and white. I'm an ass."

I peek around the corner and see him talking to his dun mare. He rubs her down with a brush, making small circles across her haunches, his hand laying lightly on her shoulder while he tells her all his problems. It instantly makes me feel like I need to comfort him for his nighttime commentary.

I giggle at his words, and he spins around so fast he loses his footing and lands against the wall of the stall, sliding down to sit on his butt, a stunned look on his face.

"I brought breakfast." I hold up the bag and the coffee. He sits in the hay and blinks at me a few times before a huge grin spreads across his face. "It seems scaring the men on this ranch is my plan for the day." I let out a self-deprecating laugh.

I see the open curiosity on his face and decide to relieve him of it. I wave a hand in the general direction of the house. "I went up to the house first, but you weren't there, obviously," I grin at his position on the ground, "and ran into some man coming out of the shed. I startled him too; he dropped his tools."

"Sonny. I'll hear about 'random women just showing up at the ranch' from him later," he adds with a chuckle.

"Doesn't happen often?" I ask, exposing my own curiosity.

"Not usually. I mean...there've been women at the ranch, but never uninvited."

I'm immediately concerned I've made a huge misstep in this plan. "Oh, I didn't realize. I can go?" I ask, wincing a little in embarrassment.

"Hell no, woman," he says, panic in his voice as he hauls himself up off the ground. "Best thing that's happened to me is you showing up to my barn. Put your stuff down on the table and come meet Daisy."

Wandering over to her, now empty-handed, he gives me a peppermint from his pocket. "It's her favorite."

I hold it out in my open palm and her giant mouth gobbles it up, making me laugh. She brings her face close to mine at the sound, her hot hay-breath blowing on my hair. I run a hand up her huge snout and she presses against it. Her skin is warm and her fur is so soft.

"She's beautiful, Cash."

"I think she agrees about you," he tells me, wrapping his arms around my middle as he lays his head on my shoulder from behind. I inhale a deep breath, relishing the man at my back, warm and comfortable. His musky scent matches the barn, earthy and grounded. "I've never seen her examine someone so closely." He squeezes me once before letting go. "I'm just going to fill her water, and we can walk back up to the house."

Carrying the bag, and sipping the coffee, we walk the trail back to the house.

"This is Lizzie's coffee," he remarks and makes a big show of moaning.

I give him a playful shove which sets him off laughing.

"Shut up. It had been a long night, and it was good coffee." I see Sonny and another man paused in the front yard of the house. Cash gives them a wave. They settle in, seeming to wait for us.

"This is the place that holds my soul, Callie. I'm never happier, or more at peace, than I am on this land." He tells me a different sort of confession than the kind I got last night. "I got Daisy when I was a teenager and we've been inseparable ever since. She's my best friend, besides Duke I guess, but I can't confess all my secrets to him." He winks at me, probably suspecting I overheard him earlier. He whistles, loudly, two fingers in his mouth. A few seconds later, he does it again.

"What are you doing?"

"You'll see." I look around and see two dogs, running as fast as their legs will carry them across the field. One, a little smaller and way more excited, the second a little slower but his tail whipping so fast it looks like it might carry him away. "Tank, Snapper, come."

The gorgeous gray and black cattle dogs run up to us so excited to see their master and make a new friend. "Meeting the whole family, am I?"

"Well, you've damn near charmed the pants off me. And Lizzie loves you. So, you may as well."

I rub the dogs in as many places as possible as they run in circles around me, rubbing against my legs.

"Sweet babies." I crouch down to get closer and the puppy knocks me down before jumping all over me. Laughing, I try to escape him.

"Snapper, off." He backs up and sits on his haunches, giving me a minute to breathe before Cash gives me a hand to my feet. "Sorry, darlin'. He's just excited."

"He's perfect. Aren't you, Snapper? Just a perfect little baby."

I think the grin Cash gives me will split his face in two.

Approaching the men, finally, I pull back a little, until I'm a step or two behind. It's something deeply ingrained in me, by Roger.

"Men don't want women who walk beside them, it makes them weak. I lead, you follow."

These are Cash's men, his workers, so I don't want to embarrass him. Cash looks at me curiously but continues walking before greeting them.

"Sonny, Lincoln. Good morning," he says, easily. I linger in his periphery. "This is Callie, she brought me breakfast."

Shit, I didn't bring enough for more people. Panic tightens my chest. I should have figured there might be more people. Is Cash going to be pissed?

"Nice to meet you, Callie." Lincoln holds out a slightly dirty, calloused hand. "Sonny mentioned some woman walking around."

Laughing, Cash responds, "I figured he would."

"Nice to meet you too, Lincoln. Sorry again, Sonny." I give him a little wave. He only grunts in response.

"Cash, the north pasture has some standing water and..."

I zone out. I mean, I'm interested, but not 'standing water in a pasture' interested. I reach down and pat the head of the dog leaning against my leg as I fully take in the land around me. The green rolling hillsides, rustic fencing with stretched wires, and barns and stables spread around.

Next to the house is a sitting area with a large grill and firepit, comfortable looking furniture gathered around it. The porch of the old farmhouse wraps all the way around and has swings and rocking chairs casually interspersed with tables, pillows creating soft places to rest. So lived-in and cozy. I see why he loves it here, I would too.

Cash grabs my hand, tugging me toward the house and breaking my contemplation.

He pulls me up the stairs and through the huge wooden Dutch door, into a large open plan house with high ceilings and warm wood. One side of the open room is a floor to ceiling wall of stone housing a fireplace almost big enough to walk inside. A soft-looking tan leather sofa sits across from it, flanked on either side by matching armchairs. Tank immediately goes and claims his spot in one. The floors are a deep, rich brown and a circular rug with a brown and red native-inspired woven pattern covers the floors in the entry, where Cash toes his boots off, setting them on the shoe rack.

I lean down, untying my own boots and placing them next to his. He gives me a satisfied look. A large, sweeping staircase to my left leads up to rooms I can't yet see. Straight ahead is a giant kitchen with a massive wall of windows looking out to the back of the house, a barn and fields visible, a few cows in the distance. A dining table large enough for twelve people fills the space between the kitchen and living rooms, right in front of the windows. There are double glass doors on either side where I can see another table and a large television mounted on a covered porch.

Cash leads me into the kitchen and through to a little breakfast nook in the back, and I sit at the small round table.

Cash disappears, opening and closing the microwave and rattling plates. He comes back, coffee in hand, a glass of orange juice in the other, two plates balanced on his arm, each containing a pastry from the bag.

"Blueberry or Cheese?"

"Blueberry, please. They're my favorite." He sets the plate down and takes the seat across from me.

If this house were a man, he would wrap you in a soft blanket, and hold you close, offering you comfort you didn't know you needed.

Chapter 13
Sad Girls

Cash

When I woke up this morning, I thought I had fucked everything up. My drunken, sloppy, texts were over the invisible line I'm working hard not to cross. Taking Daisy for a hard run this morning, when the sun had barely risen, helped reduce my stress a little. If she writes me off or isn't interested anymore because I said I want to taste her skin—I do—and I want to feel her mouth—I do so much—then I guess it wasn't going anywhere anyway.

Confessing my sins and my feelings to Daisy has become a habit of mine but hearing the tiny giggle from behind me while I did it knocked me off my feet—literally and figuratively. Seeing her standing in my barn, looking adorable in the morning air, hair in a bun, jeans so tight they look like skin, I couldn't control my racing heart.

Inviting her into my home, and introducing my animals, is the first step in this turning into something. Daisy's instant approval was unexpected but not surprising. She always knows, even before I do, if someone isn't good people. Watching her examine everything in the yard and inside solidified something for me. The women I usually bring home are impressed by the big house and ranch but are generally focused on what's upstairs and what I can offer them. I don't blame them, it's natural. But Callie has a quiet confidence and even though she's in my space, she doesn't need to claim me or it, she is just existing.

I watch with satisfaction as my Hurricane sits at my kitchen table, eating her pastry. I can't imagine anyone ever looking so right in this place. Other women have sat in that seat or wandered through these rooms but she is the first one to ever look like she belongs here.

I reach over and wipe a tiny bit of icing from her lip with my thumb, her eyes watching my movements as I bring it to my mouth, sucking on it. Her gaze heats and her breathing becomes a little heavier. I shift in my seat, trying to create some space behind my zipper.

"Want to discuss the middle of the night ramblings of a drunken cowboy?" she blurts out, her voice a little raspy.

The shift to the embarrassing subject catches me off guard and my cheeks heat.

"He blushes? Who knew it was possible." She grins at me.

"Not much gets a blush from me, darlin', but my own mortifying actions do." I smile at her, a genuine smile, not my usual flirty smirk.

"It wasn't so bad. Where should I start? Hurricane?"

"Oh." I laugh. "That's what I've been calling you in my head. From the East Coast, blew in overnight, changed everything." Her face twists, like she's unsure as to whether this is good or bad. "Except, I think it might have been the best unexpected weather imaginable." This earns a return of her smile.

She thinks, tilting her head a little, like she's rolling it around her brain. "I like it. I shall allow it," she declares and laughs.

Bowing slightly, I say, "Thank you, Queen Hurricane." I give her an over exaggerated wink. "What else?"

"Your mouth...and my skin?"

Now my ears and the back of my neck heat up under her hungry and inquisitive gaze. I don't know how to explain this one without crossing the line.

"That one seems...self-explanatory, maybe? Don't make me say it." I plead with my eyes.

"I want to hear it."

Shit.

"Well, since I tasted your mouth, I have had more than a few thoughts about tasting you..." I look her up and down, lingering an exaggerated few seconds at the junction of her thighs before raising my eyes to her mouth, "...everywhere."

She squeaks out a breath and my cock twitches excitedly in response, hoping to get in on the conversation.

Clearing her throat, she asks, "Um, my mouth?"

She gets a groan for that, and I get a cheeky smile. "Yes, your mouth, darlin'. Before I kissed you, I definitely thought about it. Since I kissed you," I lace my fingers with hers on the table, rubbing circles on her thumb, "barely a minute has passed that I haven't thought about your beautiful lips and how they wrap around...words."

Gasping, she narrows her eyes at me. "Words, huh?"

"I swear, I can't tell you how delighted I am that everything I say seems to scandalize you. You have been flirted with before, right?"

Her face falls at my comment and I worry I've said something wrong.

"Not like this and not in a long time." She pulls her hand

free of mine and I instantly feel bereft. She folds her hands in her lap and bows her head a little.

Getting up, I walk around to her side of the table, kneeling at her feet so I can catch her eyes. I find them full of tears.

"Hey, hey, baby, what's wrong? What just happened?" I'm confused; the emotional whiplash unsettles me but I will find out why she turned inward so quickly.

"It's just—just that—this can't be real, can it, Cash?" The hitch in her voice nearly knocks me down, my heart breaking for this beautiful girl and her sadness.

"Of course it can." I hold her face, keeping her eyes on mine. "This is the most real thing I think has ever happened to me. I know we just met and it's new, but this," I gesture between us, "is real, Hurricane. I want to know what happens next. Don't shut me out. Let me in." I lay a hand on her heart, begging her with my eyes.

"No man has ever made me feel the way I have felt in the last week. This town feels right." She puts her own hand against my heart. "This feels right. But," her face crumbles and tears run down her cheeks, "I'm not good enough for you, Cash. Look at me."

"I am looking at you, Callie. And I have never seen anything more beautiful in my life." I wipe her tears away. "I don't know who did this to you, but whoever it was, he didn't deserve you. Hell, I don't think I deserve you, gorgeous gorgeous girl." Planting a small, chaste kiss to her wet lips, I pull her to me until she's pressed against my chest, and I can feel her heart beating a rapid rhythm.

At exactly the wrong, or maybe right, moment, Tank pads into the kitchen and sees us hugging, deciding he is not going to miss out on the action. Nosing between us, he presses against our legs. Callie reaches down and strokes his head, a teary, wet laugh escaping.

"Where is the bathroom?" she asks me, pulling away. I point her to the door off the kitchen that leads to the laundry room with the downstairs bathroom inside.

As she disappears, I look down at Tank, rubbing between his ears, and ask him "Should we keep her, boy?" Looking up at me, he just thumps his tail on the floor.

I take it as a yes anyway.

Chapter 14
Shotgun Rider

Callie

My phone vibrating on the table next to the bed wakes me, bright and early, Thursday morning. Groaning, I glance at the clock and see it's barely seven. Must be an early rising cowboy. I blindly swat my hand and feel around for the phone before lifting it close to my face.

GRUMPY NOT-COWBOY

Wanna go fishing?

What the hell?

Grumpy. It's 7:03 AM. As in IN THE MORNING. I need my beauty sleep. I'm going to change your name from Grumpy to Sadist.

GRUMPY NOT-COWBOY

You're beautiful, enough. Calling me a sadist seems a bit of an overreaction. I guess I'll go spend my day on the lake all alone.

I'm coming.

GRUMPY NOT-COWBOY

That's what I like to hear.

Was that a sex comment or am I reading way too much into this? I'm kind of excited to find out if there is more to Duke than what I've seen so far.

Twenty minutes later, I have my hair in French braids and wear biker shorts and an oversized t-shirt that falls to my mid-thighs, and sandals. I run down the porch steps and practically skid to a stop in front of Duke's old truck. Today it pulls a tiny fishing boat barely large enough for two people.

The door on the old truck creaks as I pull it open before sliding into the cab and smiling widely. I get a small smile in return. Leaning over, I press my lips to his cheek in a chaste kiss which earns me a larger, toothier, grin.

"Good morning, Sunshine. I see you recovered from my early morning disruption of your sleep."

"Fortunately for you, I have."

Pulling away from the curb, we ride with the wind and the radio as our soundtrack, his large hand gripping mine on the seat between us.

Duke maneuvers the boat expertly down the ramp and into the lake when we arrive. He fills the boat with a cooler from the bed as well as a few fishing poles and a tackle box. I lean against the truck, watching him. He moves confidently, as though this is a regular pastime for him, and I get a little thrill that he thought to invite me. I'm not much of a fisher, but being here with him means a lot more than a proper date anywhere else.

"Come on, sweetheart. I'll help you climb in." Taking my hand, he pulls me against him, kissing me gently before lifting me by my waist and depositing me into the tiny boat, the water sloshing around us before he follows behind me. He wears a lightweight t-shirt today, his strong arms on display and a pair of swim trunks, which makes sense. I'm distracted by his pale legs that don't look like they see the sun much. Boating shoes are on his feet. This Duke is so much different than I usually see. I'm fascinated.

"What are you staring at?" he asks me, noticing my lingering eyes.

"Your pale legs," I answer, matter-of-factly. He narrows his brown-eyed gaze at me.

"It's been winter!" His tone is defensive and makes me laugh. "Hang on," he calls out over the din created by the onboard motor starting up, and rumbling vibrations spread through the boat. He shoots away from the land into the middle of the lake before cutting the engine, the sudden quiet feels unexpected.

After he gets us settled, he shows me the stash of snacks and drinks in the cooler and offers to cover me in sunscreen. He pulls a baseball cap from under his seat and, tucking a few loose strands of hair behind my ears, settles the green hat with 'Waylon's' written across it on my head.

"It'll protect your eyes; it's bright today," he tells me gruffly when I look at him a little too indulgently as he dotes on me. He helps me cast my rod and we relax. I prop my bare toes on the side of the boat and let the sun caress my skin. I should have a nice bronze glow by the end of the day.

"Tell me about where you grew up?" His deep voice breaks the silence as we sit. I haven't felt so much as a tiny nibble on my line.

"Oh," I think of what to say about home, "I grew up in a small town near the coast in North Carolina. It's beautiful there but," I make a show of looking around, "Montana might be in competition. I spent my entire childhood on the beach, like a TV show. Have you ever seen Dawson's Creek?"

"Um, I don't think so."

"Well, they filmed it near where I grew up, and a bunch of romance book adaptations. I miss it."

"How did you end up in a ditch in Inspiration?" His question is exactly what I expect. It's a reasonable thing to be curious about, but I'm not ready to tell him.

"I've been traveling for a while. My parents died a few years ago. They left me a little money, and I've been using it to travel." I feel the line I'm holding go taut and a gentle tug. "Duke," I whisper. I'm not sure why, it feels right.

"What?" He looks over at me, concern on his face.

"I think," just as I am speaking, the tug becomes more insistent and my pole is pulled, "I have a FISH!" I screech as my pole is almost yanked from between my hands. Duke jumps up and grabs it from me, reeling it in as the pole bends under the force of the obvious sea monster tugging on it.

"Duke, it's gotta be huge, right?" I ask as he struggles to reel the line in, his own pole discarded at the bottom of the boat.

"Grab the net!"

I look around, suddenly forgetting everything he explained about fishing now that there's a fish on the hook. I wave my hands around trying to figure out where the net is.

Where the hell are you? This is a tiny boat!

Spying it half under the seat I was sitting on, I grab it just as Duke starts leaning over the side of the boat, pulling the giant beast to the surface. A fin breaks through, a tan little thing.

"Give me the net." He passes me the pole while he takes the net from me. I wrestle to keep the rod from being wrenched from my hand as Duke leans over and scoops the Loch Ness monster into the net.

Holding it up, he shows me my prize. It's a tiny trout, half the size of my arm.

"What the fuck? Why is it so small?" I burst out laughing.

"It's not nice to ask why he's small, Caroline, you'll hurt his feelings."

Chapter 15
As She's Walking Away

Duke

I knew bringing Caroline fishing was a good idea. This was way better than I imagined. Seeing the excitement on her face when she hooked a fish, only for her to find this tiny trout in the net is absolutely hilarious, and I'm doing everything I can to subdue my mirth.

"So, do you want to keep your tiny fish or throw it back?" I ask her, holding it high in the air. "I can take a picture of you holding it if you want."

"Duke, you better stop teasing me, or so help me God." She looks at me with narrowed eyes. "Throw him back, he's just a baby." She plops down on the bench, crossing her arms over her chest, the most adorable pout sticking out her lower lip. Flipping the net over, I drop the little guy back where he came from.

Reaching under the seat, I pull out my waterless soap and wash up before rinsing with water from the cooler. Squatting down, I kneel between Caroline's knees and take her face in my hands.

"You're so damn adorable." Leaning forward, I take her lip between my teeth and give it a small nip. She melts into my embrace before nearly falling onto me from her bench. Grabbing her hips, I pull her down onto my lap, her knees bracketing my hips. Leaning against my chair, I pull her mouth to mine and again, we are dry humping. Instantly, all the blood, and thoughts in my head, flood into my cock.

Holding her against me, I rub my erection into her, kissing her mouth, her jaw, and her neck. Every inch of exposed skin I touch. She moans into my mouth, and I snake my hand under her shirt, caressing the soft skin of her back. Under her shirt, she wears a tank top like last time, again, with no bra. Lifting the hem of her shirt, I pull it over her head so she straddles me with her nipples inches from my mouth. I look up at her and find her eyes hooded, her pupils wide with desire. Pulling down the neckline of her shirt, I capture her pebbled nipple between my teeth and give a tiny pull that makes her gasp.

Finding her lips again, I kiss her deeply, my tongue exploring her mouth while I grab her hips, pushing her against me and guiding her movements over my hard cock. In my swim trunks, there isn't much between us and I can feel how warm she is, how slick. Her gasps fill my mouth before she throws her head back, moaning loudly, while grinding down on me. Her breathing comes in gasps now as she sets a rhythm for herself, using me for her own pleasure and it's, by far, one of the hottest things I've ever seen.

A flush starts to expand across her chest as she pushes herself closer to the edge, humping me. She feels so good against me, I bite my lip in concentration. She props her arms on my knees, pushing her bouncing breasts into my face and I nip at the skin with my teeth while she rubs her heat against me, pushing and grinding. A hiss escapes my lips as I try to concentrate on the woman in front of me. I've never seen anything more beautiful than the blush of her impending orgasm.

Don't do it, Duke. You're thirty-seven years old, if you come in your swim trunks like a teenager, you'll never live it down.

"Yes, Sunshine, you're so beautiful right here, right now. I can't imagine ever seeing anything better than this." I hold tight to her while she rocks, her movements a little more frenzied, her breaths panting out of her.

"Fuck, fuck, Duke." My name falls from her lips before she shudders, pushing against me, she collapses into me, her breathing erratic and her heart thumping against my chest.

I kiss her slightly sweaty temple and wrap my arms around her as she relaxes.

Yeah, I think bringing Caroline fishing was a good idea.

Cash coming over on Monday kept my mind off Caroline. We had a few too many whiskeys before he had to call Lincoln to come pick him up at midnight.

For the first time in a dozen years, when the subject of Cash's latest conquest came up, I had something to add. He's been talking about this girl Callie for a few days—he seems wrapped up in the possibility it might turn into something. The way he talks about her, he might be right. It seems like it's moving slower than his love life usually does; he's taking his time instead of taking her to bed. Though, according to him, he can't get his mind off her so it's probably only a matter of time.

And I told him about Caroline. Not much. It's not even anything yet. But, in my drunkenness, I told him all about the truck. How a little bubble of magic in a Montana spring thunderstorm was better than anything I have ever experienced with anyone. I'm thirty-seven years old and was married for a long time, yet I was making out and dry humping in the front seat of my truck, like a kid, on the side of the road.

I thought Cash was going to spit out his drink when I told him. Admittedly, it was uncharacteristic of me. Just something about Caroline brings out something fun and reckless, something I've been missing.

Getting married at twenty-six had been late by small town standards. Indie went to high school with me, even though she's the same age as Cash. I graduated a few years ahead of them, but our mamas had been friends their whole lives, so Cash and I spent as much time together as brothers, even though we are both only children. Hanging out at high school parties as a twenty-one-year-old, I supplied the beer and met Indie. There was never the raw passion between us that I have felt crackling with Caroline.

The fact that she wants to stay in Inspiration makes me nervous and elated. I have no idea what to do with her. By the time Thursday rolled around, I needed to see her, hence the fishing date.

After our fishing trip, I don't hear from Caroline for a few days. I don't want to chase too much or hold on too tight. I feel awkward; I thought something was happening on the boat but we've only had a few scattered texts since then. I couldn't even talk to Cash about it since he had championship finals this weekend. First place, again. The little shit. I'll never escape his ego.

Taking my phone from the coffee table, I text her.

I kind of want to say something but I'm a little lost.

Are we good?

CAROLINE

Of course, Grumpy. Why wouldn't we be?

We haven't really talked since the fishing trip. I don't want you to be uncomfortable around me or anything.

CAROLINE

I'm not. Can I come by the bar tonight or are Tuesdays also 'handsy'?

You can come anytime you want.

I pause. Consider the phrasing and decide to send it anyway. Flirting is definitely Cash's forte but I'll leave it and see if it gets anything.

CAROLINE

For some reason, after the last few times I've seen you, I believe you.

Yep, it got something. My dick instantly strains. What in the hell is this woman doing to me? It was barely innuendo, and my libido has woken up.

Like I said, happy to be of service, sweetheart.

Embarrassed at myself, I close the text thread and open a different one.

Hey, can I come by and see my baby?

COLTER

Yeah, she's waiting for you.

While I type, another one from Caroline comes through, just two words, "I bet." And if they aren't damn true. It's been a while since I've been with a woman, since before Indie left. I'm just not a casual hook up kind of guy. I've never dreamed of waking up next to a woman before but this morning, before I opened my eyes, I saw her green eyes looking back at me, sleep tousled hair a mess from me running my fingers through it.

It was a very imaginative morning.

"Dolly, Hank. Truck." They run out the door ahead of me and sit by the passenger side door, waiting for me to open it. Once we are all in, I set off down the road. I've got a few hours before I have to open the bar and it's been too long since I've been to see Lola.

The comfort I find pulling up next to Cash's truck at the old farmhouse is immeasurable. This place has always felt like home. I see him bounding down the steps, dogs hot on his heels.

"Why the fuck do you look so happy?" I joke as I grab him around the neck, knocking his hat off and rubbing his head. The dogs start wrestling in the dirt too.

Pulling himself free, he swipes his hat from the ground and throws a loose punch.

"Gotta be quicker than that, old man," he says as his soft hit lands true on my chest. "Just being an amazing rodeo champion, you know. Plus, the girl of my dreams."

He sets off at a jog toward the barn. I follow behind with a trail of dogs barking and shuffling behind me.

The inside of the six-stall barn is clean and smells like fresh hay and musky horse. It's comforting in the way home is after a long vacation.

Walking down to stall number four, with its hand painted sign bearing 'Lola,' I whistle low, and she pops her head out.

She stretches her neck to reach me, and I move closer, unlatching her stall. During my drive over, Cash must have saddled her for me. Her white hair and long gray mane are shiny and clean. Her red leather saddle, *Duke* engraved on the side, is slung over a soft fleece blanket. Grabbing her rope, I lead her from the barn.

Sitting in the saddle, I wait for Cash to join me on Daisy before we set off.

"She just shows up last week, coffee and pastries in hand, like the freaking angel she is." Cash just chats about Callie, not a care in the world. I don't listen too closely; he just wants to talk.

"She sounds pretty perfect, Cash. What's the catch?" I think back to my own girl. I haven't gotten to spend enough time with her to know if there is a catch yet, but the tension and heat between us is boiling up, quickly.

"Couldn't tell you. I haven't seen anything yet. She's got some sort of past she's working through but otherwise..." He shrugs.

"You serious about this girl? Like actually serious?" I ask him, surprised. He hasn't ever been serious about someone so it's a pretty abrupt change.

"Yeah, Duke. It's new and I don't know what will happen, but it feels different this time."

"Bout damn time."

Rubbing down the bartop again, despite the bar being almost completely empty, I get lost in my thoughts. I'm completely lost in thoughts of a beautiful blonde, in my lap, grinding on me, her arms around me, her vanilla strawberry smell all over me. Swiping my rag over the wet wood, I zone out.

Swipe.

Her sad eyes as she tears up, her pain eating her up.

Swipe.

Her joyful smile as she pointed out all the animals on our drive. Her excitement over the fish she had on her line.

Swipe.

"Grumpy, what's a girl gotta do to get a drink around here?"

I jump at the sound of her voice and she laughs, loudly, drawing the attention of the couple of men in the bar. Her eyes dance with mirth at my embarrassment and I narrow my eyes.

"Good evening to you too, Caroline. Don't sneak up on me like that."

She chuckles, a huge, happy smile on her face. It's infectious. "Duke, I was standing here for, at least, forty-five seconds before I said anything. Directly in front of you. You were facing me. Which part was the sneaking?"

"Hush." I crack a smile, my lips twitching up, slightly.

"One day, I'll get a real smile from you, Not-Cowboy."

I consider smiling but I don't. No reason I can identify, it just doesn't happen as naturally for me as it does other people.

"What can I get you, sweetheart?"

"Some service, on the bar. I mean, bar service."

She winks. Stands in my bar, propositions me, and *winks.* I can't form a thought; my mouth opens slightly. Before I can get it together, she giggles and says, "My usual, Grumpy."

I pause. I have served her exactly one drink. What was it? I turn around, perusing the wall before remembering. Pulling down the Walton's, I turn and, again, she was clearly checking me out. I smile to myself while I pour her drink.

Three whiskeys later, she's a little unsteady on her feet. She stands, her legs a little wobbly, and asks where the bathroom is. I direct her toward the door behind the counter, where I have a single bathroom, clean, not used by the customers. Sadie deserves a safe, clean bathroom when she works.

After a few minutes, she hasn't returned so I wander back to find her seated at my desk, looking at the pictures I have displayed.

I clear my throat; this time I've caught her off-guard. She looks sheepish as she makes eye contact with me. She's holding a picture of Indie, Cash, and myself from Christmas two years ago. She looks a little sad but also wistful.

"Your life is so...authentic. You fit so perfectly here. I never fit where I was. It always felt like I was being forced to fit somewhere that was too tight." She's sad again. *Tell me how to fix it, Sunshine.* "She's so pretty." She drags the word out until it feels a mile long.

"Who?" I ask, perplexed.

"*Indie,*" she says with an inflection I can't identify. Jealousy maybe?

"How do you know Indie?" I'm not sure what she knows or what she wants from me.

"She came to see Lizzie. I met her. God, she's gorgeous."

I shrug. I guess she's not wrong. I always felt like I had won a prize when I had Indie on my arm. Until the end, when it felt like a punishment.

"You don't have to lie, Duke. You were married to a supermodel, and here I am thinking I have a chance."

Shock runs through me at her words. That she wants us to have a chance and that she is insecure, comparing herself to Indie.

"I don't know what to say here, sweetheart. She's my ex. I can't change it. But don't compare yourself to her. You're you. And you *are* something special."

"I need to go. Bye, Duke." She stands, walking out of the back, through the bar and out the front door. I chase after her into the parking lot. Thankfully, it seems like she walked over.

"Wait, Caroline. Wait."

She turns to me, tears in her eyes and I'm thrown back to that night last New Year's.

"Duke, I can't do this anymore." Tears run down her cheeks.

"Indie, I don't know what you want from me. I have given you everything I can."

"It isn't enough. I had dreams. I'm stuck in this small town, with a small-town guy, who just wants to run a bar and it's suffocating me." Her retreating figure, her shoulders shaking, the pine smell of the Christmas tree that still fills the windows. I fall apart.

"Don't go."

Seeing Caroline running from me breaks me a little.

"Caroline, I can't change the past. I don't want you to be upset about things I can't control. Why can't we focus on now?"

"Sometimes, you get it, Duke, like really get it. And sometimes, you don't." Turning, she walks away, leaving me standing alone.

"Don't go," I whisper.

Chapter 16
Carrying Your Love with Me

Callie

Waking up with a hell of a hangover, I hold my head in my hands and cry. I cry for myself, and I cry for the tiny thread of hope I had for Duke and me. My head pounds and it feels like justice for how I acted last night.

I felt so happy after our day out on the boat. Cash was gone for the weekend for World Championships, which apparently is a big deal, and won.

COWBOY CASH

Wish me luck, Hurricane. This is the biggest show all year.

Good luck, Cowboy. You're a damn rodeo star.

COWBOY CASH

I'll bring home the win to you.

Holy shit, Hurricane! Did you see it? I'll call
you in a bit, it's crazy here. But I won. Beat
Wilkes. Just imagine me happy dancing. I'm
not, on account of being a cowboy and all
that, but just imagine it anyway.

Back in reality, I realize what a mistake I've made. Duke
didn't deserve any of what I did. He doesn't deserve to be
punished because Roger fucked me up. I wish I could fix it,
make it better, but everything I think of to say feels trite and
stupid. Like I'm making excuses for being an abusive drunk,
like my piece of shit ex.

I get dressed in a daze and slowly make my way down to
the dining room in search of coffee, hoping Lizzie isn't around.
Walking into the dining room, I don't find Lizzie, but I do find
Cash.

Sighing, I sit.

"What's wrong, darlin'?" he asks me, concern written in his
brow. The uncharacteristic serious look makes me feel worse. I
hurt Duke and now I'm bothering Cash. I think I have an
emotional hangover too.

"Just a headache. Let me get some coffee."

He stands up and starts to head into the kitchen. "Lizzie,
Callie has…" That's all I hear before the door swings shut,
granting me blissful silence for a few minutes. He returns and
holds out a bottle of medicine. "Here you go, Hurricane."

Taking the bottle, I nod my head in thanks and swallow
down a few pills, chasing it with hot coffee that makes me
wince.

"Thank you, Cash," I whisper.

"I won't keep you long, but I wanted to stop by and
tell you I have to go out of town. Rodeo stuff." I peer up
at him from my hiding place behind my coffee, which
earns me a sympathetic chuckle. "Damn, baby. It must

have been a rough night. Anyway, now that the season is warming up, I'll be coming and going. I'll be back on Sunday. I've got a couple of rides over the next few days, but I'll be available if you want to chat." He leans down and plants a comfortable kiss on the top of my head. "I'll be here Sunday. Don't disappear," he whispers before he turns to go.

"Bye, Cowboy," I call out weakly.

His laughter fills my ears as he walks through the front door.

The cozy, warm way he gives me updates, kisses me like he expects to do it for a long time, feels soft and normal. The heat between me and Duke burns me up.

Pulling out my phone, I open my texts, seeing nothing from Duke. Not that I expect him to have written. I walked away from him. Laying my face on the cool wood of the table, I wait for my headache to go away.

Back in my room, I gulp down so much water my stomach hurts, so much I think I can hear it sloshing around, before getting dressed. I'm supposed to start at Pete's Farm Supply on Saturday, but I have a meeting with Pete and Vickie to look at the apartment above the store that's for rent.

Realizing I'm running behind due to my late start this morning, I rush out the door and to my car. Tucked under my wiper blade is a note.

> *Hurricane,*
> *Stay safe while I'm gone. I'm still working on my chance.*
> *X- Cash*

Finding a reason to smile, I slide in the car and head to the store. I see Vickie waiting by a door at the rear of the building marked 'B.'

"Hey Callie, thanks for coming by. I'm excited to show you the apartment."

I follow her pencil skirted behind up a narrow staircase, arriving at a landing that opens into a large room that houses a kitchen, living room, and dining room. I'm surprised by how much space there is. The furniture included perfectly complements the layout. There's a large, plush grey sofa against the wall with windows across from a TV stand holding a large television. There's a coffee table, an armchair, and a bookshelf in the corner, just waiting for books.

There's a smaller four-person table near the kitchen which is bright with white cabinets and gray and black veined stone counters. The floors are vinyl plank that mirror sun-bleached wood. The whole place has a grey, white, and black theme but it's perfect for adding my own touches. I am so grateful it's furnished so I don't have to do that too.

"There's also a bedroom and bathroom through here." She leads me down a hallway to a clean and relatively new bathroom with a large bathtub I can lay in, and a small circular window. The bedroom is large, with a king-sized bed in the middle of the wall, flanked by nightstands. There's also a large dresser, a small desk, and a small walk-in closet.

"Vickie, this is perfect." She smiles knowingly, as though she expected nothing less. "Seriously, so perfect," I whisper as I wander from place to place, touching furniture and surfaces. A giddiness fills my chest. I've never had my own place before. I've only lived with my parents and then under Roger's thumb. I can't wait to buy pink pillows, paint, and cover the bed with stuffed animals. Put girly books and decorations on the bookshelf. Everything Roger hated.

After a quick discussion about moving in—whenever I want

—and writing a check—six months up front—I sign the lease, take the keys, and practically float down the stairs.

Behind the wheel of my car, I pull out my phone.

> I got an apartment. I can move in whenever.

COWBOY CASH

> Hurricane, this is the best news I've ever heard. You're staying.

I open my texts with Duke and type multiple messages, telling him my news before deleting it over and over. Closing my texts, I pull out of the parking lot and decide to head into a larger town, where they have a Wal-Mart and get some stuff for my new apartment.

I yell in excitement as I park. My new apartment.

I have an apartment!

In Inspiration, Montana.

I also have a Cash.

The thought makes me kind of sad. I almost had a Duke also.

COWBOY CASH

> Hey, if you want to watch the Rodeo, I'll be riding tonight, Thursday, Friday, and Saturday. The show is always on at Waylon's. Stop in, Duke is a nice guy. A little quiet. Tell him I sent you.

I bang my forehead into my steering wheel. I know he's a nice man. Quiet, too.

> Sure thing, Cowboy. Ride well, or whatever they say.

COWBOY CASH

> I'll win a fancy buckle just for you.

COWBOY CASH

Whatever you want, darlin'.

COWBOY CASH

That can be yours too, if you want it.

COWBOY CASH

Yes ma'am.

A selfie of him, big buckle on display, hat pulled low over his eyes, and a mischievous smile appears.

I can almost hear his chuckle.

Sitting on a settee in the lounge at Lizzie's house, my curiosity about the rodeo eats at me. Resolving that nothing with Duke will be fixed if I hide out here, I decide to go over to Waylon's.

When I walk in a little while later, I see him behind the bar, as usual, a towel draped over his shoulder. He has his sleeves rolled up to his elbows, his tattooed forearms on display. I feel a flutter in my belly at the sight of the bright colors and the strong, veiny hands, going about his tasks. Instead of the hat I expect, he has a ball cap, turned backwards on his head.

He seems different tonight, somehow.

"Hey, Duke," I say as I find a stool at the end of the bar and hop up.

"Hey, Caroline, the usual?"

"Oh, after my last performance, I think I'll just take a beer." I expect a small smile or a smirk or something. Instead, he just turns away from me and grabs me a beer. I slide a fifty across the counter which gets a raised brow. "I left before paying my tab, last night."

"Keep it." He slides it back.

"Duke, take the money," I tell him seriously. Not only does he look different tonight, but the easy banter, the joking tone, it's disappeared completely. The frostiness that's appeared instead is icing me out of the room. "Hey, I'm sorry about last night." I try to thaw the air between us.

He swipes up the money, turning to add it to the register, ringing in the drinks I had.

"It's fine, Caroline." He turns up the television hanging above him as the announcer calls out Cash's name.

The men in the bar clap for him. After his name, there are lots of acronyms I don't know. He told me about the Bull Rider's Association, but the others may as well be a foreign language. All I know is, he must be good. Like really good.

I watch as the bull erupts from the chute, my cowboy on his back. He has one hand wrapped up in a rope and the other hand thrown in the air. He wears leather chaps with tassels hanging down that swing with his movements and a leather vest with logos of various companies on it. His body moves in tandem with the angry beast. It's like the bull is an extension of his body. Or he is an extension of the bull. The movements are like a dance; they have a raw elegance I can't even begin to describe. After what is simultaneously the shortest and longest eight seconds of my life, he's pulled from the back by some rodeo guys and rushed to the gate that he quickly climbs over.

Pulling out my phone, I open our text thread.

> That was, by far, the coolest thing I've ever watched.

The whole bar watches, waiting for the scores. Ninety-three point four flashes on the screen and his name moves to the top of the leaderboard. The next highest score is ninety-one. We watch the rest of the show while I nurse my beer. Hostility and sadness radiate off Duke.

I want to talk to him, fix it. But I can't. I tried and he isn't taking it.

Once all the riders are done, they announce the winner.

"Ashley Colter, another buckle to hang on the wall!" the announcer says to Cash, who stands beside him with a huge smile on his face.

"Thanks, man. Hurricane Warning put on a good show for me." I laugh at the name of the bull before Cash holds his buckle in front of the camera. "This buckle is for my own Hurricane waiting for me at home. For you, darlin'," he tells the camera before walking off.

Smiling huge, I finish my beer as my phone starts ringing.

Cowboy Cash flashes across the screen. Leaving a ten-dollar bill, I get up, and without looking back, I walk out of Waylon's and away from Duke—again.

"Hey, Cowboy."

"Hey, Hurricane."

"That was beautiful. Like literally so beautiful. I had no idea. Seeing you up there was so cool," I tell him breathlessly.

"You at Waylon's? It's quiet."

"I left after I saw you get the buckle. You bringing it home to me, Cowboy?"

"Fuck, baby, you're killing me. I've got three more rodeos

before I can give it to you. And fuck, do I want to give it to you." I hear the meaning in his words and blush.

Just before I start speaking, I hear him saying something to someone, muffled in the background.

"Hey, baby. I gotta run. But I'll call you in the morning."

"Okay, have a good night, Cowboy."

"You too, Hurricane."

Right before the line goes dead, I hear the unmistakable laughter of a woman in the background and my stomach drops.

Calm down, Callie. You have no room to be jealous. You have a full on rom-com love triangle going on. It's impossible to not feel insecure though. I don't have quite enough confidence to overcome whatever that giggling laugh was. Cash is a hot-as-shit cowboy who just won.

Chapter 17
Don't Stop Me Now

Callie

The rest of the week passes in a blur. I don't go back to Waylon's to see Cash's riding on Thursday or Friday. I have work on Saturday morning, my first day. As promised, Cash called Thursday morning, letting me know they were traveling to Denver that day.

I don't work up the nerve to ask him about the giggles. I decide I don't have a right to, but I spend the week worrying about where his belt buckle is and if he's thinking about me the way I'm thinking about him. Lizzie shows me where I can watch the rodeo on my phone, and I see him come in second in a bout in Denver and first in Calgary. He wins in both cities in calf roping.

He's coming home with more accomplishments to his name. And I am bursting with pride.

Saturday, I get dressed in my black polo shirt with *Pete's Farm Supply* across the back and affix my nametag on my breast. Pulling on my new khaki pants, I spin in the mirror. It will have to do.

Spending the day surrounded by the local men coming and going, buying their farm supplies, I feel the comfort of a small town wrapped around me like a blanket. It's not boring or monotonous, it's homey and comforting. I visit with the baby chicks who run from one side of the brooder to the other when I come near, making me laugh, and I work out lifting food and hay, moving it around to stocking or orders. I begin to understand why the men in this town look so nice in their tight jeans and fitted tees—just moving farm supplies is hard work.

A sense of accomplishment hums deep in my bones after work—I'm finally working toward building my own future.

I decide to give Waylon's one last chance tonight, to see Cash on the TV instead of my tiny phone one more time before he comes home tomorrow.

Walking into Waylon's at just before eight o'clock, on a Saturday night, I'm astounded at the bustle and noise from the packed building. Duke moves expertly behind the bar as usual, but this time accompanied by a woman who must be Sadie. They work in perfect tandem like a well-oiled machine—with the kind of comfortable confidence that comes from working side-by-side for a long time. There's trust and history there.

He notices me sit at the bar and sends Sadie my way.

"Hey, Caroline, right? Kayla told me about you!" She smiles enthusiastically at me.

"Hey, yeah that's me. Can I get a beer?"

"Sure thing, hun." She hustles off to get the beer just as Duke turns up the television, the whole bar quieting in response. He really is their hometown rodeo hero. A quick scan tells me there are an uncharacteristic number of women here tonight, though I don't know if it's because it's Saturday or if Cash drew them in.

While I wait for Cash's turn, I catch more than a few flirty glances and words directed toward Duke, but he seems wholly uninterested. It seems the attention he gave me was a rare gift and I mentally kick myself again for ruining it.

He comes over to check on me, the first time we've spoken since Tuesday. No more cheeky texts or flirty chats over a drink.

"You good?"

"No, I'm not good." I shoot him a sour look and he narrows his eyes in response.

"Something wrong with the beer?" he asks me, like he doesn't know who I am or about the rift that's torn between us.

"No, Duke, something is wrong with us." He almost rolls his eyes, but I see him stop the movement.

"What's done is done, Caroline. I can't. I won't go through this again." He turns and walks through the door into the stockroom. I get up and follow him.

"Don't turn your back on us, Duke. Please. You didn't deserve what I said or how I said it. I'm sorry."

"I forgive you, Caroline, I get it, you've got your own shit. But I went through this with Indie, and I can't do it again."

I see the brokenness in his eyes. "This isn't like that. I was drunk and stupid."

"You want more than I have, then fine, go find it!" he yells—not with anger but pain in his voice.

I walk up to him, sliding my hands around his middle. He turns his head away from me. Reaching up, I force him to look down at me. "Duke, I don't know what will happen, but I wanted to try."

Grabbing my arm from around his back, he tries to extricate himself. "Caroline, I appreciate the gesture but seriously, I already fell harder for you than I did for Indie in half a dozen years, and if you walk out that door like she did in another month, I won't be able to handle it."

Letting him go, I step back. Hanging my head, I tell him, "You're right. You're right, I am not all in and it isn't fair to you. I'll go." I turn toward the door and Duke grabs my arm, pulling me against him. He reaches past me and locks the door.

"Wha—"

His lips slam against mine in a punishing kiss he puts all his feelings into. It's angry, passionate, hurt. It tastes delicious, and so like him. His arms wrap around me before he lifts me, setting me on top of a table and stepping between my legs. He never breaks his kiss, running his hands down my sides, he grabs the hem of my t-shirt and pulls it over my head. He glues his mouth back to mine as soon as the fabric is clear of my face.

I gasp at the sudden intrusion of air against my sensitive skin and pull at his clothes, ripping at his buttons before he takes over. He strips quickly until he's in his undershirt, his hat and shirt discarded somewhere on the floor. His kiss is searing and feels like lightning. I can smell his skin as he pulls me as close to his body as he can, his mouth leaving mine and making his way down my jaw. I wantonly rub against him, my legs wrapped around him, holding him to me.

I pull his undershirt out of his pants and up over his head as he unclips my bra, letting it fall down my arms. He drops to his knees, taking a peaked nipple in his mouth, moaning against my skin. I let my head fall back as he slides a hand up my thigh and uses his thumb to rub me through my leggings. I moan loudly and he moves his other hand up to cover my mouth.

"Shhh, sweetheart. You don't want the whole bar to hear, do you?"

I try to hold it in and fail but he keeps his hand firmly clamped across my lips. Dropping back on his haunches, his face is directly in front of my pussy. He reaches up and tugs on my waistband, a request. I lift my hips in silent answer as he yanks them down. Leaning forward, he lavishes my sensitive skin with his tongue while holding his hand over my mouth. His tongue is warm against my overheated skin, and he sucks at my clit, forcing a moan from my throat, muffled by his hand.

He slides two fingers inside me, stroking me, setting me on fire from the inside out as I move my hips in time with his strokes. He stands, leaning in close. "I can either get back on my knees and fuck you with my tongue until you come all over my face and I can taste you the rest of the night or I can take my cock out and show you what I have wanted to give you since the second I saw you sitting behind the wheel of your car in that ditch."

I stare at him wide-eyed, his filthy words causing electricity to shoot down my spine and causing goosebumps to pebble my flesh.

"Choose," he commands me, removing his hand finally.

"Fuck me, Duke."

He growls low in his throat and it's so fucking sexy, I can feel the wetness pooling beneath me where I sit on the table. He doesn't hesitate. It takes him seconds to loosen his belt and push his pants down his legs until he stands there, his chest heaving and his erection standing up between us. My eyes widen at the sight of him—he has the biggest dick I've ever seen but then again, I haven't seen many. I try to focus but get distracted by the hard planes of his stomach. I run my fingertips down his abs, and he shudders under my touch, his muscles contracting.

I wrap my hand around him and he's two fists long, at least, and my fingers almost touch each other around him. I moan and pull him to me by the hold I have on him. He grabs my hips, and I tilt my head back, looking him in the eyes.

"You ready, Sunshine?" His eyes search my face for any

hint of hesitation. I nod my head. *Yes, a thousand times yes*, I yell inside my head.

He removes my hand, places a steadying grip on my collarbone and takes himself in his other hand, lining up with me. He stares me directly in my eyes as he slowly, so fucking slowly it's agonizing, slides into me, inch-by-inch. It's slow torture. He throws his head back, his muscles straining. His Adam's apple bobs in his throat and labored breaths puff out of him. Finally, after what seems like forever, he's fully inside me. I feel so perfectly full; I can hardly breathe around him.

"Move, please," I whisper against his chest. Taking a deep breath, he leans down.

"Hold on, Sunshine. This won't be gentle. I'm in a hurry; I got a job to do. I'll cover your mouth if you can't keep quiet." He inches out, a little at a time. I clench around him, wetness flooding me. "Oh, you liked that, you're so wet."

He pulls his hips back and slams into me, forcing a cry from me despite my attempt to keep it in. His hand goes to my mouth.

"Quiet." With that, he fucks me. He pounds into me, setting a furious pace and pulling moan after moan from my lips. His cock touches every nerve ending I have, his pelvis grounding into my clit every time he slams against me. He was holding my hip, but he moves his hand toward where our bodies are joined. He pulls out slowly, looking down as he slides back in, a peaceful smile gracing his face. The best smile I've seen from him yet. He moves his body away from me, leans down, and spits toward the place where he thrusts in and out of me. I almost come immediately.

"God, I knew you would be perfect. You clenched so tight on me just now. You liked that? That's my girl." He slides his thumb through the saliva and rubs my clit, hard, causing me to buck against him. His thumb makes hard circles, smaller and smaller, as I get closer and closer. "Fuck, Caroline. You feel so good."

He seals his mouth over mine, his hips moving in time with his tongue as he moans. Pulling my head away, I try to breathe through the pleasure coursing through me. His chest heaves up and down, sweat beading across the hair covering his stomach. Reaching out, I lay my hand against his defined abdominals before rubbing across his pecs and down his tattooed arm. I pull him against me and he instantly begins peppering my neck with wet kisses. I grab his ass and bring him as close to me as I can, his muscles bunching and flexing as he pushes into me over and over.

"You going to come for me, baby?" he whispers against my ear. "Come for me, so I can come. I can't hold out much longer; you feel so fucking perfect wrapped around my cock. You're perfect. Come on, baby." His thrusts get harder, more erratic as he circles my clit. I feel my own muscles start to spasm around him and I surrender to him, screaming into the hand he has clamped back over my lips as I fall over the edge, my entire body shuttering.

"That's my girl. Let go. Good girl."

I preen under his praise. He rams into me a few more times before pulling out and stroking himself until he comes on the ground between us, a huge groan escaping him and a few muttered curses. I giggle.

The look he gives me is transcendent. He smiles a full, toothy smile. A smile I haven't gotten to see a single time in since I've known him. It's relaxed and easy.

Perfect.

Chapter 18
I Can't Help Falling
in Love with You

Duke

I think I'm falling in love with this wild, happy, sunshine woman. And it scares the actual shit out of me.

If I wanted to create the perfect woman for me, it would be her. She challenges me, demands more from me, surprises me every time she's with me. And the feeling of her wrapped around me as she comes is the most amazing thing I have experienced in my life.

I watch her as I pull up my jeans and rebuckle my belt, then pick up her clothes, turning her pants right side out. I take her little lace panties and shove them in my pocket. She gives me a shy smile.

Her pink cheeks and freshly fucked hair are already making me hard again. I swipe up my undershirt, using it to wipe the mess I made on the floor before I put my outer shirt on, buttoning it. She dresses slowly, only heightening my further interest in her body, as she re-covers it in layers of cotton. She should be in my bed, her skin wet from my kisses.

Kissing her gently, I unlock the door, walking toward my office. I toss my dirty shirt in there before pointing her toward the bathroom.

"I'll be better prepared next time, Sunshine." I give her ass a hard smack. "I think you look absolutely edible right now, but if you don't want the whole bar to know I just fucked you, you might want to visit the bathroom."

She giggles in response and saunters away.

Heading back out to the bar, I check my reflection in the mirror hanging by the bar door. Wiping my hand over my face and chin, I shove my hat on my head and push the door open. I head straight to the sink and wash my hands, looking up at the television. I missed Cash's ride, but I think he would understand.

"Cash had a spectacular ride. Sorry you missed it," Sadie says it in an entirely too knowing tone and earns a side-eye from me, which makes her laugh.

Caroline comes through the door a little hesitantly, just as Cash comes on the screen. I can barely take my eyes off her as she watches.

As he stands there, a new buckle held aloft, he says right into the camera, "I'm coming home, baby, and I have a brand-new buckle for you, Hurricane." He is so lost for this new girl he's talking to; it makes me chuckle.

I look at Caroline and take in her pink cheeks and the weird expression she's wearing as she watches him. Something about her look sets off an alarm in the back of my mind, but I can't figure out why.

She looks over at me and smiles, but it's different from before. Her phone rings from her bag on the counter and she silences it before looking back at me.

"I have to go," she tells me simply. Something happened

between the stockroom and now, and I can't figure out what it is.

"Are you okay? Did I—hurt you or something?" I whisper to her.

She shakes her head no, grabs her bag, and almost runs from the bar. Sadie looks at me oddly, like she is trying to figure out what's happening. I just shrug. I might think she is the perfect woman but she's confusing the hell out of me right now.

Chapter 19
This Kiss

Cash

My phone rings in my hand and I smile. Callie silenced me before, but she was probably trying to find a quiet place.

"Hey, Hurricane," I greet her.

"Hey, Cash." She doesn't sound as excited as usual. There's a sadness in her tone and it makes me wish I was close enough to hold her.

"What's wrong, baby?"

"Nothing, it's fine, I swear." There's a hitch in her voice that I don't like. She's crying, or she will be soon.

"I'm coming back. I'm getting in my truck; I'll be there in three hours."

"No, Cash. I'll see you tomorrow. I'm just tired. I started at Pete's today. Can you help me move some stuff tomorrow or maybe Monday? To my apartment I mean." The tone of her voice is agonizing to me. It's not tiredness, something happened.

"I'll be at Lizzie's by eight am. I'll meet you by the coffee."

"Okay, Cowboy." I'm happy to hear my nickname but the way her voice breaks on it freaks me out.

"Callie, tell me what's wrong. Did I do something?"

"No, Cash. I did." And with that, the line goes dead.

She did? What could she have possibly done?

I head to the tent and get my stuff before heading out to my truck. I don't care what she says, I'm coming home tonight. If she needs me, I'll be there. If not, then I'll see her tomorrow.

"Hey, Ashley!" I turn my head at someone calling my name and see a group of women and a couple of riders. "We are heading out for a party. You coming?"

"Nah, not this time," I answer, turning back around. Right as I get to my truck, a pretty girl in a western shirt tied above her belly button and skin-tight jeans comes up beside me. Her lips are pouty, and her eyes are smokey.

"Hey, Ashley, are you sure you don't want to come? I would really like for you to come." The way she wraps her lips around the word *come* tells me exactly what she means.

"I'm sure," I tell her, moving around her to climb in my truck.

"I could come with you then?" She attempts a seductive face, but her eyes are blue, not green and her hair isn't blonde and doesn't smell like strawberries.

"Darlin' I appreciate the effort, I do. I respect the hell out of it too, but I got a girl waiting for me at home," I tell her.

"I mean, she's not here. She wouldn't know."

"But I would. Goodnight." Climbing into my truck, I pull out of the lot, heading back toward Inspiration and my Hurricane.

I drive most of the night and get home around three o'clock in the morning. I haven't gotten any texts or anything from Callie, so I drag myself into the house, still covered in dirt from the arena and get in the shower. I fall asleep before my head hits the pillow.

A few hours later, the dogs' barking wakes me. I look over and realize it's almost eight. I jump out of bed and start throwing clothes around, trying to find something, anything, to throw on so I don't screw up my promise to Callie.

I'm dressed and out the door in record time and on the road to Lizzie's. I have a gift for Callie sitting on the passenger seat.

I burst into the dining room at 8:15, gift bag in hand, and see Callie sitting there with her coffee. Lizzie sits across from her, looking at me with her mouth hanging open, her fork halfway to it.

"Sorry, Aunt Lizzie, I'm late. I promised a certain girl I would be here at eight." I lean down and drop a kiss on the top of Callie's head before moving around the table and giving Lizzie a kiss on the cheek. "Didn't mean to alarm anyone."

"Well, good morning to you too, Cash. Congratulations on the wins this week. It's going to be a good season if this is how you're showing already."

"Thanks, it was a fun week but I'm glad I'm home." Reaching over and grabbing a plate, I load it with potatoes, eggs, and a pastry. A half-eaten pastry sits on Callie's plate as she sips her coffee. Something isn't right. Something happened while I was gone.

"Hey, Hurricane. I brought you a present," I tell her in a sing-song voice, hoping to cheer her up.

Her eyes lift to mine, and they lighten a little. "You did?"

"Yep, here you go, pretty girl." I pass the pink bag to her, excited. I bounce a little in my seat and she laughs.

"You look like a little kid."

"Just open it," I almost yell. Lizzie laughs at our antics, her eyes full of love as they volley between us. Callie reaches into the bag and pulls out the tiny box. I have to control myself not to reach over and snatch it to open it faster.

"Stop bouncing in your chair, Cash. You're a thirty-four-year-old man not a ten-year-old at a birthday party," Aunt Lizzie scolds me.

Pulling the lid off the box, Callie's eyes round and her mouth makes an adorable little O before she says, "ooh." Pulling the delicate gold chain from the box, she holds it up for Lizzie to see.

Hanging on it is a tiny little cowboy hat, and a gold bar inscribed with 'Cowboy Cash.'

"If you come to the rodeo next week, you can wear it. Please?" I change my statement to a question; I don't want her to think I'm trying to tie her down or anything too soon.

"Oh, Cash, I love it. Thank you!" Tears spring to her eyes which is unexpected. I don't know what's going on but I'm over the moon to see her face light up, and a smile just for me. I got new gloves made while I was in Denver too, they say Hurricane, but I'm not sure she's ready for that yet.

As far as I'm concerned, I won three out of four rodeos this week and championships last week so she's my new lucky charm and I don't ever want to let her go.

"So, we moving your stuff today or what?" I ask her and she nods her head.

"Let's head upstairs. You can help me get everything together."

I follow her to her room, and she holds my hand the whole way. After her gift, it feels like we're making progress again. Walking into the little corner room, I see she's spread out quite a bit in here and laugh.

"Shut up. It's a small room."

I grab her and pull her to me, kissing her.

"Fuck, Hurricane, I missed you. I wanted you there every day." When I say it, her face falls. Cupping her cheek, I ask, "What's wrong? I know it's something, so you better spill it." I don't release her even though she squirms a little.

"When you called on Wednesday, you spoke to someone in the background and then told me you had to go. As you hung up, I heard a woman giggling." She hangs her head and tries to back up. "I realize I have no claim on you yet or anything but I just—I don't know."

Finally catching on, I pull her against me again. Lifting her chin, I kiss her. I lay kisses along her jaw, around her ear and down her neck. Her breathing accelerates as she leans into me. My cock immediately stands up, begging to be a part of *anything* after almost three weeks of torture.

I lean close to her ear, my breath tickling her, based on her shiver. I press my pelvis against her so she can feel me. "Baby, I have never been so hard in my life as I have been this last week. I want nothing more than to sink inside you like I have dreamed about since I first saw you sitting at the breakfast table and heard your gorgeous moan. I've been hard since then. Nobody, and I mean *nobody*, has ever turned me on the way you do. And nobody stands a chance next to you." I suck on her pulse point before I reach around and grab a handful of her ass, pressing her so hard against me, I give an involuntary buck of my hips.

"Let me show you," I plead.

Her whispered, "Okay," is all I need to proceed.

Stepping back slightly, I grab the hem of her shirt, pulling it over her head. I kiss her collarbone and across her chest. Sliding her bra down, I grab two handfuls of her gorgeous tits.

"Fuck, these are perfect." I bite into one, then the other, leaving red teeth marks behind.

I kneel before her as she stands over me. I can see her gazing at me through the valley of her breasts and I nearly come in my pants. I take a few deep breaths to calm myself down. I kiss her gently on her belly button before unbuttoning her jeans and pulling the zipper down. I lay another kiss at the top of her pelvis I just uncovered.

"Beautiful."

Pulling her pants down her legs, I strip one leg then the other until she's standing over me in just her lacy pink panties and her bra. Sticking my face at the junction of her thighs, I inhale, pressing my nose against the fabric.

Reaching up, I drag them down her hips, exposing a sexy tuft of curls shining with wetness. I lick my lips while removing her panties completely then lean forward again, burying my nose in her, inhaling her clean, salty scent. I give a little tug on the hair, and she gasps. I look up at her from between her thighs and she has her head thrown back.

Walking her backwards until she hits the wall, me on my knees the whole time, I give one smooth lick from as far back as I can reach until I hit the top of her pubic bone.

"I like it a little bit rough, baby. I'm not sure what experience you have with that, so we will circle back, but this time you're going to get sweet Cash. Okay?"

She nods her head with wide eyes, and I chuckle.

Grabbing her ankle and draping it across my shoulder, I dive in. She tastes exactly how she smells, and I can't get enough.

"You're mine now, Hurricane. You'll wear my name around your neck, and you taste like fucking heaven. I licked it, so it's mine." She giggles at my words, and I lick, nibble, and suck until she's panting, holding my hair, and grinding on my face. She's right on the edge, but I'm not ready to let her go yet. Standing, I move her to the bed, where she lays down and I kneel next to it. Pulling her to me until her pussy is right on the edge, I put both thighs across my shoulders and surround my head. I rub my nose against her clit then run my tongue from her clit to her tight ass. She gasps when I run my tongue across the extra sensitive flesh there.

"You like that, Hurricane?" I glance up at her to see her mouth open and her eyes squeezed shut. I take my thumb and press it gently against her ass as I suck hard on her clit. She shudders beneath me. I insert two fingers, rubbing them against the top of her pussy wall, feeling for that special little spot. I rub hard until I hear her breathing change, and I know I've found it. Sticking my thumb in my mouth to wet it, I massage her ass while I suck on her and continue to rub her from inside. She squirms under me, so I stop everything I'm doing, suddenly, and she pops her head up, looking down at me.

"Don't squirm away, baby, or it all stops." I resume my movements, spitting lightly on her tight asshole before resuming my clitoris sucking. Her breathing gets harder and more frenzied, moans and the occasional 'Cash' falling from her wet, swollen lips. Pushing her further and further toward the edge, I press hard against the little rough spot inside her until her walls start to quiver around my fingers.

"More Cash, don't stop."

Wouldn't dream of it, baby.

Just as her moans reach a fever pitch, and I slide my thumb inside her tight opening, she comes in a gush all over my face. I am surrounded by the smell and taste of her. It's almost more than I can handle, and I need to come so bad, I see stars. My balls ache. My stomach hurts.

She's fucking perfect. Laying there, spread out on the bed, having been thoroughly devoured by me. I am consumed with the need to tell this woman how I feel. Climbing up her body I rub my wet face on her stomach, causing her to laugh, before I get to her face and kiss her gently, pulling her against me.

"You okay?" I ask her.

"That was…I've never…Holy shit, Cash."

Please, don't break my heart.

Clasping the necklace around her neck, I kiss the back of her shoulder before helping get her redressed. Then we pack.

We move in comfortable silence as I make a pile to return to the library downstairs and remove her clothes from the little closet, laying them on the bed for her to pack in her various bags and boxes. Once there's a small stack of boxes by the door, I start carrying them down the stairs, the books on top. Popping into the library, books in hand, I find Lizzie by the fireplace, her own cowboy romance in her hands, a shirtless man in a hat on the cover. Thankfully, being away from Callie and her delicious smell has allowed my cock to settle a little, though my balls are still aching.

Raising a brow, I give her a look. "I'm so certain *His Cattle Roping Princess* is surely just an innocent book about a man teaching a woman to rope." She huffs out a laugh before laying the book on the table.

"You hush, Cash. We old women need to keep our minds sharp. Your own little lady upstairs had a stack of books," she says, pointing at my arms.

"That she did, and I'll buy her a whole bookshop if it makes her happy."

"She's lovely, Cash. So sweet, and kind. And the way you look at her." She sniffles a little. "Reminds me of how your daddy watches your mama, to this day. He orbits around her, like she is the sun."

I sit beside her on the little settee. "I'm so grateful for everything you did for her, Aunt Lizzie. I think, if it weren't for you, she wouldn't have stayed. You gave her something in her weeks here." I put an arm around her, hugging her close. "I think I'm falling for her. And I just want her to stay."

Patting my hand, she says, "All we ever wanted was for you to find the woman who fits you and Callie is like a puzzle piece you didn't know was missing but everyone else saw it. I hope it works out. Because, sweet Cash," she pats my cheek softly, "you aren't falling for her, you are already gone."

Chapter 20
Two Princes

Callie

The aftermath of my time with Duke, and then with Cash, is devastating. Duke is dark, moody, and hard to read but his affection is searingly intense. Whereas Cash is light, and happy and shows me how he feels with every movement of his body.

I've read a lot of romance, and I've read a lot of love triangles. I don't think I can keep them both. We are speeding toward a collision I can't avoid, but I can stop now. The problem is, do I want to?

I want Duke's strong appraisal—his rough, but worshipful hands. His passion ignites fire low in my belly at a single look. We are fire when we are together, a single spark, and we are ablaze. The first time, in the truck, where the heat crackled between us as the rain pounded down, the smell of Duke's wet skin and petrichor in the air, flashes lighting the scene between us in stunning relief, is seared into my brain—the longing, the inescapable need. After his fishing trip, I was more convinced than ever that Duke could be it. The stockroom was the most amazing sex of my life thus far. He studies me, and sees me, honestly, a little too clearly. He sees my rough edges and understands them in a way we haven't explored yet. I still feel the shadow of his touch on my skin, the intensity of his gaze as he watched me come undone. The gentleness of his hold.

I also want Cash's sunshine. He's a bright spot every day. His huge carefree smile. His flirtatious nature keeps me on my toes. My heart is full of the loving and easy affection he doles out. The constant tactile communication of his hand in mine, a gentle kiss on my head, a loose arm around my shoulder is something I have never had. It's addicting.

Cash makes me feel wanted and desired in a real way, like he would welcome me home at the end of the day with a hug and a cup of tea, listen to my stories and laugh along, and be a starving man who needs me as he takes me to his bed. His sweet kiss standing by the railing eating hotdogs contrasted with the raw hunger in his eyes as he knelt at my feet and worshipped me give me a window into the man I'm just learning about. And I want more.

I'm miles away from wanting to try the children route again, but I can picture him with a little blond-haired baby running around, laughter surrounding them. So much different than the feeling I get from Duke, who feels like he would challenge me and force me to grow. These are two halves of the perfect man, if I knew how to build one.

Cash and Duke are two sides of a coin, opposites but complementary, and I don't want to lose either of them. I'm afraid, however, if I don't choose soon, the choice will no longer be mine to make. My heart shatters at the thought.

Carrying my heavy suitcase down the stairs, I see my boxes Cash brought down sitting on the floor. Tilting my head, I study them, trying to figure out where he disappeared to. I listen closely and hear murmured voices from the library.

Making my way over, I hear Cash and Lizzie speaking with a teasing quality to their conversation.

"...didn't know was missing but everyone else saw it. I hope it works out. Because, sweet Cash," Lizzie pauses for a second, "you aren't falling for her, you are already gone."

Backing away, I feel like lightning has struck me right in my chest. Thinking back to last night and Duke's words—

"...I already fell harder for you than I did for Indie in half a dozen years and if you walk out...I won't be able to handle it."

My stomach does a flip. Cash hasn't confessed these feelings to me, but I can feel them in his touch. The way he looked up at me when he was kneeling at my feet, the excitement in his posture, his voice, when he presented me with his necklace. Wrapping my hand around the charms hanging between my breasts, I want to cry.

Because, I think, I'm falling in love with them both.

Sitting in my new apartment, surrounded by my sparse belongings, I lean back on my couch. Cash left a few hours ago, citing exhaustion from getting home late. I see the little touches I picked up this past couple of days. A fluffy bright pink pillow on the couch, a large round rug under the coffee table with a flowers and bugs motif in bright happy colors of pink, purple, and teal. The black dishes I have sitting on the counter, waiting for their cabinet. The small shoe rack by the stairs.

It's not home yet, but it's a hell of a lot closer to one than I had two weeks ago. Deciding I need to address the elephant in the room, and in this town, I take my phone from my pocket and select the name from the contacts.

"Hello?" I hear her questioning voice.

"Kayla? Hey, it's Caroline. I was wondering if you guys were free for dinner? I know the bar is closed tonight so I was hoping..." I trail off, not sure how to finish the sentence. I have no idea what I'm doing when it comes to the men in my life, but maybe I can make a friend or two.

"Oh, hey Caroline. Yeah, that would be awesome. Why don't you come over here? Maybe like six? I'll text you the address."

"Perfect! I'll see you then!" I chirp happily. I hope I don't sound over eager, but I'm excited to make some friends. And these women have known the men in my life a long time, forever really. I just hope they won't be mad when I ask for their advice.

Pulling up in front of the tiny bungalow in a cute little neighborhood on the edge of town, I admire the cute blue house with white shutters and wish for something like this for myself. Remembering I finally do have something I can call my own in my little apartment, happiness and pride swell in my chest.

I ring the doorbell but don't hear the telltale bark of dogs. The door swings open to Sadie standing there, her brown hair piled in a ponytail on top of her head and her brown eyes looking at me with open curiosity. She's wearing a simple sundress, and her bare toes are painted a bright pink. I extend my hand for a shake before she seems to realize she's been staring at me.

"Shit, hey, Caroline. Sorry, that was incredibly rude. Welcome, come in." She steps back to make room for me to enter the little house and Kayla comes around the corner, a kitchen towel in hand. She's casual tonight, wearing black leggings and a tank top.

"Caroline! Welcome. I'm so glad you finally reached out." She comes over, pulling me in for a hug before backing away.

"Hi," I respond shyly, a little nervous because of the warm welcome from these women.

After a few hours, a few glasses of wine, and a belly full of spaghetti, we are settled in their cute little living room on a bright green sofa, surrounded by muted tan and white decor. I keep a very close eye on the glass of red wine I have clutched in my hand. Sadie watches me closely, like she has something to say. I don't want to confront her but tonight has been such a good night with new friends and I feel like there is something on the table between us and I want to know what it is.

Feeling emboldened by the wine, I ask her.

"Sadie?"

She turns to look at me, a slight tilt to her head. She doesn't say anything.

"Why are you...looking at me like that?" Kayla looks over at her, a questioning look on her face, before looking at me, furrowing her brow.

"Well." She sucks in a breath, seeming to gather the courage to say what she wants to say. "Look, I don't know what's going on with you and Duke. It's none of my business. But Kayla said you came to the garage with Cash Colter and y'all looked really cozy. And I'm not stupid; I know what happened at the bar on Saturday."

Kayla gasps before elbowing Sadie softly.

"No, I told you I wouldn't say anything, but she asked. I also suspect the reason you fled so suddenly after what happened is because of Cash. So let me let you in on a not-so-little secret. Indie tore his heart out and left us to pick up the pieces. Cash, Kayla, and I held that damn place together while

Duke drowned his sadness. And I don't want to sit by and watch you hurt him. He's hurt."

I sit quietly for a few minutes, the two of them equally as quiet watching me. I roll this information around my brain and realize she's right. Of course she is. He deserves to at least know. Tears start to fill my eyes, and I blink them away.

"You're right. Dammit, I've fucked up. I don't know what to do."

"Yes, you do," Kayla tells me solemnly.

In the car an hour later, I scroll to the name I'm looking for, pressing the call button. Ringing fills the car.

"Hey," he says, his voice low, tentative.

"Hey, Duke. How are you today?"

"I would be a lot better if I knew what happened yesterday."

I take a deep breath. How could that have been just yesterday? It feels like seconds ago but also years.

"What are you doing tomorrow? I have to work in the afternoon, but I wanted to see if you wanted to stop by for breakfast. In the morning. So we can talk?" I let the question hang.

"Nothing good ever follows 'we need to talk.' Yeah, I'll be there." His scared voice from the beginning of the call has a rougher, sharper edge to it now. Like he's trying to control himself.

"I meant what I said last night. I can't give you all of myself. But maybe you deserve to know why."

"Alright, Caroline, I'll be there. Around ten, okay?"

"Yeah, ten is perfect."

Hanging up, I reverse out of the driveway and head off to the store. I need supplies for this incredibly awkward conversation. I don't think I made the decision to choose Cash at any point. The fire burning between Duke and I feels too real, too ready to ignite. It's too intense.

Cash feels easier, something I'm more ready for. And I am going to have to break my own heart.

At exactly ten o'clock, on the dot, Monday morning, I'm pulling a freshly baked blueberry lemon loaf out of the oven when Duke knocks on the door.

"Come in!" I call out loudly, hoping he can hear me down the stairs as I have a whole Donna Reed thing happening with my apron and my potholder as I present my homemade food.

I hear his heavy footsteps on the stairs and see his head appear at the top. He looks at me with his usual searing intensity, and peruses me from head to toe, pausing on my flowered apron and my bare feet. He toes off his boots, and I'm fascinated by him in his socks. It's oddly comfortable, knowing under this intense, broody man is just a guy with messy brown hair and clean white socks. It's humanizing, I guess.

He gives me a half smile, not nearly as radiant as the one I got in the stockroom, but I've figured out by now he doesn't share them much and that one was special for me. In his hands, he has a bag and a cup carrier with two cups of coffee in it.

"When you invited me, I didn't know if this was a 'let me cook you breakfast' sort of situation so I brought some biscuits and coffee." He gestures to his packages, awkwardly.

Smiling brightly, I rush over and take them. "No worries, more food is better, not worse. Hey, maybe you won't like this homemade bread and freshly cooked eggs and bacon thing I've got going on."

He gives me a deadpan look that makes me laugh. I set the food on the counter and unpack the bag.

"I'll definitely take the coffee though. I can never make it as good as when you buy it somewhere, you know?" Taking a large sip, I moan a little with pleasure at the rich, nutty flavor.

Duke's eyes darken at the sound, and I clear my throat. I can't let the fire grow right now. Not in this quiet, private place.

"Let's eat," I tell him, trying to redirect.

"I would love to," comes his purred reply, which almost makes me drop my coffee, my gaze finding his and seeing a little mischief there.

"Flirt." I carry the food to the table and set two plates out. "Sit."

"She's bossy, today."

I put a hand on my hip, cocking a brow. "You better listen then."

He does. I cover our plates with food, hiding behind the tasks to delay the inevitable. We eat silently for a few minutes before he looks up at me, a piece of blueberry bread in his hand.

"This has got to be the best blueberry bread I've ever had. Seriously, Caroline. Amazing." He takes another bite, and satisfaction radiates through me at the praise. I'm apparently a sucker for Duke's praising mouth, and he seems to like it too.

"I think it's time to talk," I say. His face immediately falls, the comfortable moment interrupted, and I immediately regret bringing it up. "Before I can get to the end, I need to tell you the beginning."

With his smoldering gaze on me, I begin.

"I grew up in a small town in North Carolina, not super unlike this one but with a beachy vibe since we were near the coast. I had two amazing parents who were madly in love. I went away to college, like one does, and spent four years buried in books, studying. I graduated with a degree in English in June and I met the perfect man in September. Freshly twenty-two and freshly out of college, I was a little reckless, a little impulsive and a lot lost. And Roger seemed perfect. He was considerate, kind, and doted on me like a lovesick puppy." He watches me warily, but his face gives nothing away.

"We dated for four years before he took me to Savannah for a long weekend and proposed in front of the fountain in Forsyth Park. It was like a fairy tale and my prince was down on one knee promising to love me. Of course, I said yes. He had spent four years devoted to making sure I knew he loved me every day. I planned the perfect wedding for a year, it was stunning. We got married by the river under a canopy of calla lilies and gardenias. I loved those flowers so much. I could still smell them in my hair the next morning." I break off, my voice cracking. I see his jaw tighten, almost imperceptibly. I know this is going to be a tough conversation.

And at the end, both of us will have our hearts broken.

Chapter 21
A Broken Wing

Duke

Hearing her voice crack talking about her wedding flowers guts me. I don't know where she's going with this story or what happens at the end, but I have a feeling I'm going to fill in a lot of blanks today and answer my own questions.

"My daddy gave me away, and the day was stunningly perfect. I could not have done anything better; the sun was shining, it was warm. The reception was fun. We danced, we enjoyed our families. As the night wore on, Roger got more and more drunk. By the end, he was completely out of it. When we got back to the rooms we rented for the wedding night, it was set up for the beginning of our honeymoon, but Roger was too drunk to care or even notice. I figured out how to get out of my dress all alone, while Roger drank the champagne that was left on ice for us." She takes a few calming breaths, building up to something. I'm tense. On edge. Afraid of where this is going.

"As I climbed in bed, Roger joined me and—" Her voice breaks again, fat tears starting to fall from her lashes. I reach out to grab her hand, but she keeps it firmly in her lap. "Let's just say, he wanted more than I wanted, considering his state. He did not accept my refusal. He made it clear that I was his wife, and therefore his property and that was that. The next day, he was back to his loving, doting self. He acted like it never happened. We never mentioned it. I thought maybe he didn't remember it. It was like he was a demon, and now the demon was gone."

Fury burns in my chest, white, hot, fury with no outlet. I'm radiating with restrained anger at how a man, any man, could have hurt her. The betrayal of her wedding night. I feel the soft touch of her hand on mine, pleading with me—to calm down, to listen.

"The next four years passed in a series of incidents where Roger made it apparent that I was his. I would do as he said, I would follow his lead, I would walk behind him, always have food available for him and his friends, and my body was his whenever he wanted it. I was so ashamed that I wasn't good enough. He told me I was too fat, too unattractive, too undesirable for anyone to want me. I didn't even tell my family. I withdrew from my friends. I let him isolate and control me.

"When my parents were both killed, I inherited their estate. It wasn't a great sum of money, but it was enough. That was two years ago. They left me a note with their will saying they knew something was wrong, but I was an adult, and they trusted me to make my own decisions. The estate was in a trust and if I chose it, Roger would never have to know about it. And that's what I chose. I bought my little car, and told Roger it was the only money they left, and I let the money sit.

"I got pregnant in November." She wraps her shaking arms around her middle as she says the words. A baby. "I naively thought it would fix things. That we could fix things. In February, I was thirteen weeks pregnant and ready to tell the world. I was going to have a little baby, someone for me to love, someone who would love me back." The tears flow more freely down her face, and my eyes fill. Fuck, I wish I could sew up the hole in her heart. No one deserves to feel this way. I try to reach out, but she doesn't accept it.

"Let me finish, okay? In February, I also found out he was cheating on me." God dammit, this man is the worst kind of human. Abusive, manipulative, and a cheat. I swear, if I knew where to find him, I would hunt him down. "When I confronted him, he blew up. I told him I was leaving."

Her tears have turned to sobs now, and she tries to talk though them but it's getting more difficult for her to weave sentences into coherency.

"As I tried to leave, he pushed me, and I-I-I fell down the stairs." Her baby. The sweet baby she wanted. A tear rolls down my cheek and I swipe it away. I haven't cried in, longer than I can remember, and now I cry for the sweet girl in front of me and the life she lost. "Anyway, after a short hospital stay, I put what I could in the car and left. I criss-crossed the country for a year before I landed in a ditch in Inspiration, Montana, and a grumpy not-cowboy gave me a blanket that smells like comfort and sandalwood."

I'm lost. This is so much bigger than me. Than us. Than Inspiration.

Reaching over, I grab her chair and pull it toward me. I bracket her knees with my own, our bodies facing each other.

Reaching up, I wipe away a few tears lingering on her face before holding her cheeks and pulling her to me. I kiss each of her eyelids, her nose, her slightly sweaty, damp cupid's bow before a gentle kiss on her lips.

"Caroline, I— My mom was like you. She married a difficult man and spent the rest of her life regretting it. She brought her baby into the world, she stayed. And it breaks my fucking heart to know you lived through the things I saw my mom live through. I would have killed my dad if the farm hadn't done it first." She stares at me, openly and with curiosity. "You were always good enough. You were too good for him. And you're too good for me."

"Duke, I'm not ready to give myself to someone again, completely. I have such strong feelings for you, already, but I'm not ready to face them yet. I want to meet people. Try things out. Decide what's right for me on my own schedule. I can't continue to see you just to hurt you. You deserve better than that. You deserve a woman who will give you their entire self, without reservation."

Standing, I bring her with me. Wrapping my arms around her, I look down into her face. "Caroline, it's okay. I know I'm intense and I shouldn't have put that on you, back at the bar. I want you to become the person you deserve to be, and I want to be a person who deserves you. Don't give up yet."

"I'm seeing someone else, Duke." The words land like a bullet to my chest. I drop my arms. It's like she has slapped me.

"What?"

"I've met someone else during my time here too. And I, well, I'm not ready to settle yet. I'm sorry." I back up. I know we haven't had any talks about the two of us, so it's selfish but I'm angry and jealous.

"You're choosing him? I thought, what we have, what we were creating...the stockroom." I can't even put what I'm feeling into words. The sex, the feeling of finally sinking into her; I thought she felt it too.

"I'm not choosing anyone, Duke. I'm choosing me. I'm choosing to figure it out. I want to casually date, find the right thing at the right time. It might be you, it might be him, it might be someone different, but I don't know."

The words sound so selfish but the honest way she says

them, the pleading look in her eyes, I know this is about more than just dating, especially after what she just told me.

"I'm sorry, Caroline. I don't think I can do this. I'm sorry." I turn and walk toward my stuff, sliding my feet into my boots and setting my hat on my head, the brim pulled low across my brow.

"No, I'm sorry, Duke. I just don't want you to get in any deeper with me. I don't want to hurt you."

It's too late for that.

Walking down the stairs, I hear her sobs grow louder. Closing the door behind me, I walk to my truck, my heart bleeding in my chest. I never deserved her anyway.

Driving around aimlessly for a while, I reflect, and it's well past time I did. This thing with Caroline was new, and exciting, but I wanted to fit her. I wanted to be enough. Indie messed me up so bad at the end, I never felt smaller or more insignificant than I did when Indie walked out. I met Indie when we were so young, and stupid. We didn't know who we were, or what we wanted. By the time we figured it out, we couldn't change what we were, or what we became. I want Indie to be happy in the path she's chosen. But it has been time for me to move on and decide what I want for a while now.

And I want Caroline. I don't know how to get or how to keep her. She's thirty-two years old. She has done things, experienced life, and is ready to decide for herself what she wants. We won't have to grow up together to figure out what we want —we can grow together, a life together. I don't spare any time considering who she might be with besides me. We are adults; I don't need to know.

My mind moves back to Roger. This coward of a man—who forced himself on his brand-new wife, who abused her, and killed their baby. Thinking about him makes me sick to my stomach. If I ever got my hands on him, I can't promise he would be safe from me.

Driving into Inspiration Cemetery, I navigate toward the row where I know I'll find 'Williams' engraved on the stones. Walking through generations of my family, I arrive in front of Phillip and Jennifer Williams. Phillip Williams, loving father, devoted husband. I roll my eyes. He doesn't even deserve to be in the ground next to my mother, much less to be called her devoted husband.

"You're a fucking coward, you old abusive drunk. I was so relieved when you died. I thought we would finally be free of you. But Mama spent her whole life under your thumb, and didn't even know how to be free. You've been a dark cloud over my life for thirty-seven years, and now your ghost is haunting me through the memories of the girl I think I'm in love with." I spit on the dirt below my feet.

Moving to the right a few steps, I sink to the ground.

Jennifer Williams

She stayed when it was hardest.

She loved when it wasn't easy.

And she gave me everything good in me

"Hey, Mama. God, I miss you so much. I need you today. I've needed you for a while now. I know you spent many nights hiding your fear from me and that once I got married, you were worried I was like him. You were too strong for your own good. You were too good for us. We never deserved your unconditional love, and I'm grateful every day." I bow my head, my tears dripping into the dirt.

"She's perfect, Ma. She's everything you wanted for me. But she had a man like Phillip, and she's a little lost. I want to be worthy of her. I want to earn her love, the way he never earned yours. I want to deserve it. I wish you were here to tell me what to do."

I sit in front of the granite stone until the air starts to cool and the sun begins its descent below the horizon. Standing, I brush my pants off and lay a hand on her name, rubbing it with my fingertips.

"I love you, Mama. I will be a better man, for you. For her."

Turning, I walk away, newly resolved to endeavor to earn her love.

Chapter 22
To Be With You

Cash

Callie has been radio silent since Sunday. It feels like something has changed, but I don't know what.

I texted her on Sunday night— 'I can still taste you on my tongue.' Nothing.

I texted her on Monday—'Want to grab lunch this week? Or you can come out to the ranch and see my buckles?' Still nothing.

By Tuesday, I'm starting to panic.

> Hurricane, did I do something? I thought, well, I thought it was perfect. Talk to me.

CALLIE

> No, you didn't do anything.

Then silence again.

Wednesday, I don't text her. I stop by Waylon's after work and Duke is behind the bar.

"Hey, Duke." I give him a smile; he doesn't return it. What the hell is wrong with everyone? Is there something in the water?

"What's wrong, man?" I ask him when he puts the beer in front of me.

"Nothing, just figuring shit out."

"Since when is being a grumpy asshole to me you 'figuring shit out'?" His eyes darken at my words and I have no idea where I mis-stepped, but clearly, I said something.

"I'm not grumpy, I'm just dealing with shit. Not everything is for you, Cash. Fuck!" He throws a beer bottle into the sink, causing it to shatter.

"Woah, what the fuck? You seriously just threw that bottle?"

Duke has always been hyper aware of his temper. His dad did a number on him, and he's worried someone will think he's like Phil.

He drops his head, swearing.

"Sorry. Women will really mess everything up. They just blow in like a storm and set your world on fire. Then, tell you they are talking to someone else. And it's fucking with my head. I just want—I don't know." He blows out a breath and pulls the tequila from the wall, throwing back a shot. Then another. "Do you think it's possible to keep seeing someone after they tell you they are talking to someone else? Like, be understanding that you're not the only one?" he asks me, looking desperate for help.

"Is she cheating on you?" I respond, already angry on his behalf.

He shakes his head. "No, we never even had a discussion about what we were or whatever. It's new, you know? We only hooked up once and it was like—" His eyes widen, almost to the point of it being funny. "I've never experienced anything like it.

But after, she changed. Then she told me it's because she can't give me all of herself. And she's trying to figure it out."

I think back to my hot dog date with Callie, and how I saw she has someone else in the wings. "I think you can. I think I am right now. I'm pretty sure Callie has at least one other guy she's talking to. We aren't serious or exclusive. I want more, but she isn't ready. So, I just continue to give her my all until she decides what she wants to do. She feels...worth it, I guess."

He nods affirmatively like he gets it. "Yeah, okay. I guess. Okay." The hurt in his face hurts me to see. The days and weeks after Indie left were the hardest time to be his best friend. And I saw him his whole childhood cover for his dad. Duke spent the better part of a month drunk. Sitting in the house or at the bar, drinking day and night. Sadie and I kept this place going while we waited. One day, he just showed up, sober, and decided it was time to get on with things. And at no point did he ever look as lost as he does right now.

"We'll both get through it. Like we always have, together." I reach my hand across the bar.

He takes it, clasping our hands. "Together."

We share a few beers before I head home, deciding tomorrow is the day I get something from Callie. I thought Sunday, in her bed, was a turning point for us. The necklace, the worship. I pray it wasn't just me.

Walking into Pete's, I know there's a chance I'll find Callie. I grab a flat cart and head over to the horse pellets and load up. As I'm throwing my third bag of feed on, I hear a laugh. A laugh I recognize.

Callie.

Leaning out of the aisle trying to find her, I hear her laugh again and it's the sweetest sound. My stomach drops at the thought of someone else bringing that laugh out of her and I decide to leave her alone, for now. Carrying on to the dog food, I add a bag to the cart before heading to the register.

"Cash?" Hearing her voice, I swivel my head, looking for the source and come face to face with the woman who visits my dreams every night. And she's just as cute as I remember with her little apron on. Her khaki-colored slacks stretch across her round ass, and I remember how it felt to grab a handful. I shift a little.

"Hey, Callie. Fancy meeting you here," I tell her with a smile and a wink.

She giggles and I feel like I'm floating.

That's my girl. She comes closer and wraps her arms around my stomach, squeezing before laying her head on my chest. I pause for a second before wrapping her in my arms. I lean down a little to whisper. "Hey, Hurricane. How's my girl?"

She pulls her head up, looks up at me, and smiles. It's not quite the same smile I got before, but she looks like she's trying. Just inside the collar of her black shirt, I see the glint of gold.

Sticking my finger into the opening, I pull the shirt away from her chest, just a little and look down, seeing my necklace nestled there. The thrill of it is enough for me to pull her close again and let her feel her effect on me.

She smacks my arm, laughing as she steps out of my hold. I reach down and adjust myself, taking the pressure off.

"Hurricane, I can't even explain what seeing that does to me."

"I can see what it does to you, Cowboy. So can everyone else," she snarks, raising a sassy brow.

"You could actually see it, if you would answer my texts," I scold her playfully, wrapping an arm around her as I try and steer my cart one-handed. I'm not successful, but thankfully she grabs a handle to help me push. I want so much more from her than I think she is able or willing to give but it doesn't mean I will stop fighting for it.

"Sorry, Cash. I was just working through some stuff, but I think I'm good now."

"Good," I whisper in her ear, breathing across it and making her shiver. "Because I really really want to slide inside you and feel you come around me," I say it with barely any sound, and she turns red from the top of her head all the way down until all the exposed skin I can see is bright pink. My cock twitches in anticipation of literally anything. I'm so tired of my hand, and so ready for Callie.

"Cash," she says my name as a breath, her breathing a little heavy.

"Yes, baby?" I ask her, trying to conceal a laugh.

"Go pay for your stuff. I get off at five, wanna stop by?"

"You get off at five? You'll be off again by 5:45. Bye, Hurricane!" I wave as I walk away, leaving her in the aisle, her mouth hanging open.

Chapter 23
No One Needs to Know Right Now

Callie

Despite Cash's jokes about when I get off work, we still haven't crossed the line yet. But things are starting to feel more serious. His smile, his light, are a constant presence in my life, and in my head. We had dinner at my little table Thursday night, sitting together comfortably while we ate Chinese food—beef and broccoli for the cattle rancher and sticky ribs for me— before lounging on the couch. Lying wrapped in his arms in the little bubble of safety I'm creating, that he's cultivating, things feel right.

But in the back of my mind, Duke's face hovers like a specter, the destroyed look in his eyes when I confessed, the anger when I told my story. Things are broken between us. The fact that he and Cash are best friends gnaws at me. If I don't fix things with Duke, his hurt may hurt Cash, or I may lose them both. I don't know how to fix it though. He hasn't texted, and I haven't either. I want things to settle before I try and bridge the gap—for the feelings to be less raw and ragged.

Cash has invited me to the first event of the season nearby, a small classic in Lewistown, and I'm over the moon excited about the prospect of seeing him in action, live. Before the rodeo though, he wants me to come out to the ranch.

Standing in the store on Friday, he says, "Come out tomorrow morning. I want to take you for a ride." I raise an eyebrow at him. "An actual ride. With me and Daisy," he says with a laugh. "I mean, we could do the other thing too..." he trails off.

"Really, Cash? I would love that! Yay!" I do a little dance around. I haven't ridden since I was a kid and the idea of riding out onto his beautiful land with my real-life cowboy makes me so excited. "What time? Like seven?"

"Well, I'm up with the sun every day so really anytime but don't you want to sleep in? It's Saturday." He grins widely at my enthusiasm.

"Oh, so like...eight? I could bring breakfast," I insist, bouncing on the balls of my feet.

"Sure thing, Hurricane." Kissing the top of my head, he heads out and I settle in for a long day, anticipating tomorrow with butterflies in my stomach.

A few hours later, I'm feeding baby chicks who have grown a lot in the last week, murmuring softly to them and rubbing their little downy feathers, when the bell dings over the door.

"Welcome to Pete's!" I yell in the general direction of whoever came in, but I get no reply. Dusting my hands off, I head to the register to make sure I'm not needed.

"You good, Matt?" I ask my coworker who stands behind the till. He has this small-town cutesy charm, like you see in movies. Not too far off from the way Cash acts, except, way more innocent. He's cute and a few of the town girls pop in to see him sometimes. He's younger, mid-twenties, I'd guess.

Brown curly hair piled in a bun on top of his head and steel grey eyes. His relaxed demeanor is disarming.

"Hey, yeah. Living the small-town dream, baby," he answers as he gives me a double thumbs up and a sarcastic smile. Laughter bursts from my lips.

Mirth still flowing between us, I look up and see my ghost turning the corner, a fifty-pound bag of dog food slung over his shoulder.

Duke approaches the counter, his body tense. As Matt rings his dog food in, I stand silently beside him. Duke watches us, his eyes narrowed, shifting between my face and Matt's like he's a detective on a case.

"Hey, Duke. How's life treating you?" Matt asks as he presses buttons and processes the sale.

"Fine," Duke snaps with open hostility.

Matt's eyes widen at the edges a little. Compared to Matt, Duke is an imposing figure. Muscular and a good bit taller, hat on his head pulled low and a giant bag of food over his shoulder. I understand Matt's reticence.

"Uh, okay." Matt rubs his neck awkwardly. "Here's your receipt. Have a good one."

Duke ignores him, gives me one more long look before spinning on his heel and heading out the door.

"I'll be right back, Matt." I chase Duke into the parking lot.

"Hey, Grumpy, wait!" I command him, trying to keep up with his longer legs. He doesn't slow and his shoulders are rigid. "Duke, please. Wait." The note of pleading in my voice must touch him because he stops finally.

"What is it, Caroline?" he asks me, his voice tired, defeated.

"What is it? Why were you so...so...*hostile* in there?"

"Is it Little Matthew Gates?" he questions, pained.

"Is who, Matt?"

"The guy, the other guy?"

Without even thinking of the consequences, I laugh, incredulous. Duke turns to walk away. I grab his arm to stop him, the laughter dying.

"Matt? No. He's like eight years younger than me. He's just my coworker. Maybe my friend but that's it. I don't even have his number." I can't believe he thinks that.

"Fuck, Caroline." He scrubs his hand over his face. "I'm sorry. This whole thing has me so on edge that every man I see feels like my competition, even men I don't think you even know. I'm not a jealous man. I'm just not." He shakes his head. "But you've brought out this possessive streak in me and I don't know how to deal with it. Maybe it is better we cool off."

He turns to his truck, throwing the food in the bed before I even have time to register it.

Saturday morning, I head over to Lizzie's early, hoping she's making breakfast. She has, by far, the best coffee in town.

"Lizzie?" I call out as I get into the B&B.

"Callie? In the dining room, hun." I see her sitting at the table, breakfast spread out and the smell of her magical, rich, and warm coffee permeating the air. Nothing in the world has ever made me feel as cozy and welcome as this house. "What're you doing here this early?"

"Heading out to Colter Ranch this morning." This draws a huge smile from her. "I wanted to bring breakfast and coffee and was hoping..." I trail off.

"Of course! Anything for you." She pours me a cup in a white mug before bustling off to the kitchen to get to-go cups and a bag for some food. Coming back loaded down, she sits. "Do you have a few minutes to chat? We can catch up."

"I do."

"Well, tell me everything that's happened since you moved. How's Cash? I haven't seen him much this week, since he isn't coming to see you." Her voice is playfully scolding.

"I'll tell him not to neglect you. Things are good. Going riding with Cash today, and to the Lewistown show tonight. Work is good." I don't want to confess all my dirty secrets, but I wish someone knew about Duke. I agonize over what to do and don't have anyone to talk to. The few people I've met are on opposite sides. Obviously, Duke and Cash, but Lizzie and Bud are team Cash, for sure. And Kayla and Sadie would be team Duke.

"There was something I wanted to ask you. Strictly between us girls." She winks at me. I still, waiting for whatever this is. I know Cash confessed his feelings to her. Is she going to try and intervene? "Small towns are—well they are their own thing and nothing stays hidden for long. I don't know how things are with you and Cash, but I do know that Jim Stark told his wife that he saw you at Waylon's last Saturday. In a heated conversation with Duke Williams. And that y'all," she pauses, seeming to search her brain for the right words, "disappeared for a while."

She stops talking and waits. Letting the words land how they land and waiting for me to decide how to respond to them. This feels like a grenade landed in my lap and I can't stop the explosion. I know Cash is her whole heart and I'm so afraid of alienating this woman. I'm scared also that I'm ruining everything I'm building in this town with this back and forth.

"I was and we did." I drop my head into my hands. "Lizzie, please don't hate me."

"Why would I hate you, Callie?"

Suddenly, in a flood of words that feel out of my control, I tell her the whole story. How Duke is the first person from

Inspiration I met. How Cash blew into the dining room the first morning and brought light and happiness to my world that has been missing. About falling for both of them because they are so different and each giving me something the other isn't, and how they complement each other. I spill out my secrets about Roger and how afraid I am of not being enough and how terrifying it is that I might hurt Duke, who has been through enough, or break Cash's heart, when he seems to have finally found something he is willing to work toward.

Spitting it all out gives me perspective on my feelings and it's something I sincerely needed. The feelings are cathartic and complicated, and I feel tears welling up.

"Callie." She reaches across the table, grabbing my hand. "We all have our own paths. I want to preface this by saying I had a few romances back in my day. Bud wasn't the first man to invite me to a dance or take me out horseback riding. And, when there are a few men vying for your attention, it's easy to get lost in it, and get confused. It's okay." She pats my hand, looking me in my eyes. "It's okay to not know what to do. It's even okay to love them both. You know, because you're a smart girl, that Cash cares about you. A lot. And seeing his heart broken would be awfully rough for all of us. He's a good boy, he's kind and considerate but if he's not right for you, you'll know.

"Duke, on the other hand, is intense, and thoughtful. What Indie did to him, the town is still mad about. When she left, we all picked sides. There was no neutral ground. They both grew up in this town, and we watched their love story unfold. Duke worked himself to the bone trying to make a life. He worked ranching for our family before his daddy died, saving all his money. He bought that bar and he worked day and night to give Indie everything she could dream of, but her dreams got bigger, and his world stayed the same. No one around here wants to see him hurt again. This is a delicate tightrope. I can't tell you what to do. You will know when it's time. But take care of you first, honey." Standing, she pours the coffees I asked for and holds them out. "And Callie, you're always welcome here and at this table. No matter what happens next."

I pull her in for a hug. I needed this today. Somehow, she knew. She knew I needed her, like she needed to say her part. I didn't need permission to love them both, it was too late anyway. But knowing someone else knows fills me with peace.

Knowing that *Jim Stark* is reporting my comings and goings at the bar to his gossiping wife though, that is not comforting. I'm going to have to air all my dirty laundry to these men who have come to mean the world to me soon or the universe will do it for me.

Chapter 24
Loved By a Cowboy

Cash

When I hear Callie's little car on the gravel outside the farmhouse, I stop my mindless pacing. The dogs have been circling me all day, trying to figure out why I insist on wearing a line in the rug. Shit, do I run outside or wait for her to knock?

Why, at thirty-four years old, have I decided to become an inexperienced teenager who has no clue what to do, I have no idea. I'll just go out on the porch and greet her. Yeah, that seems natural. Moving toward the door, the motion is interrupted by her tentative knock, the dogs' raucous barking following.

I throw the door open to find her standing there, bag in one hand, coffee in the other. I take her in, from thick blonde french braids, one on each shoulder, to the gold chain around her neck that makes me flush with pleasure, the oversized flannel unbuttoned with a tank top underneath, and a pair of tight, worn jeans. On her feet are a pair of cute, but not super practical, boots.

"Hey, Cowboy." She smirks at my perusal of her as she sweeps me from hatted head to sock covered feet.

"Hey, Hurricane." I pull her to me, her arms out to protect her breakfast and press my lips to hers. I lick her bottom lip before sucking it between my teeth and biting it. Leaning back, I see her pupils dilated, and a flush across her chest. "Come on, let's eat, so we can ride. I mean, unless you wanted to consider my other offer?"

"Shameless." She shakes her head as she kicks off her boots, handing me the coffees so she can put them on the shoe rack next to mine. Is it weird I made sure there was a spot for them, purely for the satisfaction of seeing them lined up next to mine? I decide it's not. She beelines directly for the table in the kitchen, putting the bag down before coming back and sitting on the floor, crossed-legged, so the dogs get a chance to jump all over her and get their love out before we eat.

I watch as Snapper circles her, debating on jumping on her back, and Tank lays down and puts his grey grizzled face in her lap, giving her hands a few licks.

"Alright, Snapper. Settle down, silly." She laughs at him as he bounces, grabbing his snout and kissing him. It's on the tip of my tongue to confess I love her. She's so comfortable here—happy even. She fits into this place like I built it for her. Standing, she wipes her butt off and goes into the kitchen to wash her hands before sitting.

She looks up at me, still standing, holding the coffee cups, a glazed smile on my face. "Cash, you want to sit? Or maybe bring some plates or something?" She laughs at me just standing there.

"Shit. Sorry, baby." I move to do the tasks I had neglected while I watched her starry-eyed, finally sitting next to her.

Watching her bounce along, seated on my mama's old grey mare, Violet, I smile. She was so excited to see the horses—I introduced her to everyone. Daisy, of course, remembered her and searched her for the peppermints I slipped in her pockets as we walked out of the house. Violet smelled, decided she would do, and accepted a long rub down her nose. When she got to Lola, she just leaned on the gate and watched the white horse reverently, some unidentifiable emotion on her face. Almost sorrowful.

"She's a sweet girl." I click my tongue, and she moves toward me, extending her head, looking for a treat. I pull an apple from my pocket, which causes Callie to laugh.

"Where are you keeping all this fruit?"

"This is Duke's girl. She's a great rider, but he was just here riding her, so I'm going to have you ride Violet today. She belongs to Ma but since she's not here to ride her, I rotate, to make sure everyone gets time." A thump against a stall at the back causes Callie's head to raise and she looks concerned. "That's just Charger. My dad's nasty old stallion. I'm the only one who can ride him except Dad. Come down, I'll show you but don't touch, he's nippy." I tickle her side as I tell her, pulling a giggle from her.

After a visit with the ornery Charger, I show her how to saddle the horses, how to connect the straps. She marvels at all the saddles hanging up. My dad's black one is custom fitted to Charger, the pink and white one with 'Violet' written in script on the side, and the soft red leather of Duke's. She runs her fingers over the branding of his name on the side.

Once we are all saddled, we set off, snacks and water slung across Daisy's back behind me.

"So, Callie, you decided to stay for a while. What are your thoughts on Inspiration?"

"Would you call me cheesy if I said it feels like a Hallmark movie setting? Like it can't possibly be a real place full of real people?"

"No, I feel that way sometimes. When I'm gone at the rodeos, I want to return to my little peaceful existence at home, where everyone is in everyone's business and I belong. But when I'm here for too long, I start to get restless, like it's too quiet, too simple. You know?" Suddenly, my little piece of paradise feels wilder and more unpredictable, and I know it's because Hurricane Callie blew in with a snowstorm.

"Yeah, I think I do." She sighs and looks out over the expanse of Montana wild spread out before us. "I think, when I imagine what home feels like, this is what it looks like. Open, welcoming, hopeful. There is life here, and peace. Yeah, I know what you mean, Cash."

My heart beats almost painfully in my chest, at her words. At her confessing her love for my place in the world, and even though she doesn't say it, I can almost hear the love she has for us too.

As our mounts walk side-by-side, swiping the occasional long piece of grass as we explore, Callie opens up. I stay quiet, giving her the space she needs to tell me whatever she wants. I listen intently, wanting to absorb everything I can about this woman.

She tells me long stories about skipping high school classes to put her bikini on and go to the beach with her friends, dates with her high school boyfriend to a restaurant that only sells barbecued pulled pork, and preparing for hurricanes in the fall as they surge up the coast from the warm Caribbean. Experiences I've never had here in Montana.

In exchange, I tell her about throwing parties out in the

fields, a ring of pickup trucks giving us the light and music we need for our bonfires. Camping trips out into the wilderness where we attempt to avoid animals that might eat us while secretly hoping to return with a cool story. Summers spent hunting waterfalls and taking dates to Colter Falls, thinking it's so clever. And winters tobogganing and warming ourselves by roaring fires.

We find common ground in laughter and memories.

"So, Ashley Colter, rodeo king, why have you not ever found yourself a rodeo queen?" I watch her from the side, looking at her profile as she looks ahead before looking over at me and flashing a smirk.

"Honestly?" Here goes nothing. "When I started riding, I was a senior in high school, freshly seventeen, and I got popular, fast. You can't be a professional rider until you're eighteen. They wanted me on the circuit, out winning. Sponsors wanted me, but women did too. I wasn't even hardly old enough to be looking at some of these women. I think there may have even been a countdown to my birthday, at some point." By both rodeo organizers and women. "I was having the time of my life. Once I graduated and turned eighteen, I joined professional organizations and started touring. There were parties, and women available all the time. The better I got, the better it got." I reflect on those years in my twenties when I was with a different woman every night some weeks. Sometimes they were in their twenties and sometimes they were old enough to be my mother. "I learned a lot of new skills, quickly." I give her a side-eye and she laughs.

"Yeah, I think I came face-to-face with one or two, last week."

"You definitely came. And…my face was there."

She giggles, almost embarrassingly, but with giddiness under it.

"Anyway, this went on for my twenties and women threw themselves at me, but it was all superficial. They weren't actually interested in Cash, just in Ashley, and the thrill of the bull rider. By the time I got to my thirties, a lot of the thrill of the women and such had worn off, and I just wanted to be at home on the ranch. And by then, the hometown prospects had been snatched up by men who didn't spend their twenties bed hopping." I shrug. "No one has really ever interested me before now," I confess. The words hang heavy in the air, the implication clear.

"What about you? I don't need quite as involved a retelling of your love life, but you know, has there been anyone serious?" I ask her, wanting to know more about her before she turned up here. I watch her mood instantly shift, the air around us seeming to alter in a way I don't know how to explain—or even understand. "What is it?"

"There was someone serious. Something very serious."

I immediately feel nauseous. This is the dark cloud that always seems to linger just outside of grasp when it comes to Callie. The thing she has kept close to her chest, letting the pain radiate out every once in a while, but never fully revealing. I prepare myself. I know this is going to be heavy.

For the next fifteen minutes, as we navigate the fields and pastures, Callie tells me about Roger. About how in love they were, and how he love-bombed the shit out of her before turning on her the minute she said, 'I do.' She gives me a story that makes me want to stop and throw up in the bushes, before ending it with a lost baby and a trip across the country. Landing her here, where I have tried to convince her to love me, not knowing she's trying to heal her own heart.

Her need to explore, and expand her wings, be on her own, and casually date makes a lot more sense. The feelings of inadequacy that seem to mirror my own are a lot clearer now, too. I can't rush her or possess her. She needs to come to me, when she's ready.

Pulling Daisy to a stop next to a creek, I dismount and drag Callie down from Violet. Patting both horses on their rumps, they wander over and drink. Grabbing the pack I have on the back of Daisy, I open it up and pull out a blanket, neither of us saying a word. Spreading it out, I set out some waters and snacks, sitting down and patting the spot beside me. We sit quietly for a few minutes, just the soft sounds of horses and the rushing of the creek offering the music of nature, of my home.

"Say something," she begs of me.

I want to say the right thing. I want to soothe the rough edges left by someone else. I also, kind of, want to kill a man I've never met and wouldn't recognize on the street.

"Would it be too much if I tell you I would like to maim, possibly kill, Roger?" This elicits a laugh that lightens the mood slightly.

"No, I get it. I feel that way sometimes. And other times, I'm just grateful I'm sitting here, with you. But I'm also terrified. I thought, well, I believed, he was good."

"Callie, before this goes any further, I need you to know. I couldn't ever do anything to hurt you, you are safe with me. Duke lived through a life with a man like Roger and I saw what it did to him. I couldn't ever. Even if this doesn't work out, you will always be safe with me." I wrap my arm around her shoulder, and she lays her head against me. I kiss the top of it, and we sit silently for a while, just listening to the symphony of the ranch.

Chapter 25
Save a Horse (Ride a Cowboy)

Callie

Sitting beside Cash in this perfect space he has carved out for us, by the river, feels like a dream. If you asked me what I could have if I could have anything, it would feel like this. I wouldn't have been able to put this into words, but the two horses munching on their grass, tails swishing, the rushing creek with its tiny tadpoles and dragonflies, the birds chirping in the little copse of trees, this is what I would want.

Something Cash is giving me. Every day feels more right with him. He fits into my soul in a way I didn't know was possible. I didn't have to create space for him, it was there all along. I just thought it was a hole and that I was broken.

Deciding to act on impulse and not overthink, I swing my leg across his lap, straddling him, where he leans back, his weight balanced on his arms behind him. He looks at me in surprise a second before he sits up, his abdominal muscles flexing, and grabs the abandoned pack, bunching it under his head like a makeshift pillow. Placing his hands on my hips, he smiles.

"Well, hey, baby," he says, looking up at me.

"Hey, Cowboy." Leaning down, I kiss him and his arms loop around me, crushing me to his chest as he kisses me slow and deep. Not urgent or demanding but with so much feeling it reverberates through me. I feel his hips move a little below me, not pushing into me, just moving a little, like he needs an outlet for his energy.

Holding me tightly, he flips us over so he's hovering above me, his hips nestled against my thighs. Rubbing my face softly, he rests his other hand against my neck as he holds himself up with an elbow.

He kisses me softly before hovering above me once more and says, "God, you're so beautiful. It's like He captured the sky and pulled it down for me to hold in my arms." He lowers his head, kissing my neck, all over. Pushing my head back slightly, he kisses everywhere his mouth can reach, covering most of my exposed skin with his wet kiss. He gently pushes his hard cock against me, like he's testing my receptiveness.

Wrapping my legs around his hips, I pull him harder into me, rolling my hips until we are rubbing in all the correct places. He lets out a strangled whimper. It melts me.

"Okay, listen, darlin'. I'm not saying I'm not picking up the signals you're sending," he places a kiss on my pulse point, sucking the blood to the surface, "because I fucking am. I definitely am." Another kiss, another suck. I think for a second I might have a hickey, like a teenager, and giggle. "But we haven't talked about this step yet, so while I sit here, in this delicious, warm spot, we are going to take a minute to discuss."

I nod, waiting for his words. He reaches back and pulls his shirt over his head, giving me a delightful eyeful. His chest is muscular, the occasional muscle stacked on muscle, and I feel myself blush. Following the hard lines of his pecs, I caress them and lift an eyebrow, wondering how I never noticed this before.

He chuckles at my face as I study the tiny barbells that pierce each nipple. I tilt my head slightly before he leans down and whispers against my mouth, "It will get more interesting before it gets less, Hurricane."

I continue to rub my hands across the newly exposed flesh, his skin tan and smelling like the sun.

"Now, I believe I have you sufficiently interested and distracted." He winks cheekily before putting a row of kisses across my jaw. "Remember when I knelt in front of you and told you that was the time you would get sweet Cash?"

I nod my head.

"Good girl." A kiss lands on my nose. "I like things a little...rougher. I won't hurt you, unless you decide that's something you're interested in, but I'm not a gentle man when it comes to this. So, I need to know what you're okay with and not, okay?"

Suddenly nervous, I nod again, my mouth dry.

"Say it, baby."

"Yes," I whisper.

"That's my girl. So, first, have you done anything before that you particularly liked?"

"I liked you on your knees in my bedroom?"

He chuckles again. "Not with me, before."

I shake my head no. "Sex with Roger was...plain? Sort of the same every time. Missionary or from behind. I didn't have an orgasm, and he went to sleep."

The face he makes in response is funny, and I giggle nervously.

"Okay, how would you feel about this?" He puts his hand lightly against my throat and gently squeezes. I feel the immediate response in my panties. I nod.

"And this?" He adds a little more pressure while gripping

my breast, hard, bucking his hips against me, his cock straining against his zipper.

I gasp, then moan. He nods for me.

Snaking his hand under my tank top, he grabs my naked breast, and barely pinches my nipple, only applying the slightest pressure, sending a tingle across my body and goosebumps cover me. I nod enthusiastically before gasping out a half strangled, "Yes."

He exhales a labored breath.

"One last question, and I will get you out of these clothes, okay darlin'?" I watch him, wide eyed. He leans in closer, closer, slowly, so agonizingly slow, "How do you feel about"—his lips tip up in one corner and anticipation in this second builds to an almost painful level—"spitting?"

I almost combust under him at the meaning behind his words, his sexy confident swagger in the way he is pushing me to the edge, and I haven't even removed so much as a boot. But I see a little bit of fear in his eyes.

"I-I don't know."

"Okay, we can work on it. You're doing so well, baby. So perfect."

His movements become more deliberate as he studies me. He reaches into his pocket and pulls out a condom, dropping it on the blanket beside me.

"A boy scout, I see," I rib him gently, though it comes out breathy and strained.

"Always prepared." He winks at me. Lifting my foot, he removes my boot then repeats it on the other side. Reaching up, he unbuttons my jeans, lifting my hips with the movement to slide them down, leaving me lying in my panties and socks. He runs a reverent finger over my soaked panties and gives a pleased grunt in this throat.

Pulling me up slightly, he peels my shirt off me before

removing my tank top. I'm braless and his eyes widen once I'm fully exposed, just his gold chain hanging down my chest. He kisses the chain before moving to a nipple.

"Wait, biting?" He looks at me questioningly, and I give an affirmative nod. He nods back before setting about his work, sucking a nipple into his mouth. I feel his teeth close around it at the same time his fingers close around the other one. He tightens down at the same time and a gasp escapes my lips and my back bows, forcing more of my breast into his mouth, and I feel him smile against me.

"So perfect," he whispers against my skin. "I fucking knew it."

Grabbing my panties at the hips, he slides them down my legs, staring at my exposed pussy.

"So wet for me already. I love it." He dips a finger into me, running a fingertip across my clit before sliding just the tip into me, making me twitch. He sticks the finger in his mouth, licking it before he brings it back and puts it in again. This time, he holds his hand up so I can see the slick wetness coating his finger before he brings it to my mouth. He lifts an eyebrow in question, and I open.

He moves it between my lips and rubs it across my tongue, making me taste myself.

"You taste like goddamned heaven."

Standing, he pulls his buckle loose and unbuttons his jeans, pushing them down his legs before he removes boots and jeans, setting them aside. He's standing before me, a cowboy god, in tight black boxer briefs, and black crew socks. His thighs are strong with cut muscles, from the bulls. His abs are deeply defined, and a perfect V leads into his low-slung boxers, blond hair covering the center and leading into the fabric. He stands there and lets me look for as long as I want, his hand palming his hard cock. My breathing is labored, and when I finally move my eyes back to his, I can see his blown pupils, the lust raw in his gaze. He sticks his thumbs in his waistband before pushing his boxers down and kicking them off.

I trail my eyes down, absorbing the tense set of his muscles as he waits before my eyes land on his dick, hanging heavy between his thighs, bobbing slightly as he breathes hard. Just running through the tip is another metal stud, like the ones in his nipples and a tiny bead of liquid. When I see it, my eyes whip to his, and the laughter in them is enough to cause me to cover my face, blushing furiously.

"You seem so nice," I spit out from behind my embarrassed hands. This earns me a full laugh that makes his abs clench and his cock bounce.

Kneeling, he says, "I am nice, baby. Most of the time." Picking up the condom, he places it just below where he kneels, easy reach I guess, and adjusts himself so he's seated between my thighs. "We will go slow, but I promise you'll love it, especially in certain positions." His erection is commanding and distracts me where he kneels, seeming impossibly large now that it's close to me. Goosebumps break out on my skin as a cool breeze blows across us in our little bubble of solitude next to the river.

Running his thumb through my flesh, he rubs hard circles around my clit before pinching it slightly. I'm already panting and he watches every moan, every movement. Rubbing a little harder, then a little slower, then a pinch, then harder again, studying me, gathering information. Leaning forward between my thighs, he looks up at me, making eye contact across my body, his jaw works and a little bit of saliva drips down his chin and drops onto my pubic bone, and I swear it's the hottest thing I have ever seen in my life.

I try to grab him, to bring him to me, to force him to go faster but he doesn't let me win.

"Please, Cash, please. Fuck me. I want to come," I mewl, sounding desperate.

"I don't have to fuck you to make you come, Hurricane." He inhales deeply and smears the spit across my clit before beginning to rub it exactly the way I want him to, as though I showed him myself what I like.

I guess that's what all the studying was for. Hooking two fingers inside me while his thumb circles, he rubs behind my pubic bone until he hits a spot sending fireworks through me, stars exploding behind my eyes, back bowing. He lets out a satisfied whine before pressing down on my stomach from the other side, pressing from both sides. I pant, I keen, I yell, I moan, and I lose control. My thighs begin shaking as the man kneeling between them watches me, happiness written in every line of his body.

"I'm—I have to—Cash I don't—" Then I fall. I dive head-first off a cliff as I hear a moan, and I realize I'm lying in a puddle. A large puddle. The shockwaves of my orgasm continue to shudder through me as I register the embarrass-ment of what happened.

"Cash, I'm sorry, I didn't mean to." I look at him, his hand dripping, his lap wet. "Oh God." I cover my face. My cheeks are flaming, the blood hot under my skin.

His hands pull my arms away. "Hurricane, you think for one second that wasn't the hottest fucking thing? That's exactly what I was trying to do. I wanted to see if you could, and you did. You're so perfect, baby, I can't even explain it."

Laying on top of me, he kisses me deeply, nestled between my legs, his cock pressing against me. If I shift, just slightly, he will slip inside of me, where I am begging him to be. So, I do. As soon as his head slides inside, he hisses through his teeth and throws his head back.

"Baby, don't move, please. Let me just feel you against me,

for a second. *Fuck.*" He shakes a little with the effort. Sitting back up, he slips out of me. I watch, rapt, as he strokes himself a few times, the curved bar through the tip of his cock glinting in the sun. Picking up the foil packet, he tears it open, slipping it over his head and rolling it down. "You ready?"

"Yes, Cash. I'm ready." I can barely breathe before he shoves inside me, all the way to his pelvic bone. He is completely seated inside me in one smooth movement and my breath whooshes out of me. I wince at the intrusion and the fullness, and he doesn't move, his neck muscles straining and his arms shaking.

"You okay?" he asks, peering at me through his lashes, his breathing labored and panting.

"Yes."

"I'm going to move now." He begins to pound into me, forcing through all my resistance and barriers, both my body and my heart. His face red with concentration, the sweat I feel gathering in the ditch of his spine is slippery in the sun beating down. I'm enraptured by the way he just has his hand laying possessively on my neck, as he fills me over and over. He kisses and bites everywhere. I'm fairly certain there will be bruises and hickeys peppering my neck and breasts later.

Leaning up, he grips my hips in a punishing hold, fucking me hard and fast before slowing down and rubbing my clit softly, teasingly, before repeating his rough, hard thrusts. Then soft and slow. Then hard and fast. I'm overwhelmed by the sensations flooding me.

Spreading his thighs so mine are laying on them, he lifts me until I'm almost in his lap. He places one hand on my hip and the other flat on my stomach and we move slowly together, as he increases the pressure harder and harder until I can feel what he's doing. He's pressing against himself moving inside me. Pressing that secret spot inside me against the ridge of his cock, over and over, as his barbell slides against the sensitive skin.

Moaning, I fist the blanket as he sets a consistent pace. My moans grow until I am just panting, my mouth open, no sound left. It builds and builds, low in my belly, as he pushes and thrusts, pushes and thrusts. I feel pressure and the pleasure begins to flow through me like pulsing energy until he pushes me over the edge, and I come all over him. Both of us are completely soaked, covered in me.

He has the most ethereal look of complete happiness and gratification on his face. He pulls out of me, making me whimper, grabs my hips and flips me onto my stomach, pulling my hips up.

"Fuck, baby, look at this ass," he tells me as he bites me hard, causing me to cry out. He follows it with a chuckle before he slams into me again, pushing me forward, his strong hands holding onto me so I don't fall. He fucks me hard, his piercing rubbing over and over against the front wall of my pussy, the slick wetness making us slippery, sweat clinging to us. I bow my back and pant as he thrusts, his movements erratic and unsteady, his breathing labored.

One hand holds my hip, the other grabbing the back of my neck. He presses me down onto the blanket, his hand keeping me in place. Holding me tight, he slams into me, pressing so hard into me I feel him everywhere. I cry out in pleasure, coming around him, my muscles spasming as he shutters against my back, fucking me roughly. My body is trapped between him and the blanket, before he falls across my back, moaning out a long 'fuck' and digging his teeth into my shoulder.

We lay there for a few minutes, his arms around me, our breathing adding to the music of the day. The horses have wandered a bit from us but not far enough they are out of sight.

"Want to rinse off in the creek? It'll be cold but..." he trails off, moving off of me.

"Sure," I say as I stand. I want to cover myself now that things aren't sexual.

"Don't," he commands as if he can read my mind. "If you want to cover up because you're cold, or even shy, then go ahead. But don't do it because you think I don't want to see you. If it was up to me, I would keep you naked and wanting, every minute of the day." He pulls me against him and kisses my head before lightly smacking my ass.

"We will get to spanking, next time." Looking up at the sun, he sighs. "Shit, Hurricane, we gotta get back. I need to shower and get to the arena. Not that I don't want to bring your smell with me all day," I crinkle my nose, and he laughs, "but the bulls would not respond well."

Chapter 26
My Best Friend's Girl

Duke

Pushing my black hat on my head, I fix my shirt, making sure it's even. I adjust my buckle; it's a dress piece with DW engraved on it, with a little silver version of Lola, that Cash got me a few years ago for Christmas. Reaching down, I rearrange my pants until they are sitting right on my boots. Spraying on a little of my sandalwood cologne, I walk into the main part of the house, reaching down to rub Dolly between her ears, and I whistle for Hank.

I fill their bowls with their food, grab my keys, and walk to my truck. I take my hat off, ruffling my hair and set it on the seat next to me. I look over at the empty passenger seat and imagine a green-eyed girl gazing back, strawberries and vanilla filling the cab with her warmth, her sun.

I haven't been to the rodeo in a while, but I need the break tonight. I want to fix things with her, but I want her to have space too. Take a pause, let both of us breathe, and decide if this is the right thing. Riding past the *Welcome to Inspiration* sign, I head west toward Lewistown. I can't wait to see Cash on the bull. He's a showman, incredibly talented, and always captures the attention of whoever watches.

He wants me to meet Callie tonight, and I know how much it means to him. He's genuinely serious about this girl, with an intensity and focus usually reserved for me. We have always balanced each other well. Him, bright and sunny, easy going, roll-with-it and me, dark and stormy, intense, stubborn. We work well this way.

In twenty years, we've never needed to fight over women. He always attracted a different sort of woman than me. Now I'm so happy he is finally finding someone who is feeding his needs; his need for honest affection and understanding of who he really is, even if it's happening at the same time I try to stop falling for Caroline.

Pulling in the lot for the arena, I park my truck in a spot in a long row of pickup trucks. Climbing out, I place my hat on my head, adjust my shirt, and walk toward the check-in tent. Cash always puts me on the VIP list when I tell him I'm coming—better seats and usually access to the riders' tent. Checked in, lanyard around my neck, I set off in search of a drink and a place to sit.

I got here late. I didn't care much for the other events, though I see on the leaderboard Cash placed second in calf roping. Riding is next so I head to my seat and wait. Cash is riding third, just behind Miles Wilkes. By the time his scores are up, he'll know whether he beat him or not. The energy in the arena is reaching a fever pitch, boots stomping and hats waving as people try to get the bulls excited. The first rider pulls an eighty-seven, not a great showing. Miles and Steeler emerge from the chute and it's a rodeo ballet the way they move together. He's masterful at his craft and it's easy to see why he's dethroning Cash in city after city. Not every show, not every time, but enough that the crowd is on their feet.

When he dismounts and the score shows ninety-three, a huge cheer erupts from the crowd.

"Shit." That's a damn hard score to beat.

Cash is in the chute now, the beast under him doing his best to unseat his rider even behind the gate. The announcer does his spiel, calling out 'Ashley Colter,' and the crowd roars louder. I watch Cash; he dips his chin and adjusts the tail, rubbing the rope to warm the rosin. The gate swings open.

Bombardier shoots through the gate, repeatedly kicking his rear legs out. Cash flies forward over and over again, his arm flung in the air, his helmet making him look a bit bobble head-like. Bombardier takes three or four leaps, completely off the ground, tossing Cash around like a ragdoll. Cash, for his part, leans forward and back in time almost perfectly with the bull. I can see how tightly his thighs grip as he tries to keep his seat the full eight seconds.

A horn finally blares through the arena, and the pickup men run forward, dragging Cash down and away as the barrelmen dance and run to distract the bull. Cash climbs over the gate and he's free. Standing, I head to the riders' tent behind the chutes. I saw what I came to see so I want to meet Cash and Callie.

"You dirty little buckle bunny. You think Ashley would ever seriously want some overweight, hanger-on, pretender who isn't even from around here? You don't know shit about him! I've been around here for years."

I hear a woman yelling as I move toward the flap covering the tent opening.

"I don't think anything. I don't even know what you're talking about." *Caroline?* That's definitely Caroline.

"Whatever, fat slut. Why does he call you Hurricane,

anyway? Because you swallow everything down including the dinner table?"

I can see Caroline from behind, her head hanging down. She's got on tight jeans and her brown boots. Double braids trail down her back, and there's a cute white hat on her head. She's wearing a t-shirt, but I can't see if it says anything from this angle. She looks more beautiful, and appropriate, than the woman yelling at her who wears white short shorts, white boots, and a white hat covered in jewels, a pink shirt tied up at her waist. She has an equally sour-faced comrade beside her, sneering at Caroline.

Coming up and standing just behind her shoulder, I give both women a dirty look. "What's going on, ladies? Isn't this the riders' tent? Where are your lanyards?" I hold mine up for them to see. Caroline spins around, her jaw dropped.

"Who the hell are you? You're not security," the one in white snaps at me. They both look at me, stubbornly but also unsure.

"I'm here to make sure you're not harassing people who are supposed to be here. Security!" I call out, and they rush over. "Please escort these—what did they call you, sweetheart?"

She mumbles, "Buckle bunny."

"Yeah, these *buckle bunnies* out of here." Once they've been removed, I stare at Caroline. The realization of what just happened, and what *is* happening, hits me like a lead ball through the gut.

"Hurricane?" I ask her and she nods her head, slowly. A little frightened but I don't think of me. More, of the situation she has found herself in. "Are you Callie?" Again, she nods.

"Caroline, you've got, maybe, thirty seconds before Cash comes through that door. Start talking, please."

"Callie is my nickname. I'm sorry, Duke. I didn't—"

"Hurricane!" I hear Cash's exclamation as he bursts

through the door. Rushing to her, he sweeps her up in his arms and pulls her in for a kiss. A comfortable, sweet, I-could-do-this-for-the-rest-of-my-life type of kiss. A familiar kiss. "Oh, Duke, what's up man?" He holds out his hand which I accept, never taking my eyes off Caroline, or Callie. Or whoever-the-fuck she is. "You met Callie?"

"Yep. Sure did," I say, my eyes locked with hers. The fear is there again.

"Cool. Come on, darlin', I gotta accept my buckle and I wanted you to stand with me. I'll be back, Duke," he tells me, beginning to pull her to the tent opening.

"See ya, Caroline." I wave, a little half-heartedly.

Cash stops in his tracks and turns his head, looking at me curiously, before looking at Caroline. He volleys back and forth a few times before he continues to pull her out, a little less enthusiastically.

I turn on a heel and march out of the tent, directly out of the gates, and to my truck. Getting in, I slam the door behind me and slam my hand, hard, down onto the console, creating a large crack.

"Fuck!" I scream before ripping out of my parking space and heading back toward town. Tears stain my cheeks as I drive, fury filling my chest. I can't tell where the destruction to my heart ends and the anger begins. I have never been so thoroughly consumed before. I told Sadie to expect me after the show, but I can't tonight, I just can't. Slamming my truck into park in front of the house, I storm through the door and out into the gym I built in a shed. I strip off my hat and shirt as I walk.

Roaring through the door, I slam my fists into the heavy bag hanging in the corner. And I slam and slam and slam until I feel blood dripping onto the floor. Bending over, I put my bleeding hands on my knees, sucking in labored breaths. I thought I knew what a broken heart felt like, but I was wrong. *So fucking wrong.*

I head back in the house, towels wrapped around both hands and stick them in the sink, turning on the water. I hiss at the pain and it's still nothing compared to the giant hole that has appeared in my chest. I grab a bottle of whiskey from my liquor cabinet, throwing the unopened bottle of Walton's I bought for her into the fireplace—it explodes in a shower of glass and alcohol. The dogs both yelp and retreat to another part of the house to hide from my rage.

I feel bad, but not enough to calm down.

Opening the Jack, I pour it directly into my mouth, and swallow huge gulps. Shaking, I set the bottle down. I stare at it, breathing heavily, trying to wrap my head around the last hour and what has gone so horribly wrong.

Did he know? Cash wouldn't do this to me. He knew how much I was starting to care about Caroline; he wouldn't have done this on purpose.

She knew though. She knew Cash was my best friend, my oldest friend. She knew because I told her myself. She played me, she played both of us for lovesick fools.

I was falling in love with her and the person I was falling for, I'm not even sure she exists. I can't even lie to myself. I wasn't *falling* in love with my best friend's girl. I am wholly and completely so in love with her to the point that right now, I can't breathe around the pain.

Feeling the whiskey starting to warm my veins and blur my thoughts, I lay down on the couch and let the storm take me away.

Hurricane, indeed.

Chapter 27
The Less I Know, the Better

Cash

"See ya, Caroline," I hear Duke call as I pull Callie through the tent back toward the arena.

Caroline? I stop walking and turn toward him. I take in the utter devastation on his face and his hand raised in a really sad imitation of a wave. I look to Callie and see the brokenness mirrored there. I look between them for a few moments before the announcer calls out my name and I turn and continue through the door, pulling Callie behind me. I swear in those twenty steps or so, I can actually hear my heart breaking.

"Cash?" she whispers as we walk but I don't acknowledge her. As soon as we are in the arena, I plaster a smile on my face. It's my costume to hide the absolute nuclear bomb that just landed in the tent.

"And who is this, Ashley?" the announcer asks, trying to make this look like anything resembling a normal interview.

"Oh, this is Car-Callie. My Hurricane." I stare into the

camera. "She swept in overnight and destroyed everything." I take the buckle and turn and walk back to where I came from.

Walking through the tents and out into the night air, I can hear the soft steps of Callie behind me. We rode together so I have to take her home. The last place I want to be is trapped in my truck with her though.

Climbing up, I place both hands on the wheel, facing forward while she gets in. I don't look at her. I don't speak to her. I turn the engine over and begin the drive back to Inspiration. The only place I have ever felt at home now feels like a war zone. We ride in silence, not even breathing loudly. Pulling up to her door at Pete's, I put the truck in park and stare ahead, hands on the wheel. I'm pissed, like well and truly pissed, but I don't for one second want Callie to be afraid of me.

"I'm sorry," is all she says as she removes her seatbelt, opening her door to climb out.

"He's my best friend, Callie," I say in return. When the door shuts behind her, I see her necklace laying on the seat.

The moment I gave it to her was the moment everything changed for me. I thought she was it. The woman I could hold onto. Wake up next to. Raise a family with or have a thousand farm animals if she wanted that instead.

I feel the tears prickling my eyes as I retreat into myself. I thought it was finally my time to claim a real piece of happiness. Every interaction, every event feels fake, like I was being manipulated.

Arriving back at the ranch, I walk in and hug my dogs, letting my tears dampen their fur and imagine I can still smell her on them from this morning. Only this morning, my dream girl sat in my kitchen. Now, I am alone, being swallowed by what could have been. My dream became a nightmare faster than I can even digest. I give myself time to grieve, to wallow. I collapse into myself for a few moments, flinching away from the thoughts flying at me at a thousand miles an hour.

Now, a million small things jump out at me. Her about-face last Saturday when I called after she watched the rodeo at Waylon's. Her wistful look when she met Lola, rubbing her fingers over Duke's name branded on his saddle. How sad she was the same days Duke was. It's all pieces of a puzzle I was too blind, or too unwilling, to put together. The chances of us both meeting the perfect girl, days apart, who happens to not be from around here? We were both so blinded by her that we didn't see the signs right in front of us.

She never told me who she was talking to, but she did tell me she was seeing someone else. I can't hold it against her. I thought we were building something real. Something worthy. But I can hold it against her that we had a dozen conversations where I talked about Duke. I told her about him and Indie, about our childhoods, and she never even indicated she had ever heard his name before much less that she was intimately familiar with him.

The pain slices through my chest. The fear, the anger.

Pulling my phone from my pocket, I see I have no notifications. I open my thread with Callie and scroll back, smiling sadly at the laughter we shared, the jokes. How a curious flirtation had transformed into something real.

Switching to my chats with Duke, they are short, to the point, the way my best friend often is. Mostly just texts about coordinating events, when to come or go. Scores from Rodeos and hockey games. The sum total of over thirty years of friendship.

I've never competed with Duke for anything; we've always had different interests. We liked different women and did different things but always stood side by side when it mattered. He is the cloudy sky to my sunshine, and we have always balanced each other. I refuse to let a month-long romance, no matter how sure I am that I've already fallen in love with her, come between us.

> Duke, we need to talk.

A few hours later, I've had half a dozen beers and almost as many swigs of whiskey from the bottle I keep in the back of the cabinet and my head swims. Drunk texts are never the answer, but I don't want to leave the door open. Opening the Callie texts I type, "We're over," and delete; "I can't believe this," and delete; "I love you, but I can't do this," and delete.

Finally, I settle on—

> Caroline. Callie. Whoever. This is it.

Sending my text off into wherever it is that texts go, I drag myself upstairs. I shower quickly before lying on my back, spread eagle, and beg for the pain to go away before the ceiling spinning lulls me to sleep.

Rolling over in the morning after something disturbed my sleep, I glance at the sun and realize it's well after midmorning and I haven't slept this late in years. My next thought is of a beautiful green-eyed girl sitting on a horse, walking beside me, forever. I think these peaceful thoughts, a smile on my face, until the truth of my life slams back in and I groan, dragging myself up. My head pounds, and I cup my face in my hands.

Today, I walk into the world after the hurricane.

Chapter 28
And the Healing has Begun

Callie

I have screwed things up so incredibly royally that I'm almost afraid to leave my house, that I have to come face to face with what it looks like.

Hours where I sulk in bed, avoiding the world, turn into days. After work, I pour my own Walton's and ginger and drink until sleep overtakes me; that turns to weeks—where instead of being surrounded by new love, I nurture myself and learn to love me.

The sweet sunny end of May becomes the warmth of June and then July. July, as the sun is high above me, under the giant blue sky of the Montana plains, I decide for this to be the last time I allow my self-imposed heartbreak to break me further.

I walked out, I left Roger, I took my autonomy and myself back. I rebuilt myself into the image of the woman I thought I should be. I was funny, relaxed, and engaging. I fell for two men who wrapped me up in their love—Duke's like a raging wildfire searing my soul, tumultuous, passionate, Cash's like a warm blanket, and finally coming home. Inspiration fed my soul with its welcome, it's kind people and slow lifestyle. I immediately fell into and became one with them.

By the end of June, it stopped tearing my chest out when I saw Cash's truck, a second shadow in the passenger seat. I tried to stop the tears and the frustration. I have no one to be mad at but myself and I have punished myself enough.

By the beginning of July, it didn't crack my soul open when Sadie mentioned at dinner that Duke has been taking more nights off than usual but didn't specify why, but she suspects he finally met someone. While the hole in my heart wishes I was bringing Duke joy, it is filled a little with the knowledge that maybe he is finally healing himself. I finally return to Mable's, knowing it's the place where I sat with Cash and had lunch the first week. I sit at a booth and avoid letting my gaze slide to the barstools where we sat and laughed. I go to visit Lizzie and stay for breakfast. We dance around the subject of her nephew, who she loves like her own child, knowing we are all healing from the gaping wound of the sweet month of May.

That late spring month where we made love by the creek, and I discovered what it feels like to be cherished and wanted. The month where I sat perched on a table in a stockroom while the grumpiest bartender in Montana held his hand over my mouth and poured his love into me.

I learned a lot about myself, about what being alone could do for me that summer. I hiked into the mountains and hills. I hunted for waterfalls, the way Cash mentioned doing. I visited Colter Falls and laughed that Cash thought he was clever. I sat in my car and cried as the rain poured down and I remembered a perfect bubble of bliss when Duke and I explored each other and our passion the first time.

I put myself first and didn't beg for forgiveness. I didn't grovel or decide it was one friend or another. I let them have each other, the way they should have, had I not gotten in the middle. I stepped back and let my heart be broken because someone was always going to be hurt. Instead of hurting them more, I let myself be hurt. In this, I am the agent of my own destruction.

Not only did those men each feed a part of me I didn't know was starving, I gave them each a version of me they needed too. I needed a strong protective man to hold me close and make me fight every day to grow and Duke needed a bit of lightness and levity to draw him out of the serious life he had boxed himself into. I also needed a man who was wholly devoted to bringing a smile to my face, the kind of man who jumps up and down in his seat waiting for me to open a present, and Cash needed a woman who listened and saw him, for him, not for what he could do for me—to me.

If I had managed to convince Cash to give it a go, it would have broken Duke and Cash. Their friendship was worth a lot more than our tiny flame of love. If I had devoted myself to Duke, it would have ended the same. No matter what I did, we were all going to suffer. I made everyone suffer. And now, I'm finding myself.

In July, I mustered the nerve to visit a tattoo shop in Billings with a drawing I did myself.

"What's it represent?" She tilts the drawing this way and that, laying it on my bare arm.

"Down here, by the wrist, is where I grew up, a small beach community in NC. This tiny candle flame is a spark of a life that never was. As you move up, it represents me driving across the country. The snowflakes are for the big snowstorm we had back in April, the storm that changed me. The bucking bull is for the rodeo, and the hurricane is for a storm that blows in overnight, and changes everything. The whiskey tumbler, a glass of something neat, at the end of the day. And the little creek there? That's where dreams are whispered. And finally, a thunderstorm by my shoulder. Because sometimes you have the most clarity about the world when you can't see it at all." Tears fill my eyes as I show her everything and how I want it placed. She covers me from wrist to shoulder, my skin changing, becoming something different, the way I have.

Lying in my bed, staring at the ceiling, I contemplate what happens now. I'm halfway through my six-month lease and I feel just as at home in Inspiration as I did the first week. When something is right, you just know it. It's what Lizzie was trying to get me to understand, decision making, especially the tough ones, isn't linear. It's steeped in uncertainty and sometimes regret, but when it's right, you know.

I wasn't ready for what I started with either of the men of May, and I didn't yet deserve the reverence, the care they gave me. Hurt people hurt people. And I am no longer hurt. I'm recovering, and I will be okay. I know this feeling that has settled in my chest, the crack where the love I received from them lives, won't last forever. And one day, just maybe, I'll be ready for my heart to belong to someone else. But I will never regret what it felt like to open myself up to someone new and honestly feel like I deserved it.

A gentle but insistent knocking fills my space. Peering at the clock, 12:34, I can't for a second figure out who might be here at this time of night. Confusion fills me but betraying optimism does too. Maybe it's Duke or Cash come to, at least, talk it out. I haven't even gotten to tell them how it happened.

Moving into the living room, wearing nothing but a thin camisole and sleep shorts, I peer out the window at the parking lot, but I only see my car. My heart starts beating, faster and faster.

The knocking becomes more demanding. I stand frozen at the top of the stairs. Running back to my room, I grab my phone. I don't want to call 911 if it's not an emergency. I open my text thread with Duke, figuring a late-night visit is more likely to be him than Cash.

> Are you at my door?

GRUMPY NOT-COWBOY

No.

Fear fills my chest as the knocking continues. It doesn't stop. It's a staccato beat, just pound...pound...pound...pound.

"Who is it?" I yell down the stairs, my voice quivering, cowardly. There is no answer. My phone dings. I slide the screen open.

GRUMPY NOT-COWBOY

Why? Is everything okay?

Before I can type out a reply, my door swings open and I duck behind the stair wall.

Chapter 29
Ain't No Sunshine

Duke

Swigging back another sip of beer, I rest the toes of my boots on the edge of the firepit. Leaning back, looking at the big sky, I take in the millions of stars and think of the millions of possibilities that exist. The fact there are potentially endless options in infinite universes, and I get the one where I fall in love with the same girl as my best friend.

It was a month before I felt like dragging myself out of the hole I had dug and reached out to Cash.

"Hey Duke," he greets me at the door of the farmhouse, looking as worse for wear as I felt, and probably looked.

Pulling him in for a hug, I say, "Hey Cash. Sorry it took so long." If I regret anything, it's making my best friend of thirty years wait a month, under a gauntlet, to know I wasn't mad at him.

He sighs. "I know, brother, this sucks."

We spent two hours that day talking about life, and Caroline. We each detailed exactly what happened, how we met her, when, the events that led up to the rodeo. Satisfied Cash would never have done this to me on purpose, I was able to examine everything else more clearly.

I found out about her troubled past a week before he did. He knew she was talking to someone else, me, well before I did. Telling him about the day in the truck, he winced but remembered me texting her while they were at lunch. The night we fucked in the storeroom and she changed immediately after? I, now, know it was because Cash was on the television dedicating his win to her. The day I came to her apartment and she confessed to having someone else in her life? It was the day after they crossed the physical line in their relationship.

I try to look at her actions objectively; I've been trying for months. Hearing Cash's whole story and comparing it almost day to day with mine, I see her more clearly, too. She wasn't trying to hurt us. She wasn't some horrifyingly precise manipulator; she was a wounded girl who wanted to be loved. Cash and I got caught in the crossfire. Our relationships each grew organically, and they fit the two people who were in them. Cash and I viewed her differently.

To him, she was a storm, unpredictable, exciting, but she also fit his life. She seemed like the ranch was where she belonged, and she slipped right in. With me, she was sunshine; she brought light and warmth to the cold expanse of my future, and we were gasoline lit and fueled by passion. She could have landed with either of us and it would have been the right person. And every damn day since I have wished Cash had not walked into that dining room at Lizzie's the day after I met her. I met her first, and fuck, did I want her to be mine.

I *want* her to be mine. Not a day has passed since our collision at the rodeo that I haven't wished she had chosen me. I know it's selfish, and wrong. So fucking wrong. But I wanted her to choose me. And yet. I also know Cash needed her, needs her now the same as then. He needed someone to see him for the man he is, without the glamour of the rodeo, just him on his horse, being him. Someone else who sees him the way I see him, as worthy.

But Cash did walk in that day. He did pursue her, and she reveled in it. She deserved happiness—deserves happiness. Every time I think back though, knowing weeks before I talked about Cash, Cash told her about me, and she didn't say anything. She didn't address it. Secrets like this can't stay buried. That morning at her apartment when she cried as I threw a tantrum finding out there was someone else, I think she was realizing there was no way out. She was in a corner.

Now, Cash has gone back to his playboy lifestyle, a shield he ducks behind every time something gets hard. He has fucked his way through everyone left in town, and any girl who has approached him at the rodeo. He's still hurting, still burying his pain and all I can do is sit by and watch.

The only time I ever said anything was in early July.

"Cash, seriously?" I ask him when I show up on Sunday morning for a ride and find him still in bed, two women wrapped around him like a blanket.

"What the fuck, Duke?" he yells back, barely stirring.

"We are supposed to ride today. And yet..." I trail off, letting him fill in the blanks.

"Yeah, well maybe I feel like something different," he says, grabbing the tiny brunette and pulling her mouth to his. I storm out, a stream of giggles following me.

I've counted at least a dozen, maybe more, but I haven't seen a single blonde or a woman with curves with him since our shared blonde goddess tore our hearts to shreds.

I have decided to finally do the thing years of begging from Indie and her subsequently leaving couldn't do. I learn about myself, outside of Inspiration. I hired a second bartender. I spent the month of July going to rodeos with Cash, visiting nearby cities, ranging further and further out. Pushing the limits of how far I can drive.

Every time I went for a hike or found a new site to see, I would think of the excitement in green eyes and hear easy laughter. I remember that drive, back in May, when the rain created a cocoon for us on the side of the road. But that isn't what I remember most clearly that day—I remember the radiant smile she wore as she pointed out the window of the truck at every animal and interesting sight along the way. I know she would love to go and explore with me. If I saw the back of a woman, blonde hair streaming down, a hat shoved on her head, I would hope she would turn around and Caroline's face would smile at me.

In actuality though, I only visited the feed store when her car wasn't in the lot. If I did see her anywhere, I turned the other way. I stay on my side of town and let her have hers. The heartbreak in this town is shrinking it by the day and I'm starting to worry I will need to find a new place to settle just so I can walk down the street freely, my head held high, and not feel my heart cracking. I spent a decade walking these streets by Indie's side and when we broke up, I happily, and easily, shared this town with her, the awkwardness wearing off quickly. But one month by Caroline's side and Inspiration is a three-block war zone. I can't take the chance of allowing the bomb in my chest to detonate by seeing her on the street.

I haven't seen or heard anything about her meeting anyone or seeing anyone else. She seems to be imposing rules on herself about staying single for a while, and honestly, I respect it. We all jumped in too fast. She was too soon out of things with Roger and needed to heal herself. The kinds of wounds he inflicted on her didn't heal when the bruises went away. I hope Cash and I helped though, that we fed her soul and healed her wounds, just a little. She may have hurt us in the process, but she needed what we had. She needed to know she was enough.

My phone dings on the table next to me, it's late, has to be after midnight. I pick it up to read the text.

CAROLINE

Are you at my door?

Why would I be at her door at, checking the time, 12:36 am?

No.

Sitting my phone down, I lean back again.

"Who was it?"

His voice across the fire startles me. I was so turned inward, I forgot he was there. I hesitate. I don't know if I should mention the ghost that haunts us.

"Caroline."

"Oh." His voice takes on a sadness that hurts me to hear. His brow furrows. "You've been talking to her? Without telling me?"

"No. This is the first time she's reached out since the rodeo. It's weird actually. She asked me if I was at her door."

"Huh? Why would—wait, someone is at her door, someone she isn't expecting?"

Picking up my phone, I type a quick message.

Why? Is everything okay?

I send it and stare at the messages, waiting for a reply. I hear Cash's movement before I feel him leaning over my shoulder. I see she reads it, and the bubbles pop up, she's typing.

They stop. We watch. And watch but no text comes through.

We sit in silence for a few minutes before I glance up at Cash and see the same look of concern on his face.

Dialing her number, it rings once before going to voicemail.

"Something seems...off," he whispers.

"Let's go." I stand and walk directly to my truck, Cash behind me. Once I'm behind the wheel, I lean over and pop the glove box open, nodding satisfactorily when I see what I'm looking for.

"You really think we will need that?" Cash nods his head toward the weapon.

"I hope not."

Spinning tires out of his driveway, we speed toward her apartment.

It takes twelve minutes, a drive of usually twenty. Pulling in next to her car, I see there are no other cars in the lot.

"I don't see anyone," Cash says as I peer up at her windows. There's only a single light on in the living room, but no other indications of anything.

"She's up; the light's on. I sure hope we don't feel like idiots." Grabbing the .44 Magnum from the glove box, I climb out. I check the cartridge and the safety, before sliding it in the pocket holster and into my pocket. Cash closes the door slowly, like we are on a secret mission. I don't bother with the stealth, slamming my own door and he jumps. I would have laughed under normal circumstances.

Rounding the truck, he whispers, "What now?"

"Now we go to the door, see if we hear anything. Maybe knock? I'm not sure, this is my first rescue mission." I look at him sidelong.

We walk to the door and stand there, anticlimactically, while we wait to figure out if something will happen.

"The door looks intact so if someone is in there, she let them in," I tell him, studying the lock. I give the handle a jiggle.

"What if, it's like a boyfriend or something, and we are just hovering outside the door like creepy stalkers?" he asks, his voice full of tension, and a little fearful. I can't tell what he's afraid of though in this proposed scenario.

"Well, she shouldn't have texted me. I was fine where I was."

I take out my phone and call her again which goes straight to voicemail this time.

"Seriously, Duke, I don't know what to do. We are just lurking around, but everything seems fine." We stand there for another minute, maybe two before both of us hear a thud and a muffled cry.

"That's it." Pushing me out of the way, Cash raises a single booted foot, and holding onto the doorframe, kicks the door through the opening.

I follow Cash through the door and the apartment seems silent. We both wait at the bottom of the stairs, and I draw the gun from my pocket, holding it at my side, safety on but my finger hovers above it. I can just faintly hear crying, like a sniffling, trying to stop the tears, crying. Then a furious whispering.

"Call the police," I whisper to Cash as I squeeze past him in the small entry. I hear him pull his phone out and a slight metallic ting. I glance over my shoulder and see he's got a blade out, his pocketknife. Anything is better than nothing, I suppose.

He whispers the address before hanging up and we start slowly ascending the stairs, on edge, trying to figure out what's happening. Once we reach the top, I peer over the half wall that surrounds the stairwell. Her lamp is knocked over and a pink fluffy pillow is on the floor. Everything else seems in place. Moving toward the hallway, the muffled crying gets louder but sounds like her mouth is covered, and I swear, it better be her own hand covering it or I will kill the person it's attached to.

I wave a hand to keep Cash close to my back, clicking the safety off, as we approach her closed bedroom door. Her crying gets louder and so do the whispers. They are male and angry and it's pissing me off. My hand shakes, and my back shudders. My heart pounds so hard I feel it in my entire body. Cash's hand rests between my shoulders, calming me, and I briefly wonder if he can feel my heart. I square my shoulders; there will be time for falling apart later.

There is only time to get our girl, now.

Chapter 30
Run for your Life

Callie

"Shut the fuck up, or I will knock you out," he tells me, the blade of his knife pressed into the hollow of my throat. My hands are pressed to my mouth, sweat running down my temple, tears flowing over my knuckles. I shake in fear, adrenaline flooding me. My vision is blurry, and I can't tell if it's tears or I'm about to pass out.

My hair is twisted around his fist, causing me to lean back to make space between us. Pulling his other arm back, a solid hit lands to my jaw, forcing a cry from my lips. Tilting sideways from the blow, he releases my hair, and I fall onto the sofa before slamming my side into the coffee table. Pain shoots through me before he twists his hand in my hair again and pain prickles my scalp. Dragging me down the hallway by the hair wrapped around his fist, I hear the front door slam against the entry way wall as someone forces their way through it. Relief floods me, breaking through the terror.

Pushing me into the closet, he follows me in, closing the

door behind us. I cower in the corner, my breaths shaky, sobs ripping out as I frantically cover my mouth with my hands, trying to keep the sound in. Grabbing the back of my neck, he pulls me in front of him—a shield. His knife, long and glinting in the sparse light, presses against my ribs. My chest expands and falls rapidly, and I'm on the edge of panic. I can't suck enough air through my teeth. I can't breathe. I can't think.

The edge of my vision goes from blurry to black.

"Callie, I will kill you. Calm the fuck down."

My lungs are tight, my fear controlling me. My skin is clammy, slippery. My shirt is stuck to me. My flesh is covered in goosebumps; my hair prickles. My heart racing, time seems to slow, agonizingly slow. The tip of his blade pierces my side, just enough to bring a sting of pain. His hand around my throat tightens as I strain my ears, trying to hear them, trying to find them in the apartment but all I can hear is my heart pounding. The sound of it is deafening. The darkness is too suffocating. His breaths are too harsh in my ear as his body presses against mine. I feel sick, I might throw up.

Breathe.

Breathe.

Breathe.

Chapter 31
Last Kiss

Cash

My hand pressing into Duke's back, I use him as a grounding force as we approach Callie's bedroom door. It's gotten quiet behind the door, and I don't know what it means. I try to take a few deep breaths to calm my heart but it's racing out of my chest at what we may find on the other side.

Duke reaches out to turn the knob and my senses are on high alert, for anything. I can faintly hear cars out on the street. I can feel my skin stretched over my muscles. I can feel the flannel under my fingertips, the knife in my other hand, the handle slick with sweat. I can smell the adrenaline rolling off us mixed with the sweet smell of Callie in the air. I see Duke shaking under the weight of our actions.

Raising his gun, he pushes the door open, stepping through in a quick movement, finding nothing. Looking around, he clocks the open bathroom door and the closed closet. We move in lock step toward the closet. There's shuffling and labored breathing behind the door. Reaching out, his hand shaking so much he can barely grab the knob, Duke pulls the door open, gun raised in front of him.

Despite being on edge from the moment I realized what the text on Duke's phone meant, I am not prepared for what we find. The entire scene is thrown into stark relief, from Callie's shaking, nearly naked form wearing only a short tank top and tiny sleep shorts, to the dark-haired man behind her, his hand wrapped tightly around her throat, a large knife pressed to her side. I zero in on the blade as the tip presses against her, a tiny bead of red welling. Her knees are knocking together, and she has both hands clamped over her mouth, fear in every line and shudder. She whimpers and the man tightens his hand. I can see the ligaments in his hand move slightly as he strains. Tears are running down her cheeks, her hands covered.

"Oh, a fucking cowboy," comes from the mouth of the man, disgust and anger twisting his features. He stares me in my eyes, completely having disregarded Duke as a non-threat. "You been fucking my wife, cowboy?"

Roger.

I can't even formulate a reply to his words.

"Roger," Duke breathes beside me. "Look at me, you goddamned coward. I've been fucking your wife. Look at me!"

Callie's tears increase and her eyes start rolling.

"Don't worry baby, you're going to be fine. Okay, Hurricane, don't worry."

"Don't speak to her!" Roger roars at me, before looking back at Duke. Tilting his head, he scoffs, "Oh you're a dirty fucking whore, Callie. I should have known. Actually, I did know. Disgusting."

Pointing his gun at Roger's head, in a low and lethal voice, Duke says, "Take your hands off her."

"She's my wife. Just because she's been here on both your dicks doesn't mean she isn't mine. Right, baby?" He rubs sweaty hair off her forehead before laying an angry kiss on her temple. Her eyes widen in fear before she winces.

Taking her hands from her mouth, her chin wobbles before she says, "Roger, just leave them. Roger. It's okay. I'll do whatever you want." Her voice is hoarse as she tries to breathe. He continues to squeeze her throat until her eyes start to roll back, her eyelids heavy.

"Like I would want you after this. Dirty Cunt." He bites her, hard, on her shoulder causing her to cry out.

I lose all semblance of control and step forward.

"I'm going to kill you, you fucking coward. Hiding behind a woman." Knife out, I move toward him and Duke places a restraining arm around my middle.

"Just a pretty little piece of ass. A little fat for my taste." He pinches her stomach, hard, and a pained whimper escapes her lips.

"Let her go." The fury in Duke's voice even makes me step back. He's shaking, like a man holding a monster under his skin. "Now."

"I will, I will. Let's see if she can still keep you warm." And he slowly, so slow, slides the blade he has pressed to her side through her ribs. Her eyes widen as he pushes. Time seems to stop as he continues his slow push until the long blade has disappeared into her side completely. I hear boots stomping across the floor. He flings her limp body at me, and I catch her, sinking to the ground as I hear a single shot ring out in the small closet.

"No!" I scream as I crumble to the floor, the woman I love cradled in my arms. I feel Duke collapse next to me. "Baby, Hurricane? Callie, please!" I crush her body to me, so warm, so soft. I sob into her chest, the knife protruding from her side glaring at me, angry I didn't do enough to save her. Blaming me.

"Caroline, please wake up baby girl, please." I hear Duke, I see his blood-soaked hands feeling for a pulse, terror in his eyes. "Baby, please." His voice cracks as he pleads with her prone body, running his hands over her neck, her face.

I feel a tap on my shoulder and look up into the eyes of a paramedic. I know him. My brain won't tell me who he is though. I'm cold. My body shakes. My teeth are chattering.

"Cash, let me see her. Come on."

I sob as I hug her body to me, feeling her blood soaking through my clothes, the puddle expanding on the floor around us.

"Cash, let her go," Duke tells me, trying to move my fingers where I grip her. I look at him, my eyes wide. He looks shell-shocked, his face a mirror of my own. I release her and the paramedics lift her gently from my lap.

"Please be careful with her. Please," I whisper through tears as pain rips through my chest. I lay back on the carpet as they take her away. I roll my head to the side and see police have filled her room, one leaning over Roger, checking his pulse, as blood flows out of a single shot, in the center of his chest.

Sitting up, my head swims, my sight blurs, and I fall back to the carpet, everything going black.

Chapter 32
Don't Take the Girl

Duke

Watching Caroline fall to the floor, Cash wrapped around her body, I feel like the heart in my chest stops beating. Aiming my gun, I squeeze the trigger. I've never even pointed a weapon at another person. Until this very second, I wasn't even sure I would be able to pull the trigger if I needed to. The anger in my chest is visceral; it's a physical presence filling me. I don't stop to consider what I've done as Roger falls, lying in the corner of the closet, blood flowing freely from a single hole in his chest. The terrified scream that erupts from Cash drags me to my knees.

"Caroline, please wake up baby girl, please," I beg. I check her pulse, weak, barely beating. I watch the blood seep from around the knife sticking out of her. "Baby, please." I hear the paramedics. My hands can't find purchase on her, slipping every time I try to grab her.

Please. God, please.

Cash holds on to her like a drowning man, the pain pouring

off him in waves as he begs her to wake up. Touching her hair, her face, her chest. She doesn't breathe. She doesn't move. He holds her close as the paramedics try to get to her.

Mickey, a man I've known most of his life, kneels next to Cash and lays a hand on his shoulder, trying to get to Caroline.

"Cash, let her go," I tell him forcefully, trying to remove his hands from her. My hands are coated in her blood and I'm smearing it across her body and Cash's. He finally releases her, and they pick her up, careful not to jostle her too much, protecting the knife that now acts as a dam for the blood trying to flow out of her.

"Please, be careful with her. Please," Cash whispers as they strap her to their stretcher, stabilizing her, taking her pulse, inserting a needle into her. Blood is dripping from her onto the floor. There's more blood outside of her than in, I think. Cash sits up, looking around before his eyes roll back and he collapses.

I fall on top of him. "Cash, Cash, come on buddy. Cash, don't do this."

An officer kneels next to me. "He's okay, just in shock. Give him a minute."

I sit back, pulling my knees to my chest and laying my head on them.

They are taking the woman I love down the stairs, strapped to a stretcher, her life leaving a red trail on the floor as they go. My best friend is unconscious on the ground. A man is dead beside me.

I don't even know how to think around the enormity of the situation.

"Duke, we have to get a statement from you, and from Cash, when he comes to," the officer, Billy, tells me.

"Not now, Bill," I respond, my own voice so devoid of emotion, I wonder if I'm even in this room at all.

"Yes, now."

I stand. I need to go to her. I need to make sure she's alright.

"No, I have to go to the hospital. We have to go. We have to know if she's okay," I tell him, my voice growing increasingly panicky as I consider she might not make it. I sit back down. I shake Cash. I try to stand; it doesn't work. I reach my arm out in the direction they took her. I hear the sirens get further away. "Where are they taking her, Billy?" I ask.

"I'll tell you after you make your statement, Duke."

I fly to my feet and grab his lapels. "Tell me!" I cry, tears flowing down my cheeks.

"Duke, I know emotions are all over the place right now but if you don't take your hand off me, I will have to cuff you. You have to make a statement before I can release you." He stares me directly in the eyes. "I can either bring you to the station or you can tell me here. But there is a woman with a knife in her side and a dead man over there. And *you* have to tell me what happened."

I see Cash moving around, trying to sit up. I crouch down. "Cash, come on buddy." I help him to his feet, and he takes in my frantic eyes and my tear-stained face.

"Is she dead, Duke?"

"I don't know. I don't know," I tell him, my breathing shallow and fast.

"Cash, Duke, come out here, so we can talk away from," he waves his hand at the blood, "all of this."

Cash's breathing catches as he looks around, looks at me, looks down his body, blood covering both us and all the surfaces.

"You killed him, Duke."

"He might have killed her," is my response as I walk out, following Billy into the living room.

It takes two hours of sitting at her little dining table before the police are satisfied. We washed up as best we could before we sat down, and I watched Caroline's blood swirl down the drain and my throat felt like it was closing.

I shake Billy's hand, and he clamps a hand on each of our shoulders.

"I'm real sorry for what happened here tonight, guys," he tells us the hospital she was taken to but doesn't tell us anything else.

We head out into the night which is quickly becoming early morning. The sun will be rising in the next hour or so and I am so bone-deep tired, into my soul, as I walk with heavy steps down the stairs that are covered in blood, through the kicked in door, and to my truck. I had to surrender my gun to the police, for forensics. I climb in behind the wheel as Cash joins me. Everything feels disjointed. Out of order. The smallest things sticking out in my head.

Leaving the lot, I see Vickie and Pete pulling in. I don't stop as we head toward the hospital. They've already transferred her to a trauma hospital in Billings, which means, at least she survived the trip. The sun lightens the sky as we pull into the parking lot. I climb out, and unbutton my shirt, trying to remove some of the blood from my body. Cash and I look like murderers. And maybe I am. I can't feel guilty for it.

"Good morning," I tell the woman behind the reception desk as she takes in our appearance and her eyes widen. "We are looking for Caroline Pearce. She was brought it on a med-evac from the Inspiration Clinic?"

Her eyes register recognition. "Oh, yes of course, they said you would be coming. Head up to the fourth floor. They can tell you more there."

"Is she okay?" Cash asks quietly from beside me.

Her eyes soften at his question. "I'm sorry, sir, I can't tell you anything down here. Please head on up."

In the elevator, I press the 'four' button, reading the chart above it. Fourth Floor – Trauma/Intensive Care Unit. I shove my knuckles between my teeth, biting down to stop the sob creeping up my throat. Cash stands close to me, his shoulder touching mine as we step out of the door together and head toward another desk.

"Mr. Williams? Mr. Colter? Let me call the doctor; the police called ahead to say you were on the way. Have a seat," a woman dressed in scrubs tells us before we even fully approach.

"Please, is she okay?" Cash begs her.

"The doctor will tell you everything."

"Ma'am with all due respect, I saw her wheeled out with a knife in her side hours ago. We drove all the way here and no one will even tell us if she's alive. Please just tell us that."

She listens to me, to the pleading in my voice. She types on her screen, moving her mouse around.

"She's alive. Now please, go into the waiting room. I'll have someone bring you something to change into."

Chapter 33
She's Got it All

Cash

I'm wearing paper clothes in a sticky plastic chair in a waiting room that smells like disinfectant and fear, and I have never been so relieved in my entire life. The doctor's assurance that, for now, Callie is okay grants me the ability to take a full breath for the first time in hours, since the firepit. Sitting there, looking up at the stars, seems like a lifetime ago.

After a short lecture that he isn't supposed to tell us about her condition, he gives us the bare minimum. Her parents are dead, her husband is also dead. As far as we know, there isn't anyone else. No one but us.

So, for now, she's alive. She had surgery but she's alive. She isn't out of the woods yet, and she hasn't woken up. But she's alive. And, in thirty-four years, no words have ever made me happier than those.

"Y'all can sit with her if you want," the nurse behind the desk tells us once visiting hours start.

"Thanks." I smile at her, and she blushes. My phone

vibrates in my pocket and pulling it out, I see it's a call from Lizzie.

"Hey, Aunt Lizzie," I answer.

"Oh God, Cash? Thank God. Are you okay?"

"Yes, I'm fine." I can hear the tiredness, the weariness, in my voice.

"What happened at Callie's house? Of course, nobody will tell us anything, but they called Vickie and Pete, you know. And they told me she was taken in an ambulance. And the police—" I look at Duke as he eyes me from his seat. Lizzie just goes on and on about what she heard but I don't have the energy or desire to entertain the gossiping hoards today.

Duke holds out his hand, so I give him the phone.

"Lizzie?" he interrupts her. "We are at the hospital." Pause. "Yes, everyone is alive." Pause. "Yes, both of us." Pause. "Okay, we will call you later." Hanging up, he hands me my phone back.

"Thank you," I tell him, full of gratitude.

"Let's go see our girl." Suddenly, the last two months don't matter anymore. The nights spent crying, the women I used to hide my pain, the drinks. None of it matters. All that matters is that the girl we love is hurt and dammit, she deserves to know she's worth it.

I sit on one side of the bed and Duke sits on the other. We both hold a small, cold hand. She's pale, a shadow of a bruise on her jaw, a less shadowy one on her cheek. There's a ring of livid purple bruising around her throat. The IV snaking around her gives her antibiotics and fluids. All the blood has been washed from her flesh but her pale color looks like she could use some more in her body.

She has a new tattoo covering her entire arm. Duke and I studied it closely as we sat, and we cried as we each found ourselves in the pictures. The storm cloud and the whiskey tumbler are Duke. The bull and the little creek are me. She chronicled her journey to us and our journey together in bright colors and it made us both a little sadder knowing no matter how hurt we were, she was just as hurt. We had each other, but we left her alone.

We can't change anything about the last two months, but in this hospital room, we pray for her safety and beg God for the chance to prove to her that we deserve her, even if we have to do it side by side, shoulder to shoulder. She feels worth it. The same thing I told Duke all those months ago when I talked about Callie, before I knew everything.

She feels worth it.

We sit vigil by her bed, only moving to use the attached restroom before returning to grab her hand. We talk to her, we tell her how sorry we are, what idiots we are, and how lucky we are to have her, any part of her. The nurses bring us water and snacks, giving us pitying or curious looks, depending.

When visiting hours are over, an older, matronly nurse comes to us to say it's time to go.

"Can we sit in the waiting room?" I ask her.

"No, you'll have to leave and come back tomorrow. We will take care of her."

"Just a few more minutes, please," Duke requests.

"Fifteen more minutes gentlemen, but that's it. Rest and quiet is important for healing. You can come back at eight o'clock tomorrow."

After she leaves, we say our goodbyes.

"Goodnight baby, I want you to wake up, okay? Can you wait until we get back though? I want to be here; I don't want you to be alone anymore," I whisper to her, leaning in and kissing her brow.

"Goodnight, sweetheart." Duke kisses her other brow, moving a few strands of hair away from her face. "Don't worry about us out here. Sleep as long as you need. We will be here." He whispers something inaudible in her ear and when he stands back up, tears fill his eyes, but they don't spill over.

Walking out of the hospital to Duke's truck, I realize I have no idea how to navigate this. What do we say? What do we do?

"I was just going to head to a hotel for the night. Is that cool? I know you don't have your truck, so you're sort of at my mercy, but Inspiration is too far away," Duke says in the quiet cab, glancing over at me.

"Yeah, that's perfect. I don't want to leave yet. We need to be here. Want to grab some dinner though? Maybe we can... talk?"

"Yeah, okay." He pulls into a small Mexican restaurant across from the hotel he put in his phone.

We are seated across from each other in a small booth, munching on tortilla chips. We are just watching each other and it's comically awkward.

"More than thirty years of friendship and we can't start an awkward conversation?" I joke as I take a sip of my water.

He shrugs. "We've never needed to have a conversation to navigate what happens when the girl we both love wakes up from her ex-husband's murder attempt." His dry sarcasm is a balm to me and reminds me that even if this is uncomfortable as hell, we can figure it out.

"Correct. You killed him, for her. Dammit, you're going to win." I plop my forehead down on the table, sighing loudly.

"You truly are so dramatic," he tells me, rolling his eyes.

Our food arrives and I tear into the burrito, the first thing I've eaten in almost twenty-four hours. "Nobody is winning, not right now. We have to focus on not losing her first. Let me ask you a question." He shoves rice in his mouth, swallowing before continuing, "If she wakes up tomorrow and decides it's both of us. Or that she can't decide. What are you going to say?"

Leaning back, I chew slowly, thinking. I never considered we would be here, having this conversation.

"Hypothetically, because it comes down to what she wants, but hypothetically, are you asking if we could share her or if we could both date her until she chooses one of us?" I just need some clarification from him, where his head is.

"I'm asking you what your thoughts are on either of those possibilities. I am telling you that I cannot, will not, walk away again unless she doesn't want me." His answer is straightforward and matter of fact, the exact thing I expect from Duke.

"Okay. So, let's focus on her waking up, getting better, and then let her decide what she wants. Agree to follow her lead?" I hold out a hand, and he takes it.

"Agreed."

We are waiting in the fourth floor waiting room at eight o'clock on the dot the next day. We made an emergency shopping trip at a twenty-four-hour Walmart after dinner so at least we're wearing clean clothes today.

"Y'all can go on in," the nurse tells us. "Probably another long day sitting."

We don't care if we are just sitting, watching her sleep. We've missed enough time.

"Good morning, Hurricane," I greet her as we enter the room.

"'Morning, Sunshine," Duke says at the same time.

I'm mildly entertained we have both adopted weather nicknames for her, and how different they are. It doesn't feel so bad, knowing he's there. I may have to share her a little, if that's what she wants, but I can't imagine a better man by her side than him. Including me.

I pull her necklace from my pocket, holding it up.

"Now, Callie, since you're in this bed recovering, I won't put this back on your neck where it belongs, but I have it, okay, baby? When you wake up, it's yours."

"How do you have that? We haven't been home yet." Duke looks at me curiously.

"It's been in my wallet every second of every day since she climbed out of my truck."

"I can't believe you are worried for one second that I would 'win,'" he tells me, deadpan.

We spend the remainder of the day the same as yesterday.

And the same as tomorrow.

And the day after.

On the fourth day, we sit quietly, each holding a hand when the machine connected to Callie starts beeping, loudly, scaring both of us.

Duke runs into the hallway yelling, "Help, something's wrong. Please, help."

A nurse runs into the room and studies the machine before pressing the button, silencing it.

"Nothing's wrong honey. She's waking up."

Chapter 34
Independence Day

Callie

Everything hurts.

My head hurts.

My chest hurts.

My arm hurts.

What is beeping?

BEEP. BEEP. BEEP.

Is it my alarm? What do I need to get up for again?

BEEP BEEP BEEP.

"Nothing's wrong honey, she's waking up." Who is that?

My eyelids feel glued shut. Am I hungover? How much did I drink that I can't remember drinking at all?

I manage to unglue one eyelid; the white tile ceiling is confusing. I don't recognize this place. I close the eye.

I smell the air; I need a clue. Disinfectant. Flowers.

Something rustles and I turn my head slightly. It hurts to move. I wince.

"Don't move, baby. It will hurt."

I recognize that voice. He comes to me in my dreams.

"Cash," I croak out of my dry throat.

"I'm here, Hurricane. Don't try to move. Don't talk. Just relax." It's then that I feel his hands wrapped around mine. The points of contact are warm and vital. I squeeze his hand and get a squeeze in return.

"Hey, sweetheart. You squeezed my hand; I've wanted you to do that for days."

Wait. "Duke?" My voice is scratchy but comes out a little clearer.

"Yes, Sunshine, I'm here." He squeezes my hand again.

I try to open my eyes but it's so difficult. I give up, breathing heavily from the effort. I take a few deep breaths before there's another voice.

"Caroline? Can you hear me?"

I try to nod but it hurts. "Yes," I breathe instead.

"I'm Dr. Jones. I need to examine you. I'm going to ask your friends to leave and then I will need to check you over while we chat. Can you open your eyes?"

Squeezing both of their hands, I hold on.

"Doctor, she doesn't seem to want to let go," Cash tells the man.

"Stay," I croak.

"Okay, they can stay. If you would just move to one side of the bed, please." I hear more rustling, and the sound follows Duke from my side until he and Cash are both touching my arm on the same side.

"Okay, Caroline. Can you open your eyes?"

"Hurts," I try to say.

"Hey Tina, can you grab me a bottle of warm saline and some clean gauze?" he tells someone. "Okay, we will come back to that. I'm going to just move your gown a little and check your wounds. Do you remember what happened?"

"No." A breathy whisper. It's getting easier now.

"Well, you were assaulted. I will let the police explain that part. But your injuries have been quite extensive." He unbuttons my gown at the shoulder and moves it open, shielding my breast but exposes my side. He gently probes my ribs, and a hiss of pain escapes my lips. "You had a punctured right kidney, a lacerated lung, and a gallbladder bleed. We managed to control the bleeding in your gallbladder. We did have to remove the kidney as the damage was too great, but the good news is you can live with one. You will meet with a nephrologist, a kidney specialist, as soon as you're feeling a little better to explain what this means. Your lung was punctured but seems to be doing okay post-surgery."

As he lists off the various injuries, I hear the breathing of the men beside me become shallower and at one point, Duke removes his hand which had started shaking.

"Thank you, Tina. I am going to just apply some pressure with warm saline to your eyes and see if we can help get them open, okay?" I feel the wet cloth placed against my eye, warming me. Once he's finished, I try to open my eyes again and I am successful this time.

A kindly looking man with gray hair leans into my field of vision. It's a little blurry but if I concentrate, he comes into focus. "It's so good to see those green eyes open, Caroline. I'm just going to continue my exam while I ask you some more questions, okay?" I try to nod again and wince.

"Don't try to move your neck. You have some significant bruising to your trachea and the neck tissue which will make talking and moving your neck difficult for a few more days. It should get better every day. Now, let's see." He probes my shoulder, and I whimper. "Yes, that is quite sore I'm sure, but it's a flesh wound and didn't require stitches or anything so it

should be feeling better soon. Bite marks can be so painful."
Bite marks?

Honestly, I have no idea what has happened. I can't remember anything. I have a missing kidney, a punctured lung, a bite mark, and a bruised throat.

"What day?" I ask, pushing my sore throat to its limit, hoping my point comes across.

"It's Thursday, Caroline. You've been asleep for five days. You came in on Sunday morning around three am. Okay, I will leave you now, but I am scheduling a follow up CT scan to check for any rebleeding in your abdomen and to check on the healing of your lung and gallbladder. Tina will take good care of you." And then, he's gone.

I'm laying almost completely flat so I move my hands, feeling around for the buttons I know must exist.

"What can we do, Caroline?" Duke asks, leaning over me so I can see him.

"Up, please."

"Okay, Caroline, I'm going to raise the head just a little at a time, let me know if it hurts," Tina tells me before slowly lifting my head and the rest of the room appears.

"Okay," I tell her when the angle starts to be too much.

"Great, let me just get some vitals and I will be out of here."

"Can she have, like, water or something? For her throat," Cash asks her.

"Of course."

Once she's gone, Duke returns to the other side of the bed and they both sit. We exist in silence for a little while and I am dying of curiosity about what happened and why they are both here.

"Duke," I whisper, and he jumps up, leaning over slightly.

"Yeah, baby?" Hearing him call me baby makes me want to melt into the bed, but I have no idea what any of this means. I slide my eyes toward Cash and see him watching me earnestly, affection in his eyes. He doesn't seem to care that Duke called me baby or is here at all. What happened? What landed me in this bed and what happened while I was asleep?

"What ha—" My voice breaks halfway through the word, and I feel a tear run down my cheek. Duke wipes it away. He looks at Cash and they stare at each other for a few heartbeats before Duke begins his story.

After he finishes, ending with me being stabbed and them coming to the hospital and sitting with me for four days, I ask, "Roger?"

He again pauses, looking at Cash again as though they are having some sort of private communication that I am not privy to.

It's Cash that speaks this time. "He's gone, darlin'. Like, forever."

"Dead?" I croak.

Cash flinches from the word, and Duke looks a little peaked.

"Yes," Duke answers. It is so bizarre seeing them together and being one side of a conversation. Not finishing each other's sentences exactly but working so closely together to have this conversation that one seems to know where the other will need them.

"How?"

Duke rubs his neck. Cash fidgets a little awkwardly.

"How?" I ask a little more forcefully, but it still comes out weakly and cracking.

"I did it," Duke whispers, almost too low to hear. "I'm sorry, Caroline. He hurt you and I lost control. I'm sorry." His own tear drips onto the mattress near our joined hands.

"Come here," I command, barely above a whisper. He leans down until he is close to my mouth, turning his head so I can get close to his ear. "Thank you." I try to lift my arm to wrap around him, but I'm weak and so tired, so it just kind of bumps him and he chuckles slightly.

Lying my head back, I drift off to sleep.

The next few days pass in uneven periods of waking and sleeping. My neck feels better every day and soon I can talk in full sentences. Repeat tests show I'm healing well but it's a long road. The police stop by and ask for a statement, which is hard the first day, but the memories return day by day.

By day four, I can remember every minute of the home invasion/attempted murder. Realizing he came all the way to Montana to murder me is a sobering thought; I never even considered this as a possibility. When all the information becomes clear, I can finally tell the guys what happened before they got there.

"I heard him knocking and it was getting scarier, so I texted you. I was also going to text Cash, but I never got that far."

"Why would you think I would be at your house in the middle of the night banging on your door, Caroline?" Duke asks me, clearly perplexed.

"I didn't. It was just, well, when he started knocking it was gentler, urgent but not scary. And since I really only know the two of you well enough to show up and knock on my door, it was just the only thing that made sense, I guess," I tell him, confessing without words there are no other men who would have shown up. The slightly pleased look on Cash's face indicates he understood what I didn't say.

"Okay, so then what?" Cash leads me.

"After you replied back, asking why, I was trying to tell you someone was banging but he got through the door at that exact moment, and I was too scared to keep typing." I remember it now, in such vivid detail, it's as though it just happened moments before.

"How did he get in? When we got there, the door was closed and locked," Duke questions.

"I'm actually not sure. I feel pretty certain I locked it, but I may not have. I don't know." I shudder, the fear of those moments snaking up my spine. "Once he was inside, he came upstairs and grabbed me."

"How did he find you? How did he recognize me as soon as he saw me? He didn't even know who Duke was."

"It was so weird. He looked right at Cash, ignoring me completely. But if he had been watching you or something, he would have seen both of us." There's curiosity but also hurt mingled in Duke's question.

"He saw us on TV. No idea why he was watching a rodeo from Lewistown, Montana but he said he saw you and I after the rodeo, when you won and told national television I destroyed everything..." I trail off, my voice softening.

Sadness fills Cash's face at my mention of those events.

"I know I hurt you, Callie; you hurt us too. I never wanted to bring you pain, but I can't apologize for it. I am sorry I dragged you in front of the camera, knowing afterward I was going to leave you alone. If I had been with you, or you with me, that night, things would have been different," Cash says, spilling his heartache and pain onto my soul.

I see the opening, the gap, where I can confess and tell them I'm sorry. The time when I can smooth over the pain and heartache and explain myself. But I don't take it. It isn't fair to either of them if I give them a blanket apology. They each deserve the time to talk to me alone. So, I carry on with my story. "He grabbed my hair and pushed me to the floor, straddling me. He hit me across the cheek." I saw stars when he did it and I thought he was going to knock me unconscious.

"Then he pulled me up and yelled for a while about the apartment and me leaving, and you, Cash. He punched me in the jaw at one point, which made me fall to the floor. I think that's when you got there because he hauled me up by my arm and dragged me to the closet. You know what happened next." I don't tell them he kissed me, roughly, and threatened to make me his wife in all the ways that matter again since I had let another man inside me. It would hurt them more and I've done enough.

"The doctor mentioned yesterday he thinks they will discharge you in a few days so we will need to head back to Inspiration in the next day or so," Cash informs me. My heart splits in half. I'm so grateful they came for me. So thankful they sat by my bed. "Why are your eyes filling with tears, Callie?"

"I am just so happy you came for me and that you've been here. Thank you. Do you think I could hire a car to drive me, or maybe someone would be willing?"

"What the fuck are you talking about?" Duke asks me, harshly.

"So I can get home? Although I don't know where home is. Do you think I still have a place to live?"

Cash and Duke make almost identical faces, furrowing their brows before rolling their eyes.

"I'm sorry, sweetheart, not to be rude, but I killed a man for you a week ago. *Killed.* And you think I was just here for fun and intend to just...leave?" Duke is incredulous and the look on his face is so comically offended that both Cash and I snicker, earning a frown.

"Well, you said you had to leave?" I'm confused.

"Yeah, because we went on an unplanned impromptu rescue mission while we were sitting around the fire and are in

Duke's truck. We can't even get you home unless you want to spend the drive squished between us with a shifter between your legs."

"Do not respond the way your face says you want to. You're injured, Caroline," Duke scolds me before I can even put words to the thoughts that are clearly written on my face. I giggle, and both their faces soften.

"We discussed it last night, before bed," Cash adds.

"Before bed...?"

"Yeah, at the hotel?" Cash seems confused by my confusion.

"Listen, I haven't spent a lot of time thinking about this whole situation but you saying 'before bed' conjured an interesting picture, okay?" I snicker at him, crinkling my nose.

"Simmer down, Callie. We have separate beds. And you called *me* shameless. I swear." Cash rubs his hand down his face, his cheeks a little pink at my implication.

Duke looks at Cash, tilting his head just a little, then rubs the week of beard he's grown. "Sorry, sweetheart, he's just not my type."

"Oh, for fuck's sake. Can we focus please?"

Duke exhales a laugh at Cash's words. It's a real live, deep, throaty laugh and it makes my heart sing. He's so reserved but it seems he saves his joy for Cash which is such a cowboy bromance thing.

"Anyway," Cash continues, "we talked. Before we went to our separate beds and hugged our *own* pillows. And one of us snored. It wasn't me." Duke rolls his eyes. "We are going back to Inspiration and swapping Duke's truck for mine. It has a backseat. That way you can ride up front, and Duke can watch over us from his perch in back."

Duke lets out a beleaguered sigh, as though this is all too much for him.

"I can ride in the back," I volunteer.

"No, you can't. You need to be able to lean back. I'll be behind you to help you however you need, and Cash will drive the speed limit and get us home. And, I have no idea the state of your apartment, but we think it will be best if you stay with Cash at the farmhouse for a bit. Just until you're back on your feet."

"You *both* think it will be best?" I'm sorry, these men are jointly making decisions for me now? "I actually think you two need to tell me what is happening here. The last time I saw you, before you busted in like white knights, you hated me. Rightfully so, but I am just confused."

Looking between them, I wait to see who will break first. Surprisingly, it's Duke.

"Look, Caroline, this isn't the ideal place or time for a conversation as serious as this. We can't do confession hour while you're injured. We *will* have the conversation, but can we please just get you home, settled in at Cash's, and then go from there?"

"Yeah, Hurricane." Hearing his nickname for me warms me from my toes to the top of my head. "Big conversations are needed, and I would like to have them at home. Will you let us take you home?"

I nod. "But only if Duke is there too. It's the three of us or it's nothing."

Duke looks at Cash and they do the silent communication thing I've noticed a lot these last few days before Duke nods.

"Okay, I'll be there, Sunshine."

Chapter 35
Free and Easy

Duke

"I meant what I said when I said I would be there until she doesn't want me to be," I tell Cash on the drive back to Inspiration. The doctor thinks he will be sending Caroline home tomorrow, and we have work to do before she gets there.

She was sad to see us go this afternoon but it's a few hours' drive home and we need to get the house ready for her, stop by her apartment and get her some clothes, swap trucks, sleep and get back, all before visiting hours start.

"Okay, but 'it's the three of us or nothing' sounds really...ominous. Are we in a throuple? Are you my new boyfriend?" Cash bats his eyelashes at me.

"Shut up. I honestly don't know if any of us know what the hell is going on. If it's worth anything, I don't actually think that's what she meant. I think she is trying to figure this out, just like us, and the only way to do it is if we are together."

I drum my fingers on the wheel as we cruise toward town.

Pulling up Sadie's number on my phone, I listen to it ring a few times before she answers.

"Hey, Boss. How's Billings?" She's been taking care of the dogs and the house while I've been away.

"I'll be back tonight so just check in on the dogs this afternoon. Sadie, I appreciate you doing all this."

"How's Callie?" News travels fast in a small town and while everyone doesn't know the exact events from that night, they know enough to fill in a fantastical story for what they don't know.

"She's good; they are sending her home tomorrow. I'll probably be at Waylon's this weekend. Thanks again."

As I hang up, Cash speaks up, "Did you know they are saying you and I burst into her house, guns blazing?"

"That's honestly better than the real story of us sneaking around like cat burglars."

He snorts out a laugh. "Are you okay, you know, with everything?"

He means the shooting. We haven't talked about it. We've tap danced around it while we worried about everything else going on. But now, since Caroline is coming home and is on the mend, I don't blame him for wondering.

"Yeah, I think so. Like, prior to that moment, I never considered I would need to use it for protection, even though that's the reason I had it in the truck. I've taken all the classes, you know? And we've been hunting our entire lives. But I've never actually pointed a weapon at a person." I exhale heavily. "I guess, I'm glad I had it, and I could bring myself to use it. Using it to protect the girl I love? Worth it, I think."

He nods his head sagely. "Speaking of the girl *we* love, how do we tell her that?"

"We don't. Not yet. She just went through something awful. I think supporting her through it is showing her how we feel but she doesn't need the burden of the obligation to confess her own feelings. Besides, she might choose one of us."

"I know. And when she picks me, don't hate me, okay?" He laughs as he says it.

I reach out and punch him on the shoulder across the cab.

"Ow." He rubs the spot. "Damn, Duke, it was a joke. You been working out? I'm going to have a bruise."

"Like I said, dramatic."

By six am, we have accomplished a long list of tasks. We picked up Dolly and Hank and brought them to the ranch, along with some of my clothes and things since I'm sticking around. Now there are twice as many obnoxious dogs.

We went to see the state of things at Caroline's apartment and discovered the door was fixed and we could go in and get some of her stuff. We just threw everything we could into a few suitcases we found. The clothes in the closet, we left, but we got socks, pajamas, leggings, t-shirts, and panties.

Cash set Caroline up in the room across from his and I'm next door. I have the hall bath, but the guest room has its own bath. Cash would have probably given up his room if it didn't. He wants everything perfect.

"She won't want to sleep in your man-whore bed anyway," I tell him as we bring her bags into the guest room.

He looks a little contrite. "You think I should buy a new bed?"

"For God's sake, no. Just wash your sheets, you heathen. And spray some Febreze. Actually, open the windows. It smells like musk and pussy in there." It doesn't, but I like the embarrassment he wears. "Do you think the room will do for her?" I follow up as I put some of her soft things from her own bed onto this one. Lifting a cute little stuffed animal to my face, I smell the strawberry and vanilla scent that always clings to her.

Since being in the hospital, she doesn't smell like that anymore. I went into her bathroom and grabbed her shampoo and conditioner as well as other toiletries. I don't know which one makes the smell, but I want it back. We aren't going to unpack her things; she will want to do it, but we put out a few things to make her feel at home.

"I wish I knew what kind of food we should stock. I didn't even look in her kitchen." Cash wanders around, picking things up and moving them before moving them back. "Oh, she loves the coffee at Lizzie's. I'm going to go get her some so she has it here. I just want her to be happy, Duke."

"I know, me too."

Climbing up in his, honestly, stupidly high truck, I look over at him and it seems like we realized the same thing at the same time.

"Dammit, Cash, why is your truck so fucking stupid?"

"Duke, I've never needed to transport someone who couldn't climb in here." We sit there trying to figure out how to solve such an absurd problem.

"Got it." Pulling out my phone, I scroll to K.

"Hello?" she answers on the third ring, her voice heavy with sleep.

"Kayla? Good morning."

"What the hell, Duke? Its—6:45 am and in case you didn't remember, my wife worked until one o'clock in the morning at *your* bar and now you're calling me this early?"

"I figured you would be up, you know, for the garage."

"What do you want?"

"We have a problem. You know how Cash has this stupid ass truck up in the damn sky?"

Cash smacks me and I smirk at him.

"Yes?"

"And my truck doesn't have a backseat. Well, we need to get Caroline today and bring her home. Can we borrow a car?"

She exhales a long, loud, tired-of-this-shit kind of sigh before telling me to meet her at the garage in half an hour.

"This...Kayla." Cash gives her a long look. "This is a minivan, Kayla." He looks personally offended that he is trading his jacked up pickup for a minivan.

"Ashley James Colter, you two fools woke me up and dragged me from my warm bed before seven in the morning, begging for help, and now you're complaining about the help I am offering?" She crosses her arms, leveling him a look.

"Nope, absolutely not. Thanks, you're the best!" he yells as he goes around to the driver's side and climbs in.

"Seriously, you're a lifesaver," I tell her.

"I know, I know. You owe us. Take care of her, Duke. And tell her to text me."

"Sure thing."

Driving down the highway a few hours later, Cash gushes over his newfound love for a minivan, "I have to admit, it does drive smooth. And the gas mileage, amazing."

"Great, you can trade in your truck for one. Maybe throw a couple car seats in the back."

"Look at all the storage in this thing!" he tells me, popping things open and pressing buttons.

"Cash, just drive."

"You're mean." He pouts.

A laugh erupts from me. I hope beyond hope I get to have the girl I love and my best friend. It will kill me if I have to choose.

Back at the hospital, we find Caroline sitting up in bed, a tray of food in front of her. Her smile is radiant when we enter.

"Hi." She gives a little wave before biting into a piece of toast.

"Hey, Hurricane." Cash drops a kiss on the top of her head.

I'm struck by how comfortable their affection feels, how casual. Caroline and I have always been like fire. All or nothing. But we never managed to make it to the comfortable, warm blanket stage—the gentle hugs and cuddling before falling asleep. The little kiss before walking out the door. It makes my heart ache to see it. I want that for her, with her. "Brought you something." He holds out his hand and the necklace dangles from his fingers.

"Oh my god, Cash!" she exclaims, reaching for it.

"I'll do it." Moving her hair, he clasps it behind her neck, kissing her shoulder gently.

Nudging him out of the way, I lean down and press a gentle kiss to her mouth. No expectations, no lingering, just a small kiss. She gasps a little and her lips part. It physically pains me not to deepen the kiss and drive into her mouth, tasting her. I lick her bottom lip just slightly before standing up.

Her breathing comes out a little erratically and her cheeks flush. I wink before taking my usual seat next to the bed. Cash smiles at the two of us, radiating pleasure. I want to be as at peace as he is. When I watch the two of them, I'm not jealous he's next to her and I'm not. I just want a piece of their affection for myself. I want to learn how to love her the right way.

I will learn to love her the way she deserves. Even if that love is returned by only half of her heart.

Chapter 36
No One Else on Earth

Callie

In the afternoon, the doctor finally comes in and does one last check. He gives me, what feels like, a thousand discharge instructions. I'm told to rest for another week with no strenuous activity for another two weeks. He gives Duke and Cash a look with narrowed eyes as he puts emphasis on "at least two weeks." They both watch him with rapt attention like they don't want to miss a single instruction.

I have no concerns about them adhering to the rules. I suspect I will be fighting the bonds of the rules before they give in.

"Where in the world did you get a minivan?" I ask Cash after I've been helped into the car. I wanted to stand and walk the last few feet in the loading zone, but Cash pushed me right up to the door and Duke damn near picked me up and placed me inside. I didn't do anything. They are like a couple of doting old women.

"Duke borrowed it from Kayla. Apparently my truck wasn't a good choice."

"Oh yeah. I could barely get in and out when I wasn't hurt. Good thinking, Duke." I give him a sweet smile. His eyes soften and he runs a finger down my cheek.

"Anyway, it's actually a really nice car. Look at the storage!" Cash exclaims, opening some hidden compartment. Snorting out a laugh, I side eye Duke who just rolls his eyes.

"If you say so. Let's go home, I'm tired and want to rest in a real bed."

"Sure thing, Hurricane."

The long drive flies by with classic rock flowing through the speakers, Duke and Cash both tapping their fingers or whistling along. I watch them and notice the ways they are the same despite how different they are. Duke is more relaxed with Cash around, like Cash fills some sort of part of him that was missing. Cash is his happiness. It makes me want to cry, knowing no matter how much I adore Duke, I wasn't seeing essential parts of him when it was just us.

Cash is light, and free, like the sunshine he is. He orbits Duke a little, like Duke's grumpy cloud balances his bright sunny day. During those early days of dating, I remember thinking these men were two sides of a coin, each giving me something the other wasn't. But I was missing the whole picture—they aren't two sides of a coin, they are two halves of a whole person and together they form someone who was created for me.

At the ranch, Cash pulls the van right up to the stairs, onto the grass. Rolling my eyes, I wait patiently for my nurses while they huddle by the door, whispering as though they didn't have a spare second to consider getting me out of the vehicle, up the stairs, and inside the house.

"Okay darlin', we are going to help you out of the car and

up the stairs. I'm going to go put the dogs away first, so they don't jump on you. Be right back." He runs up the stoop and into the house.

"Come on, sweetheart. Let's get you sorted." Duke grabs me under my arms and turns me so I can be helped up. Sitting there, I stare into his eyes, and he watches me. "What?"

"Nothing. I just missed looking at you is all." His face transforms into a look of love and softness I've never seen before.

Clapping, Cash says from the door, "Alright, let's do this."

A man under each arm, they lift me gingerly, and my feet barely touch the floor as they help me up, one step at a time. I grunt a little at the effort and they both furrow their brows. Once we are in the entryway, they take turns removing shoes and hats while I breathe heavily through the pain shooting up my side at every movement.

I look fearfully at the stairs to the second floor where I know my bedroom is.

"Fuck this," Duke says beside me, drawing my attention. Stooping a little, he carefully picks me up into his arms. Carrying me bridal style, he moves toward the stairs.

"Wait, Duke, I'm too heavy. I can do it."

He looks at me incredulously, with an angry set to his mouth.

"Don't ever talk that way. You're perfect." And up the stairs we go. He carries me straight through the door of my room and lays me gently on the bed. His breathing comes a little faster but otherwise, he doesn't seem overly exerted.

"Are you okay?" I ask him, afraid I've hurt him somehow.

"He's fine, the brute. I could have done it. I didn't want to steal his thunder though; I know how important it is that he's big and strong," Cash remarks as he walks into the room behind us, showing off a bicep in his short sleeve shirt.

"Not all of us get manhandled by thousand-pound animals

just to prove we can. Some of us have practical uses for all this." Duke gestures to his body. Looking at them standing side by side, ribbing each other, I take in their differences. I never compared them to each other before.

Duke is a good three inches taller than Cash, but they are both over six feet. He's long and lean, but there is quiet strength in the lines of his body, his arms strong and his stomach flat. Despite vividly remembering how he felt moving inside me, I've never seen him completely naked and gotten to look at him.

Cash is shorter, more compact but his musculature is more defined, louder. Where Duke's is quiet but powerful, Cash's body is all hard lines and screams power at you. The way he moves is confident and comfortable. Remembering how he stood over me on the creek bank, allowing me to look him over, brings blood to my cheeks.

"Something on your mind, darlin'?" Cash asks me, a knowing smirk on his face. My face feels hotter, my neck and chest turning red, and Duke chuckles.

"Leave her alone, Cash. She's just an innocent, shy, little lady."

A full laugh explodes from Cash at his words.

"Yeah, if you say so." My mouth drops open at the casual way they are most certainly talking about the fact I have had sex with both of them.

Duke begins a little tour, telling me where to find all my things, about the stuffed animal he brought from my apartment, my clothes in the suitcases that they will help me put away if I need. I'm again reminded of two old ladies settling me in. They are nesting, both overly concerned about what I need and want.

"Can you guys do something for me?" I ask from my place on the bed, propped up by more pillows than I thought one man would ever have in his house.

"Anything," Cash breathes while they watch me eagerly, waiting for a task.

"Go away. I want to take a nap. All your fidgeting is making me nervous." I smile a huge, sunny smile.

"Alright, but here is your phone." Duke lays it on the bedside table. "Call either of us if you need anything. We'll be downstairs. My room is just next door," he knocks on the wall, "just on the other side. Cash is across the hall."

"Thank you, both of you. This is too much, but I appreciate every second."

Cash comes to me first, leaning down to whisper against my lips. "Nothing is too much; you deserve everything," he says, before kissing me chastely and skipping out of the room.

Duke leans over me, smelling delicious, making my nostrils flare. "Sunshine, you can't look at me like that. Doctor's orders." He skims a hand lightly up my leg, under my blanket, and my breath comes out in pant. "I promise to make it up to you." Kissing me, gently at first, he slips his tongue in between my lips, tasting my mouth. He moans in his throat. "Fuck, I can't wait." Turning, he follows the way Cash went, pulling the door closed behind him.

Leaning back against my pillows, I take in the room I've been assigned. I wonder idly how many bedrooms are up here. I've never seen the second floor and didn't get a chance to inspect when Duke carried me up. The walls are painted a pale, calming blue. There are landscapes in dark frames on the walls, pictures of Montana's plains and a few of horses out at pasture. I recognize Daisy and Violet. The black rearing stallion must be Charger. On the dresser is a younger Cash, on a bull.

The furniture, a simple headboard, matching dresser, and two nightstands, are knotty pine and large, exactly the sort of thing I would expect on a ranch. There are wide double windows looking out on the front yard, and I can see the horse barn off in the distance. Gauzy white curtains cover the windows. Through the partially opened bathroom door, I see double sinks with white counters and darker blue cabinets. There's an expansive glass shower with blue and grey tiles and multiple shower heads, with my brand of shampoo and conditioner on the small shelf.

Under the soft blue sheets, I stretch out. The quilt looks handmade in shades of blues, greens, and browns. Did Cash hire a decorator? Maybe his mom before she got sick? Everything is so cozy, the way Cash feels, and coordinates well. I snuggle down into the pillows until I feel enveloped by their soft warmth. I close my eyes and drift off to sleep.

"Should we wake her up?" I hear Cash whisper. My mouth tips up in a smile.

"No, she's recuperating. She needs sleep."

"But it's been hours." He's whining. I try to stay still so I can listen.

"You aren't a baby that needs to be entertained. Are you seriously pouting? I'm leaving." I hear Duke leave.

"Hurricane, I'm bored. Maybe I'll just talk to you while you sleep. Seeing you in my house, it's like magic. I've missed you so much." I feel his hand resting on my foot. I try to remain frozen. "Don't tell the grumpy guy but having both of you here? It's perfect. I can't wait to hold you in my arms. The dogs have been losing it at the bottom of the stairs. I think they know you're here. Wait until I tell you some of the outlandish tales from the town about what happened. And the gossip, you wouldn't believe. You don't have to tell people anything when you're in a small town full of imaginative busy bodies. They are saying we were at yours having a threesome when a man broke in and Duke shot him, while naked!"

I can't control it, and I break out in a fit of giggles.

"Caroline Pearce, were you eavesdropping?" he says in mock outrage.

Fully laughing now, holding my side, I wheeze, "Stop, stop, I can't laugh this much. You were talking to *me*! How could I be eavesdropping?"

"Because I was talking to unconscious you!" he says, acting confused.

Duke comes through the door, smiling. God, his smile is glorious, even more so because I know it's rare. "You woke her up? You really are an infant!"

"I didn't. I don't even know when she woke up. She just started laughing." He holds his hands up in surrender.

"Can someone help me up? I need the bathroom." Both men spring into action, trying to figure out how to help.

"It's my turn, Duke, you carried her up the stairs."

"Because I'm stronger than you."

"You are not."

"Stop bickering—you're like an old married couple. Give me your arm, Cash." Pulling myself up, I wince as I take a few steps.

Duke steps forward. "Caroline, I can carry you." He reaches for me, and I bat his hand away.

"I appreciate it, but I really need to be able to pee by myself. For my dignity."

They both roll their eyes.

Cash's eye light up with mischief. "It's not that different than—"

"So help me God. Do *not* finish that sentence if you know what's good for you." My face burns, probably bright red.

"What? What did I miss?" Duke looks between us.

"Nothing!" I say loudly just as Cash says,

"Oh, just that Callie can—"

"Shut up, Cash!"

He puts his hands up again. "Okay, okay."

Duke frowns.

I shut the bathroom door in both their faces.

We spend the week of forced rest reconnecting and creating new memories.

One day was spent entirely playing different card games.

Another day, we did some online shopping since I refuse to wear anything from the closet of my apartment.

One or both of them stand vigilant guard over the bathroom door as I shower. I know they would help but I need to get the independence of at least bathing. Cash brings me books and Lizzie's coffee. I spend hours looking out over the ranch and getting lost in steamy romance novels, knowing that my own romance is happening around me.

I'm impressed by their cooking abilities every day. I shouldn't be surprised by men who live alone and care for themselves, but I am, nonetheless. Cash brings Tank and Snapper up to visit. Snapper acts like a fool and Tank lies at the foot of my bed, his grey head laying on my legs.

I feel better enough to put my clothes away and to walk slowly around the second floor, peeking my head into bedrooms. I discover Duke's bedroom is the same as mine except his walls are a muted yellow and he shares a hall bath with a fourth bedroom. The fourth bedroom is pink, Cash informs me he wanted me to have the pink room, but I deserved my own bathroom, so I got the blue room. I have no idea why he has so many bedrooms or why he chose the colors he did.

There's an office up here as well but instead of bookshelves and art, there are hundreds of medals and belt buckles lining the walls around a desk that houses the ranch ledgers. I'm in awe of the evidence of his talent and amused by the pictures that line a table; pictures of him on bulls, accepting his first Championship buckle, and his parents.

But the ones I love the most are him with a tall gangly teenager, then a filled-out, lean man. Duke and Cash by the creek, splashing around. Duke at Cash's graduation. Both of them on horseback, surrounded by steers. It's a tiny glimpse into the entire life they had together before I stormed into it.

I reach the last door in the hallway. Cash's door. It feels intrusive even though he told me to look around. His bedroom, his space, where I know he has had more than a few women and I've never even seen behind the door. I turn and walk away. I'll leave it for another day.

"Callie!" I hear Cash calling so I lean over the stair banister and see him standing in the living room. "Hey, pretty girl, don't you think you've been upstairs long enough? Wouldn't it be nice to come down here?"

"Stop yelling!" Duke comes from the kitchen with a towel over his shoulder that reminds me of nights at the bar. "Want me to help you down the stairs, sweetheart? We can have dinner down here tonight."

"Yes, please," I tell him enthusiastically. I'm going stir crazy up here.

Once they have me seated in a chair at the little table, Tank at my feet, and three dogs zooming around the living room, Cash brings me a glass of lemonade. "Sorry, Hurricane, no whiskey for you; you're still on meds." He puts down two tumblers of the rich amber liquid before disappearing again.

Duke places a serving platter piled high with green salad and grilled salmon in the center of the table, while Cash puts a basket full of bread next to it. My plate is piled high and we all sit together, eating and laughing. I feel more content than I have in months.

We sit together and it's like a family takes shape around me. We discuss the adventures I got up to when we were apart. I tell them about the hiking trips and falling deeper in love with

Montana every day. About the tattoo and how I picked every-thing and how much those days together meant to me. I dissect my thoughts about the two of them being incomplete without the other. I make sure to mention I visited a doctor about birth control which causes Cash to grin widely and Duke's cheeks to turn slightly pink.

"So, Sunshine, I've got some bad news," Duke tells me, a serious look on his face.

I put my fork down and fold my hands in my lap. "Okay?"

"Lord, don't look so afraid. It's not that bad. Neither Cash nor I have worked in almost three weeks. Now that you're moving around a little, we are going back to work."

"Oh," I say, dejected. I mean, of course it makes sense, but I love what we have here.

"Callie, I work on the ranch, I'll never be more than a ten-minute ride away. And we already talked about it. Duke will be here during the day while I'm out there. I'll be back here before he leaves for the bar. You'll never truly be alone and nothing else is changing."

I raise my head, hopeful.

"Did you think I was leaving?" Duke asks me.

"Yes. You don't live here. Eventually, you'll have to go. And I'll have to find a place to live. This feels like a temporary bubble, and I don't want it to pop."

They both reach out, simultaneously, each of them grab-bing a hand. Cash's hand is warm, and he rubs gentle circles on my knuckles. Duke's hand is large and swallows mine. "Let us worry about that. For now, I'm on day duty and Cash will be here at night. As much as the idea pains me." His joke lightens the mood. I squeeze both of their hands.

Chapter 37
I Know She Ain't Ready

Duke

The first morning Cash heads out on horseback at six am, I walk by Caroline's room to find her sitting and watching him trot away on Daisy.

"You okay?" I sit beside her.

"Yeah, I'm fine. It's so beautiful out there, it's painful. I can't wait until I can go for a ride. Oh Duke, Lola is stunning. I forgot to tell you. I don't think she liked me, but she is stunning."

"She's just shy. Once you're up for the walk, I'll take you out there; she will warm up. Want some breakfast?" I pull her to her feet, and she trails me, a little slower, down the stairs. Tank and Snapper are out with Cash so it's just us and my dogs. It feels so right, just being with her.

Cash expressed a little concern over the new arrangement, but I think it's going to be important we each spend a little time alone with her and she gets to spend some time without us both hovering.

She sucks in a breath, like she's preparing for something. I flinch a little. She seems happy but I'm always going to be a little on edge, I think, not sure what's in her head as far as we are concerned.

"Duke, can we talk?"

"Of course." Dread fills me but I try not to let it show on my face.

"I just, well I want to say I'm sorry. The way things went down? It wasn't right."

I hold up a hand to stop her. "Sweetheart, it's okay. Cash and I already talked through it. We know what happened and we already forgave you."

"That's great that y'all worked it out, but I didn't. I don't deserve forgiveness until I say what I need to say. I didn't know what I was getting into when I met you. You're hard to read, even harder to get close to. It was confusing but the more time I spent with you, the more I craved our fire. Our passion." Her eyes are alight with feeling as she speaks. "You fed a part of my soul I didn't know was starving. Our desire for each other made me feel like I was wanted in a way I never have been. I needed you so much. And I regret it every day that I betrayed that."

Kneeling in front of her, I place one of her hands over my heart. "Caroline, from the moment I laid eyes on you, you were in my dreams—behind my eyelids every time I closed my eyes. When I couldn't control myself anymore, I took you in my storeroom and gave you everything I could, not knowing you were going to become the sun around which my world revolved. You deserved better than a quick romp in the dark and I intend to make it up to you. But more than that, you deserved to be given everything." Kissing her fingertips, I lay my head against her stomach.

Looking up at her, I continue, "When I saw you in that closet, my broken heart healed instantly. There isn't a single day, for as long as you'll have me, that I won't strive to prove *you are mine*."

I pull the little box from my pocket, and she inhales sharply. Handing her the little blue box, tied with its white ribbon, I sit back on my heels.

"Open it," I order her.

Pulling gently on the ribbon and letting it fall away, she cracks open the box and a giddy smile tugs her mouth up.

"Oh Duke, it's perfect!" She pulls the delicate silver bracelet from the box, its tiny charms jingling. "Oh, a little fish for our date! And a storm cloud." Her cheeks pink at the memory. "This one is just a little cup?"

"They didn't have one of a beautiful girl perched on a table, panting for me, so that one will have to be the bar." I wink, and her laughter fills the room. "Put it on."

She holds out her arm and I loop it around and clip the little closure.

Tugging gently on the gold chain hanging from her neck, I say, "I couldn't let Cash be the only one you wear."

"Silly boys."

We spend the rest of the day lounging on the sofa, her soft leg lying in my lap as I rub her foot. Every once in a while, she rubs it against my dick, and I immediately harden.

After the third time, my balls are in so much pain I can hardly sit here anymore. "Sunshine, I need you to stop that. I haven't been inside you in months and I'm going a little crazy. You aren't cleared for anything strenuous for a few more days. I'm already jerking off every day and I wasn't planning to before work."

Her giggles make me smile. She sits up and leans over, bringing her mouth right to mine. "Sorry, Grumpy."

Picking her half up, I lay her back on the couch before

hovering over her. I push my pelvis into her and press my hips against hers, rolling them just slightly.

Leaning down, I skim my mouth from her collarbone, up her neck, and latch my lips to her ear, tugging gently. She lets out a long, throaty moan and I thrust against her again.

"I cannot wait to sink inside you and feel you come on me. But before that—" I thrust gently against her again, and she mewls beneath me. I lick up the column of her throat. "I'm going to fuck you with my tongue until you beg for mercy. Okay, baby?"

She nods breathlessly and I sit up, returning to my side of the couch, pulling her foot back into my lap.

What seems like seconds later, Cash bursts through the door.

"Honey, I'm home!" he bellows and Caroline squeaks.

He looks at me, all serious, and Caroline's blush high on her cheeks and narrows his eyes. "Doctor said!" He points a finger at me accusingly.

"I didn't do anything. She's the one who won't keep her feet to herself." His gaze drops to the foot in my lap then swings to her face. Laughing, she covers her face with her hands.

"Naughty, naughty," he scolds her before leaning over the back of the couch to kiss her. "Heading up to shower, be back in fifteen." He bounds up the stairs, taking them two at a time.

"See, you got me in trouble." Rubbing circles on her ankle, I move my hand slowly up her leg. I massage her calf then her knee. I knead her thighs before placing my palm flat against her legging-clad pussy. "Fuck, sweetheart, you feel pretty wet. You good?" I taunt her.

She whimpers and moves her hips against me. I press down with the heel of my hand until she lets out a little moan, her eyes rolling.

"Sorry pretty girl, can't do anything about it for"—I pretend to check a watch—"four more days. Doctor's orders." I hear Cash's bedroom door open.

Standing, I adjust my dick as it presses into my zipper before giving her a chaste kiss. "Gotta get dressed for work, maybe take my own shower." I pass Cash as he thumps his way down the stairs.

"You look awfully flustered, Hurricane. You okay? Are you in pain?" I laugh quietly to myself as I head into my bedroom to get ready for work.

Chapter 38
(Everything I do) I do It for you

Cash

Finally having some alone time with Callie feels like falling into a warm embrace, I've missed her so fiercely.

Serving her the steak I grilled up with a potato, we sit outside and have dinner on the deck.

"How was your day without me, Hurricane?" She looks a little unsure how to respond. "Listen, this is as new to me as it is to you, and to Duke. None of us have ever had to navigate something like this before. If you had fun with Duke, you can tell me."

"I had a good day. We had fun watching movies and stuff. I just don't want to hurt anyone."

"If there was ever a man in the world that I was jealous of being with you, around you, it wouldn't be Duke. I know he's a good man. And there is every chance you end up with him as there is with me. But he deserves happiness too, so I don't begrudge him chasing it."

"Cash?"

"Hmm?"

"I need to tell you something."

The words feel like a lead stone just dropped into my stomach. I lay my fork and knife on the table and give her my full attention.

"I'm sorry. You didn't deserve what I did. I didn't set out with the intention to hurt you or Duke. By the time I realized you guys were friends, best friends, I was already in too deep. I knew I couldn't keep it from you both forever; it was inevitable. But I just wanted to for a little longer before I was forced to choose or lose you both. So, I'm sorry."

"Fuck, Hurricane. You have the most amazing, kind, pure heart. I know, *we* know, you weren't trying to hurt us. Can I tell you a secret, just between us?"

She looks at me curiously. "Yes."

"After the rodeo, after my initial hurt wore off, I wanted to run over to your house every single day. You're the only woman I've ever felt this way about. I don't want to stress you out, and Duke said I shouldn't even tell you. But fuck, Callie. You're the only woman for me."

Her mouth opens in a silent 'O.'

"I love you, Caroline Pearce. I'm sorry to just spring this on you, and you don't have to return it, I just need you to know. I have loved you since the first time I took you out. I was in love with you at Lizzie's when we packed your stuff, and I was head over heels that day by the creek. I thought I lost you in that closet and I don't know if I would have survived it." The memory of that day causes tears to spring to my eyes which I swipe away with the back of my hand.

She has a stunned look on her face, then it crumbles and tears fill her eyes and spill down her cheeks.

Standing, I round the table and squat in front of her. "What Callie, what is it? I'm sorry, I didn't mean to upset you."

"Nothing's wrong really, I just—" Sobs tear from her chest.

"Callie, what in the world?"

"I just, I love you too, Cash. So much. But..." She doesn't finish her sentence, and she doesn't need to. My heart damn near explodes out here on the porch. I want to cover her from head to toe in kisses, lavish her with love until she pushes me away.

She's worried about Duke. Worried about what this means.

"Don't worry about Duke, baby." I kiss the tears on her cheeks. "I promise, nothing has changed. Actually, this weekend, we're going to his house to get more of his stuff and make this living arrangement a little more permanent. Nobody is leaving."

More tears roll down her face, and Tank whines at her feet. Out of all the dogs, he's the most obsessed with her. He just wants to lay on her all day. He must get that from me. She reaches a hand down and rubs his head, soothing his anxiety.

"I know we are just getting into the swing of things here and returning to work but, uh..." I rub the back of my neck with my hand, trying to figure out how to bring this up. Her wide, wet eyes watch me. "The rodeo season is winding down, but I have a couple more appearances to make before the end of September. Then we settle into winter. So, I will be gone in the next few weeks, off and on."

She sniffles a little but doesn't say anything.

Laying in my bed later, I stare up at the ceiling. Things have gotten infinitely more complicated but also simpler. Duke and I have the woman we love right across the hall from us— this is what every man could want. But we have to traverse the complicated relationship we are in and what the future holds.

Duke has been my best friend for more than thirty years but now, my heart is twice as large to accommodate someone new and I want to explore exactly what this means.

Chapter 39
On The Road Again

Callie

Lying in bed, I stare out the open curtains to the bright stars shining over fields and pastures. Happy isn't even the word I would use to describe the pure, all-consuming joy I've felt recently. Spending my life in this place could be enough for me.

They could be enough for me. Am I brave enough to take it?

They aren't making me choose right now; they don't even seem to care when they see me intentionally *not* choosing. At the end of this week, I will have my body back. It will belong to me again. Roger won't be in control of what I do—the same way he hasn't been in charge of who I am for so long.

If I decide to turn my life into a romance novel and choose to love them both, what will happen? We can remain here, in my gorgeous slice of peace tucked away on the ranch. But Cash is a public figure, and we live in a very small town. Judgement is definitely a possibility, though any woman who has seen Cash and Duke side by side surely can't judge me.

I'm going to keep them. Both of them. This can be our future if I'm brave enough to try and keep it.

GRUMPY NOT-COWBOY

Goodnight, Sunshine. It feels good to be back behind the bar, but I would rather be with you.

Night night, Grumpy. I'm lying in bed, thinking about you.

I send a selfie of me, in my oversized sleep shirt, hair messy, lying in the millions of pillows on my bed.

I hear a gentle knock on my door along with the ping of an incoming text.

"Come in," I call out as I wiggle down further into the bed.

"Hey, Hurricane, I just wanted—what are you doing?"

"I'm snuggling. This bed is so comfortable and so many pillows. It's like a nest." I giggle.

He probably thinks I mean a bird's nest, but that's only because he's never read an omegaverse novel. He jumps onto the end of the bed, and I squeal out in protest.

"No boys in the nest!" I yell from under my pillows.

"Not even if I do this!" he yells as he dives under the covers, lifting my shirt and blowing a raspberry on my belly button before capturing a nipple between his teeth.

"Ah, stop," I tell him playfully. It tickles but also sends tingles from my ears to my toes. Suctioning his mouth around it, he pulls it deep and hard before letting go with a *pop*, making me giggle more.

"I just wanted to say goodnight, but you're so damn cute." He climbs up my body until he's beside me, wrapping his arms around me. He turns me slightly, my back to his front, his hips pressed against me, his cock wedged between us.

He kisses my neck gently where his chain hangs. Capturing my wrist, he studies the bracelet before he kisses there too.

"Do you think this can work?" I ask him quietly as we cuddle in the dark.

"What, us? I hope so."

"No, all of this. All of us." I hide my head a little in the pillow, so my words are slightly muffled. "All three of us. I don't want to choose. I can't. It will destroy me."

His arms tighten around my waist, holding me closer, while being mindful I'm still healing. "I suspect it would kill us too, baby. I can't speak for Duke, though I have spoken to him quite a bit, and I don't think either of us is interested in forcing your hand. We may be in a bubble right now, but no one has power over us, except us. Why don't you talk to Duke about it? For me, I'm as content to share you with him as I can be. I just want you to be happy."

"Goodnight, Cowboy."

"Goodnight, Hurricane."

I don't feel him crawl out of my bed but when I wake up at one-thirty, Duke leans over me.

"Hey, Sunshine, I just got home, and I wanted a kiss goodnight. Sorry I woke you."

I smile broadly at him. "I'm happy you came. Lay with me?"

He unbuckles his jeans and pulls them down his legs and pulls his shirt over his head, putting both on a nearby chair, laying his hat on top.

"Scooch," he tells me, so I make room, and he climbs in, lying on his back. I cuddle into his side. With his long arm wrapped around me, he pulls the back of my shirt up, exposing my skin. We lay together in the quiet with only the bright light of the moon illuminating us. He draws gentle circles on my flesh, soothing me to sleep.

It's so opposite lying with Cash, who fidgets and snuggles. Cash is warm and all hard lines that surround me completely. Duke is a little softer but calmer too. He's perfectly still except his hand on my back. I rest my arm on his abdomen, curling my fingers into the hair there, causing his muscles to bunch and release periodically. It makes me feel whole, complete, to have gotten both of my men in bed with me tonight.

Duke's rubbing slows, and his breathing deepens. He's falling asleep and my heart explodes with joy at having him here. Cash cuddling my back would make this better, perfect.

"I love you," I whisper almost inaudibly into the dark.

He freezes for a minute before pulling me more on top of his body, kissing the top of my head. "I love you, Caroline," he whispers back, just as quietly.

Again, the differences in our declarations of love are stark, but they feel right, for each man.

The rest of my forced rest week is much the same. Cash has to leave on Saturday morning for the rodeo and won't be back until Sunday afternoon. I think he's a little sad he will miss the end of my 'rigorous activity' restrictions, but nothing can be done, it's his job.

We sit and have breakfast together, the three of us, on Saturday morning before Cash leaves. Gathered around the little table, with what seems like piles of dogs at our feet, we feel like the family we're creating.

"So," he drags the word out about twenty letters long and Duke rolls his eyes. "It's been two weeks since you came home." The casual use of *home* as it refers to all of us makes my heart sing. "How do you feel?"

"Perfect. Good as new. Well, almost. I'm not going riding anytime soon but for the most part, I feel so much better." It's been four weeks since the incident and my body has bounced back.

"Speaking of riding." He side-eyes me. "While I'm riding bulls, you two kids have fun." He grins, cheeky.

"I do still have to work too, you know," Duke responds, his face concentrating on his eggs. He's clearly not as comfortable as Cash with joking about sex in front of me, about me.

"I know, but listen, I'll be gone for the night. Y'all can watch the show. Then, because I'm the sexiest man alive, you won't be able to control yourselves."

I throw a blueberry at him. "Yeah, okay." I tell him, laughing.

"Can I come down to the bar, Duke? To watch the rodeo?"

"Why would you think you have to ask, Sunshine?" He looks at me with curiosity. "You don't have to ask; you can come anytime you want."

"That's what she said," is Cash's snarky reply.

Duke and I swing our eyes in his direction, both wearing the same face of exasperation. He laughs back.

"Okay, I will then. I like it there."

"Alright, Hurricane, I gotta run. I love you!" Pulling me from my seat, he wraps me in his arms and kisses me. Deep and consuming, It's only seconds before my belly is alight and I crush myself against him, feeling him harden against my belly. Extricating himself, both of us breathing hard, he says, "Whew, sit back down. The first time we are back together, it can't be me bending you over the table in front of Duke." And with those parting words, he sweeps out of the room. I hear him putting his boots on before the front door opens and slams behind him.

Duke watches me silently as I take my seat, my cheeks surely pink.

"What do you want to do with your day before I head out later?" Duke asks me as we sit, the room suddenly silent and a little colder without Cash.

"It feels complete when we are all together," I tell him, a little sadly.

Grabbing my hand, he says, "I know."

Sitting on the porch in the afternoon sun, I decide to bite the bullet and ask Duke what has been on my mind since I spoke to Cash about our unusual situation.

"Hey Grumpy, can we talk?" I look over at him, relaxed in a rocking chair.

He looks momentarily concerned but replies, "Sure, Sunshine," all the same.

"I was talking to Cash and—"

"Don't listen to anything he says," he tells me with a laugh.

"I asked him about our...situation. About all our situations." I trail off somewhat, unsure of how to continue.

He stops rocking and rises to join me on the porch swing.

"What exactly is your concern, Caroline? Let me help." He's stoic as always in that comfortable, present way. He wants me to feel better, to not worry, and I love that.

"Can this work? Between us?" I ask him.

"What do you mean? I'm sorry, Caroline, but I'm going to need you to spell it out for me. I want to answer the right question, not volunteer the wrong thing."

"I can't choose, Duke. I am in love with you. And I'm in love with Cash. You two are so opposite and everything feels so right." Tears fill my eyes at my confession. I'm terrified of pushing either of them away, of hurting them. Duke is sensitive and has been hurt before and my fear of hurting him is the reason I'm in this to begin with.

Holding my face, he kisses the tears off both my cheeks before running his thumbs under my lashes. "Sunshine, I have never, in thirty-seven years, been happier than I am at this exact moment. I don't pretend to know the answer to any of these questions or how we will figure this all out, but I can promise you, with certainty, you are it for me. If this falls apart, then I will move on, but there is no way I'm leaving until you tell me to. That's exactly what I told Cash when you were in the hospital." He hugs me to his chest before holding me at arm's length to look into my face. "This was my idea, Sunshine. Making a go at it. I want this."

My heart swells with joy at his words. I've never felt loved the way I do at this house, on Colter Ranch, in tiny Inspiration, Montana and I refuse to allow this peace to be taken, no matter the circumstances.

Getting ready to head to the bar later, I'm a little nervous. Duke and I spent the day just being together, hanging out, working through some of my concerns. Tonight, we will watch Cash ride, after we will come home, and that's where the nerves come in. The only time Duke and I have ever been together was quick and rough on a table in a storeroom and it was one of the most mind-blowing orgasms of my life. What will happen tonight?

Duke, as usual, is just being his normal self, unsmiling, as he gets ready. He pulls his boots on and slides his hat on his head, his brown hair curling around his ears. He bends down and pulls his dogs into a hug before kissing the tops of their heads.

"Alright everyone, your job is to protect Sweet Caroline. Okay? She is the queen and needs her soldiers to keep her safe since Cash isn't here." They thump their tails on the floor in tandem. "Perfect."

I cover my mouth with my hand to hold in the laugh that's threatening to burst free, and he grins at me. His smiles are so rare, they feel like a special offering when I get a genuine one.

"I'll be there in a few hours, before the show," I tell him.

"Okay, sweetheart. I'll be behind the bar. Want me to order you some food for when you get there?"

"Yes, please." I beam at him.

He pulls me in for a kiss, and when I slip my tongue between his lips, he pushes me against the front door, trapping me with his body. Pulling my knee up to wrap around his hip, I stand with just my toes on the ground. One hand under my thigh and the other wrapped around the back of my neck, Duke kisses me like a man parched and I'm the only water available. My body responds like lightning, the fire that has been burning low and hot flares between us and we burn in it together.

He presses his hips to mine, his cock pressing against me, drawing a moan from my mouth. I tilt my head back and he moves to my throat, sucking and biting. He lifts my other leg and wraps them both about his narrow hips, his hands grabbing my butt to hold me up. We are panting into each other's mouths before we pull apart. I stare into his eyes and see the desperation there.

"Fuck it, I'll stay home. We can go upstairs," he whispers against my lips.

"No, we are going to watch Cash." Pulling him harder against me, I kiss him gently. "It will be worth it, Grumpy."

At my words, he steps back, dropping my feet to the floor,

and nods his head before grabbing his keys. "Bye, sweetheart, I'll see you in a bit." He grabs my face, one more chaste kiss laid on my lips before he says reverently, "I love you."

"I love you too." And I close the door behind him.

With four hours to kill, I decide it's time for an 'everything' shower. Gathering my supplies, I spend the next hour primping and prepping for the weekend filled with my men after way too long being restricted. Pulling on tight skinny jeans and a tank top, I buckle my belt, with a new fancy belt buckle at Cash's insistence, and plop a white hat on my head.

I decide to finally investigate Cash's room. He told me I could, but it was intimidating before now. Pushing the door open, I wander in and see his giant bed in the middle of the room, unmade. The excessive number of pillows seems to be a thing with him; I think his bed has more than mine. Diving into them, I snuggle down and take a selfie where you can barely see me peeking out.

> Hey, Cowboy, so many pillows. I may need to claim a new nest.

COWBOY CASH

Hey, Hurricane, that looks comfy but awfully lonely. I can't wait to be buried there, in you.

I mean WITH you.

He follows this with a winking face, and I laugh out loud.

Walking around, I pick up little trinkets and put them back. There's a little wooden bull on his dresser amongst colognes and discarded scraps of paper. Plus a few random belt buckles. Dirty clothes fill the hamper and spill onto the floor. A messy cowboy.

Deciding to be super nosy, I pull open the drawer on his bedside table. I find a half-empty bottle of lube, a few cock rings which I raise an eyebrow at, a handful of golden foiled condoms, and a tiny bullet vibrator. Well, we will need to get rid of all of that, I think, sliding the drawer closed.

In the second drawer, I find an assortment of letters and pictures of fans, mostly women. The pictures are a little inappropriate. Mixed in with the souvenirs, I see a few pairs of panties, none of which are mine. I feel sick to my stomach at the sight.

I turn and leave the room. I know it's hypocritical, considering our current situation, but a stash of women's underwear and half-naked, or fully naked, photographs feel like betrayal. Is he still seeing these women? When did he last fuck someone else? I want to cry at my stupidity for thinking I would be enough for a man like Cash. He's a fit, handsome, rodeo cowboy and I'm me; chubby, damaged, and not good enough. This is my fault; I should never have looked in his drawers.

Just another man I'm not good enough for. Duke's ex-wife is damn near a super model and based on the pictures in Cash's drawer, I'm not his type either. Sitting on my bed, I let the tears fall and consider my options. Am I the naive one here, thinking these men could possibly want me? My apartment is a no-go. Grabbing a bag from the closet, I throw a few days' worth of clothes in and head downstairs. My brain wages war on me, screaming at me that I've never been good enough. Why should now be any different?

The dogs whine as I get my boots on, my bag by my feet. Tank lays down, resting his head on my bag and my heart breaks a little for the peace I felt here. Those girls were right, all those months ago. I don't deserve a man like Cash—or Duke.

Walking out, I toss my bag in the backseat and get behind the wheel, thinking through my options. I don't think I can go to Lizzie's; I have no doubt she would let me stay there until I found something more permanent, but it isn't fair to her to put her in the middle of Cash and myself.

Driving out of town, I hope I'm making the right decision. It's going to destroy my heart to leave the men I love but they deserve better than a broken woman who is barely recovered from her ex-husband when the options before them are better. Cash deserves to find a woman without so much baggage to carry and Duke, my Duke, he deserves actual sunshine, not me pretending to be okay, caught up in the excitement of a new romance.

This will be better for them, even if it kills me.

Chapter 40
Stand by Me

Duke

I can't believe I get to have her in my bed tonight. Or her bed. Whatever works for her. I just want to hold her in my arms, wrap myself around her, and never let go. Pouring drinks for the regulars and chatting with Sadie, I watch the minutes tick by for her to show up and bring the sunshine into my bar.

At a little after seven, I call over to Mable's and place an order for a grilled cheese and fries for Caroline. It should get here around the same time she does. The rodeo is on the television above the bar and Cash should show around eight-thirty or so. She's finally off the medications so she can have a drink if she wants.

"Boss, you're fidgeting like a high school boy going to pick up his prom date. What the hell is going on?" Sadie asks.

"Nothing, I'm fine. Worry about yourself." I pull the towel off my shoulder and start wiping down the already clean bar.

"Okay, grumpy pants." Her snarky comment causes a few

men at the bar to snicker in response. I ignore them, going back to my clock watching.

Seven-thirty comes and goes and she's not here. A little bit later, the food shows up and I put it on the counter behind the bar.

Seven-forty and she still hasn't gotten here.

Seven-fifty.

> Hey Caroline, I got some food here for you, when you going to get here?

She reads it but doesn't respond. Must be driving or something.

Another fifteen minutes passes and she still isn't here.

> Hey Sunshine, I'm worried now. Everything okay? Cash is up in twenty minutes.

Eight-fifteen.

Eight-twenty.

I decide to call her this time.

"Hey, this is Callie, leave a message."

"Hey Caroline, it's almost eight-thirty. I was expecting you an hour ago. I'm really worried now. Please call me back. I love you."

I look up at the show and hear them announce Cash. Leaning against the bar, I watch him ride. It's beautiful as always. The countdown timer in the corner counts his eight seconds.

Six-seconds, he flows perfectly in sync with his bull.

Five-seconds, they dance like it's choreographed, his talent on display for the world.

Four-seconds, the tail of his rope is loose and whipping around.

Three-seconds, the tail whips him in the face. The crowd 'ooooohs' in response.

Two-seconds, the great beast beneath him does a double rear, pushing him back, the tail of his rope flying around and Cash loses his hold, flying off into the sand. His arm somehow lodges under the flank rope, getting trapped against the body of the raging animal. The barrel-men rush toward Cash to pull him free, his arm twisted at a sickening angle. They pull him while the fighters try to distract the bull.

As soon as they pull his arm free, Cash collapses to the ground. The thousand-pound bull sees him fall and stomps on top of him, catching him across the abdomen with his hooves. The bull is pulled away as Cash lays in the dirt, unmoving.

"What the fuck?" I hear from behind me, though I have no idea who it is. The camera pans away from Cash's prone body as the announcer discusses the wreck. I feel my mouth hanging open, but no words come out.

I feel a hand on my arm and Sadie's voice. "Duke, are you okay?"

I don't respond. I just pull my phone from my pocket. I don't know if I should call Caroline to find her or Sleepy to figure out what's happening with Cash.

I settle on Sleepy.

"Duke," he says by way of greeting when he picks up.

"Tell me he's alright, Sleepy."

"I can't do that. I don't know." My heart sinks at his words and I walk into the back room, leaning over the slop sink in case my stomach decides to empty itself.

"Is he...where is he? What's happening?" I plead for any piece of information.

"They just loaded him up. They are taking him to Regional. It don't look good."

My stomach has had enough, and I cough before vomiting into the sink. I heave over and over until I collapse onto the floor, my head between my knees.

"I'm going now, Duke. I'll let you know." The line goes dead, and I stare at the phone in my hand.

Where the hell is Caroline?

Dialing her number, it goes to voicemail again.

I can't even form words when it's time for the message. Tears run down my face, sobs erupting from my chest in giant hitching breaths.

Cash is hurt.

I don't even know how to write anything else. I can't figure out what to write. How do I put any of this into words? My phone rings in my hand, Caroline's smiling face appearing on the screen.

"Hello." My voice is hollow, wrecked. I can barely breathe through the pain in my chest.

"Duke? What's wrong? What happened?"

"Where are you? You weren't here. He's hurt, bad. And you weren't here." My voice is defeated, but I have to keep myself calm to have any sort of conversation.

"I'm sorry, I'm sorry. I'm coming now. Tell me, what happened?"

"Cash, the rodeo, the bull." My words don't make much sense, but I can't. I just can't. I start sobbing all over again. I feel Sadie wrapping her arms around me, and I sob into her shoulder. She pulls the phone from my hand.

"Hello?" she says.

"Oh, Caroline. Yeah, I know what happened. Cash fell and got trampled. He didn't get up. Um, I don't know what happened after that. Duke is real tore up though. Yeah, I'll tell him."

Hanging up, she slips my phone into my shirt pocket. "She said she is twenty minutes away. What happened Duke?"

"Sleepy said they took him to the hospital. It doesn't look good." A fresh wave of nausea overtakes me, and I start heaving again, but there isn't anything left. I just drool onto the floor, between my bent knees. My body shakes with sobs as I try to clear my head for just a moment, to figure out what happens now. I sit on the floor of the backroom and cry and cry and cry until I feel a different set of arms around me.

"Come on, Duke. We have to get up now." It's Caroline's soft voice I hear.

"Caroline?"

"Yes, Duke, I'm here. We have to go to him, he needs us."

I nod and allow her to wrap her arms around me and hoist me to my feet. She leads me out of the bar to her car and bundles me inside, helping me belt myself in.

"Where do I go, Duke?" she asks me quietly, getting her GPS ready. I tell her the name of the medical center and she sets off. It's completely silent in the car except for my hitching breath every once in a while. It takes an hour but sooner than I realize, we're pulling into the lot.

Somewhat calmer, I pull my phone from my pocket and check for messages; I have nothing. I dial Sleepy.

"Duke." His normally deep voice sounds empty and strained.

"Where is he, Sleepy? We are here at Regional."

"I'm in the first floor waiting room. Come in." And he hangs up.

Caroline comes around the car and opens the door. We walk side by side, her hand clutched tightly in mine as we walk. She squeezes mine reassuringly, but I don't feel any better. I won't feel any better until this is over and I know that Cash is okay.

Approaching Sleepy sitting in the plastic chair in the blue-walled waiting room where everything smells like disinfectant, I don't miss the reflection of Cash and I in an almost identical waiting room when Caroline was in the hospital.

He stands as we enter the room, his face thirty years older than the last time I laid eyes on him. His shoulders are slumped, and his soul seems empty.

No.

"No, Sleepy. You can't tell me what you're about to say. NO!" I yell. I don't need his words; I can feel them already.

"It's not good, Duke." He sits heavily in the chair, motioning me to take the one next to him. "Three broken ribs and a punctured lung, a broken femur, and a broken arm." I hear Caroline gasp beside me. "But he hit his head, hard, when he fell. He hasn't woken up and his heart stopped twice on the way here."

Broken, soul-crushing sobs come from Caroline, and she covers her mouth to try and hold them in. I want to cry with her, I want to, but I'm numb. The pain is so overwhelming I don't even think I have the capacity to feel it anymore.

"His mama and daddy are on the way; they'll be here in about an hour. I was waiting for them."

We sit in silence, only interrupted by Caroline's breathing and muffled cries. I take deep breaths, convinced that if I don't fall apart, it will be okay. We will all be okay.

"Sleepy?" I hear Cash's mother as she rushes into the waiting room.

"Hey, Mrs. Colter. Mr. Colter," he says.

His mama pulls me in for a hug, causing me to lose my grip on Caroline's hand as I'm enveloped. "Hey Duke. I'm so glad you're here." She gives me a wearied look, her eyes red-rimmed from her tears.

Caroline stands and recaptures my hand, leaning heavily against me.

"Mrs. Colter, this is Caroline." I don't explain who she is, I don't have the energy to decide what to say.

"Oh Callie, aren't you Cash's girlfriend? He told us all about you."

Caroline's face crumples at her words. Mrs. Colter's gaze takes us in, standing side by side, a little closer than appropriate for me and my best friend's girlfriend, her fingers entwined with mine. She doesn't comment, of course, but on the other side of this, there will be questions.

"Yes, I'm Callie." She holds out a hand for a handshake which both of Cash's parents accept.

"I have to go meet with the doctor, but I will come right back," Mrs. Colter says and rushes from the room.

Sitting back down in the uncomfortable chair, I feel Sleepy's eyes on me. I raise my gaze to meet his. His steely glare volleys between me and Caroline, and I can see the thoughts swirling in his eyes. We stare at each other for a few long moments until he seems to make a decision and opens his mouth to speak.

"Okay, I spoke to the doctor." Mrs. Colter rushes into the room before Sleepy gets out whatever thoughts he had formulated. I see him shake his head slightly, like he's clearing away his calculations.

"Dr. Kines says most of the issues aren't a huge deal. He needs surgery on his arm, and they are hoping to do it today. They already did an emergency repair on the lung and everything else looks good in his abdomen. He has a brain bleed which is why they are watching him so closely and why he hasn't woken up yet, but they are hopeful."

I reach out and squeeze her hands that are knotted in front of her. She sits heavily on a squeaky blue chair, her husband beside her. He wraps his arms around her shoulders and holds her close.

Looking at Caroline, I see relief in her eyes but also, a lot of fear.

"It's okay, sweetheart, he's going to be okay." I wrap my arm around her, pulling her in and kissing the top of her head.

"I know, I can't believe anything else. I just, dammit, Duke. Hasn't the last month been enough?" she speaks quietly but I know the other people in the room are listening.

Lifting her chin until she's looking me in the eye, I say, "We will be discussing where you were and why the hell you weren't at my bar. I don't know what happened, but we will come back to this. For now, let's focus on Cash. He needs us."

She nods her head slightly, her chin trembling. Leaning my forehead against hers, I whisper against her mouth, "I love you."

Tears fill her eyes and fall silently down her face. "I love you too, Grumpy."

"When can we see him? When does the doctor think he will be awake?" I ask the room.

Mr. Colter eyes me. "We can go in after the doctor is done in there. But I don't think it's a good idea for you two to be here when he wakes up. I don't know what the hell is going on here, but Cash has made it pretty clear that he is in love with Callie," he tells me, crossing his arms as he watches us. "I refuse to watch my son have his heart broken because his girlfriend is fooling around with his best friend while he's unconscious."

Caroline gasps from beside me. "Sir, it's not—"

"All due respect," the look he gives her is full of zero due respect, "buckle bunnies have been chasing my son for fifteen years. I know one when I see her. And this thing with Duke, while my son lays unconscious in the hospital, is trashy. I would like you both to leave."

More tears run down Caroline's face, and her breathing comes heavier as she tries to figure out what to say.

"Cash deserves better than a backstabbing best friend and a slutty girlfriend. Please leave," Mrs. Colter whispers from beside her husband.

My heart breaks at the fact these people who have known me for more than thirty years think I could do something like that to Cash. Standing to my full height, my shoulders back, I refuse to be shamed by this man.

"Now, watch how you speak to her. I'm not pleased with what you're saying but I will not stand for you calling her names. And if you think I'm unhappy about it, you wait until Cash wakes up, and *dare* call her a slut to his face." My chest heaves with anger. "I dare you to say it again." I level Cash's dad with a look.

"Alright, alright." I feel Sleepy's hand on my chest, as he symbolically holds me back. I wouldn't hit Mr. Colter but I'm almost mad enough to. "We don't know anything about the situation but the way I see it, if Duke was two-timing behind Cash's back, it seems unlikely he would choose the waiting room of the hospital to do it. Let's just keep the focus where it belongs for now."

"It's not what you think," Caroline says quietly beside me. I know she wants to hold onto me for support, but I also know she is probably afraid it will make things worse. I am not.

Wrapping my arm around her waist, I pull her against my body, lifting my chin. "Cash will explain, until then, keep your feelings to yourself."

We sit in tense silence for a while before a nurse in light green scrubs comes into the waiting room and tells us the doctor said we can go in now. Following her down the hallway, I clutch Caroline's hand to mine.

Entering Cash's hospital room is terrifying, and I almost fall to the floor again. I've held it together since my breakdown at the bar but seeing my best friend lying in the bed is too much to handle. There's a tube coming from his throat, connected to a machine pushing air into his body. Wires and cords snake out from under his blanket. His blond hair falls over his brow, his eyes closed as if he's simply asleep. His arm is wrapped and supported, with surgery scheduled for later today. Another tube winds out of the side of his gown, draining fluid from the site of his collapsed, punctured lung. I see Caroline run her fingers over her shirt, where I know she has a scar across her own ribs.

"It's okay, Sunshine. You'll have matching scars; it'll be cute," I murmur into her hair, and she lets out a small huff of laughter before the tears start again.

We all stand around and watch the machines monitoring his heart and his oxygen, the machine making a *shoo-a shoo shoo-a shoo* sound as air flows into his body.

"Is he on life support?" Caroline asks and Mrs. Colters nods affirmatively.

"The doctor says it's just until they know the extent of his brain injury. He's sedated. They are going to do a repeat CT scan later to see the progress, but it will likely be a day or two before they know how it's healing."

"Oh," is her only reply as she walks closer to the bed, grabbing hold of his hand, being mindful of all the tubes and things. Leaning over, she kisses him softly on his forehead, brushing his hair away. She speaks softly in his ear, words we cannot hear. Lifting his hand, she brings it to her cheek, holding it there before her shoulders begin shaking. Gently putting his hand back on the bed, she returns to my side.

We all approach the bed in turn. When I get close, I kneel beside him and lay my head on his hand. "Brother," I whisper against his clammy skin, my voice breaking. "Come back. We need you. Caroline and I need you. Tank and Snapper. Daisy. We can't do this without you. Come back." I stay there longer than I plan to, eventually feeling Caroline's hand on my shoulder.

Standing, I wrap my arms around her, putting my chin on the top of her head, and just cry. Tears for so many things run down my cheeks. Taking her hand in mine, we walk from the room. Sitting back in the cold, plastic chairs we let his parents have some time alone.

"Where were you, Caroline?" I can't wait anymore. I need to know.

"I got scared," she whispers, her voice barely audible.

I twist my body to see her face. "Scared? Scared of what?"

"Of this. Of us. I saw something that wasn't meant for me, and I got scared."

What the hell could she have seen while I was at work?

"What was it, Caroline? I can't help if you aren't telling me things. You can't run away."

"I was in Cash's room, being nosy. It was so stupid. I shouldn't have even been in there, but he said—he said I could look around. I opened his bedside table and there was," her voice breaks and tears fill her eyes, "photographs and underwear, other women, Duke. Beautiful women. Skinny, supermodel women." Her confession sends a stab through my heart.

If he wasn't already on his deathbed, I would kill him myself.

"Fucking idiot," I say in response.

Her tears fall faster, and I realize a second too late that she thinks I'm talking about her.

"Not you, Sunshine. Dumbass Cash. Listen, this is something you're going to have to talk over with Cash, but I can tell you with certainty he forgot they were there. He should have thrown that shit out but what I can tell you, Caroline, is that Cash loves you more than anything I have ever seen. If I was a better man, I would have stepped away from you a long time ago. But I'm not."

"You don't think he...you know, is still doing anything or that he cares about them?"

Running footsteps interrupt our conversation and I look up to see multiple nurses pushing a cart and a doctor all rush through the door to Cash's room. Standing, I go to the door just in time to see Sleepy and Mr. and Mrs. Colter ushered into the hallway as the door slams shut behind them.

Mrs. Colter collapses in a heap of hysterical crying on the floor with her husband kneeling beside her. His face is one of utter devastation.

"What is it? What happened?" I yell into the corridor.

"The machines just started beeping and a nurse came in and called a code blue on her phone. I think his heart stopped," Sleepy tells me, his face haggard and worn, deeper lines marring his brow than the last time he was in the bar.

Picking up his wife, Mr. Colter carries her into the waiting room and sits in a chair with her in his lap, rubbing circles on her back. We all sit in silence and stare at the closed door to Cash's hospital room, the entire space holding its breath. After too many minutes, the door opens, and I jump up to see what's happening.

Two nurses wheel Cash's bed out into the hallway while a third nurse slowly depresses and inflates a bag attached to the tube that goes down his throat. They roll him slowly down the hallway as Dr. Kines approaches the waiting room.

"Mr. and Mrs. Colter? Cash's heart stopped again; we aren't sure what is putting so much pressure on it but I'm afraid it might be the brain bleed. We've been monitoring it as closely as possible, but the neuro team thinks there may be some blood pooling in the brain stem which could be affecting his heart. We are going into surgery. We will let you know."

"Is he going to be okay?" comes Mrs. Colter's quiet voice from her husband's lap.

With a grave face, he says, "I can't make any promises right now. He's in rough shape."

Chapter 41
Mommas Don't Let Your Babies Grow Up To Be Cowboys

Callie

It's a full twelve hours of us sitting in relative silence, the occasional movement or errand to get coffee the only change to the tense atmosphere, before a new doctor we haven't seen before comes.

He pulls his scrub cap from his head as he enters the room, exhaustion evident in the line of his shoulders.

"Family of Ashley?" he says as he enters.

"Yes, yes that's us," Cash's mom says as she stands, smoothing down the rumpled clothing she's been in since yesterday.

"Great. They will be bringing him up soon; he's just in recovery. We had to evacuate a blood clot on his brain stem, but I think he's out of the woods now. I wouldn't be surprised if he wakes up today or tomorrow. We are removing life support since he's showing signs of breathing on his own."

The urge to throw my arms around this stranger over-whelms me but I wrap my arms around Duke instead. Tears of happiness flood my eyes, and I see the emotion reflecting back at me from four other sets of eyes in the room. Mrs. Colter doesn't ignore her desire to hug him though as she barrels toward him and hugs him, sobbing her thanks.

He smiles kindly before leaving.

Twenty-four hours later and none of us have had proper meals or a shower in two days. We are running on fumes and faith, but no one wants to leave his bedside and miss him waking up.

His mother and father sit on one side of the bed, Mrs. Colter with her hand wrapped tightly around his. Duke and I sit on the other side. I hold his hand, and Duke rests his hands heavily on my shoulders. We are all exhausted and weary. But ever so hopeful.

Standing to stretch, I wrap my arms around Duke's abdomen, holding him tightly against me, as he kisses the top of my head.

"Nearly dying has got to give me an advantage, brother," Cash's scratchy voice makes me spin back to him so quickly I lose my balance and nearly fall into the bed. "Careful, darlin', I'm happy to see you too but please don't kill me."

I laugh as I try to breathe through my relief at seeing his eyes open, a smile on his face.

"Oh my god, Cash, I never thought I would be so grateful for your snarky comments," I huff at him.

"Cash, my boy, my baby," Mrs. Colter sobs from her side of the bed at seeing her son wake up and launch immediately into teasing.

"Hey Mama, hey Dad. Hey, Sleepy." He gives a little head

nod to his trainer across the room who looks, for all his unemotional posturing, like he's breathing for the first time in days.

"What day is it? Sunday?" he asks the room.

"It's Monday night, Cash," Duke tells him, leaning over to hug him slightly.

"Well shit. Sorry, Mama," he apologizes for his language and we all laugh a little. It feels so good to relax for even a second.

"Y'all look rough. You been here the whole time?" He looks Duke and I over from head to toe.

"Of course, we wouldn't be anywhere else," I say.

It takes a full week before Cash can get out of bed completely unassisted and comes home. During his week convalescing, he was forced to explain our unorthodox relationship to his parents, much to their dismay. His mother did apologize to Duke and I, but I could tell she still wasn't convinced.

It's another two weeks at home before he climbs the stairs on his own.

Duke and I have reserved any forward momentum in our relationship because it felt wrong to revel in each other's bodies while Cash was unwell.

The time has come for me to have a conversation with Cash now that he's downstairs lying on the couch. It feels too much like a mirror into what I went through. Duke has gone back to work, quicker this time since he trusted me to care for Cash in his absence.

"Hey, Cowboy, how's it going?" I plop onto the couch next to him.

"I've had to hang up my ropes for now, Hurricane. Not much of a cowboy anymore." His voice is filled with pain.

"Just because you aren't riding bulls and roping calves doesn't mean you aren't a cowboy. You still have the ranch."

"I know. I sent my official retirement to the association today. Everyone knew it was coming but it feels final now that it's out there."

"I'm so fucking proud of you, Cash. You've created a legacy worth remembering and now you'll focus on the ranch." I climb into his lap, holding my own weight so as not to put any on his injured leg. I kiss him deeply, pouring all my love into him. I feel him harden almost instantly beneath me. "There is something else I need to talk to you about. Since we are sharing."

"Anything, baby." He nuzzles my neck, his scruffy beard scratching me.

"It's about the panties and nudes you keep in your nightstand." I drop the comment into the room, and he immediately goes rigid. He doesn't move for what feels like ages.

"Uh—" He rubs his face awkwardly. "Shit. Listen, I forgot—"

"No, you listen. I know you were far from saintly before me." I cock an eyebrow, daring him to respond. He stays silent. "But now that there is a me, and an us, I need them gone."

"They would be already if I remembered them. I haven't wanted anyone else but you."

Kissing him again, I grind against him a little.

"Good. Now would you like to make out? Maybe a little heavy petting?" I giggle against his neck, and he laughs.

"I may die."

Leaning forward, I capture his lips with mine. He thrusts his hips up the best he can with his cast, and I feel him hot and hard beneath me. Deepening the kiss, I suck on his tongue which pulls a moan from his throat.

I climb off his lap, and he frowns up at me from his position sunk into the couch. Reaching a hand forward, he tries to pull me back, but his casted arm is useless, and I laugh at his efforts.

"Nope," I huff out as I sink to my knees onto the rug in front of the couch and his eyes widen.

"What are you..." He trails off as I run my fingertips under the hem of his t-shirt, slipping them into the waistband of his basketball shorts.

"Can you lift your hips?"

He raises just enough for me to slide his shorts down his thighs and over his cast, and I let them pool around his ankles. His large cock springs free, bouncing in the space between us, the tip glistening with a small bead of moisture, the little ring at the tip shining.

"Fuck, Hurricane," he murmurs before leaning his head back on the couch as I wrap a tentative hand around his shaft and give it a tug. "This, uh, won't take long." He huffs out a laugh.

Lowering my head, I give a soft lick to the crown, tasting him for the first time. A breath hisses out between his teeth as I look, intimidated, at the large cock I hold in my hand, unsure of what to do with the shiny silver barbell.

Looking up at him from my position kneeling between his knees, I ask, "How do I..." I gesture with my head toward the piercing.

"Anything. I don't care. Whatever you want. Fuck, this view of you is the hottest thing I've ever seen."

I laugh at his response before dropping my head back down and wrapping my lips around him, pulling him as far into my mouth as I can. The metal feels weird on my tongue but doesn't get in the way. I push myself to the limit, gagging slightly, before popping my mouth off his length and gazing up at him.

He watches me intently, his mouth open, excitement lighting his eyes.

Placing a kiss against his head, I dip down and run my tongue from the base all the way to the tip, along the ridge, causing his dick to bounce comically. Sucking him into my mouth, I swallow as much of him as I can fit, and wrap my fist around the base, setting a rhythm.

Cash winds his hands into my hair, wrapping it around his fist as he pushes himself further down my throat, his breaths coming out in labored pants. Gazing up at him, my mouth stretched open around him, I catch his eyes. He groans low and long in his throat before his hips start moving and he proceeds to fuck my mouth, holding my head in place as he does everything he can to thrust.

"Fuck, fuck, fuck," falls from his lips in a sensual mantra, causing wetness to pool in my panties. "God. Fuck, baby. Yes." More words gasp out of him as his cock swells in my mouth, his release close. Reaching up, I cup his balls and tug. A long, low moan flows through his lips as he tightens his hold on my head, pushing me past my limits. My eyes fill with tears and gag.

"I'm going to come, baby. Tell me where. Where, Hurricane?" He releases his hold slightly on my head so I can pull my head off him, if I choose. Instead, I press further down, forcing more of him into my throat, and squeeze his balls gently.

A gasp pushes through his lips and his hips buck as he fills my throat with warmth, his orgasm shuddering through him. His breaths huff out and his chest heaves as he releases me, flopping back against the sofa.

Finally feeling like I cleared the last of the issues between us, I feel settled. This place feels like home, and I daydream about waiting for my cowboy on the porch at the end of the day before sending my bartender out into the evening to serve the locals their beers.

Chapter 42
Forever and Ever, Amen

Duke

It's been a month since the accident, and things are starting to fall into a rhythm around the ranch. Cash, while still on crutches, is at least making his way on his own up and down the stairs and seems to be in good spirits. It broke my heart to see the hollowness in his eyes when he realized his rodeo career was over.

It's not an easy thing to watch your life's work go down in a single eight-second span. Once he put in the paperwork for his official retirement from the rodeo circuit though, it was a turning point for him. He's focused on rehab and building the ranch into something bigger and better, though I don't for one second think he's done completely. I suspect in the coming years, he will be in the arena coaching some up-and-coming rodeo cowboy, like Sleepy did for him all those years ago.

We're all healing and figuring this out together but there's never a day that passes I don't feel more resolute in the knowledge that this, Caroline, and me, and Cash, are it for me. And I love her more every day.

"Hey, Sunshine." I lean down and press a kiss to her sleepy mouth as I sneak into her room when I get home from the bar.

"Hey, Grumpy," she replies, her voice heavy with sleep as a small smile tips up her lips. "Lay with me?"

Unbuckling my belt, I push my jeans down my thighs and leave them in a pile next to the bed before pulling my t-shirt over my head. Squeezing in beside her, I give her a gentle nudge to push her over, which she reluctantly does.

"You gotta give me a little space, sweetheart." I laugh to her.

"You could just lay on me," she replies, her voice mischievous.

Raising an eyebrow that I know she can't see in the dark, I reply, "Oh, really?"

Instead of replying, she wraps her warm body around mine and plants a few wet kisses against my chest, before moving her mouth up to my throat and sucking the skin between her teeth. My cock, which was already interested in these developments, fills with all the blood in my body, pressing against my boxers. Rolling to my side, I maneuver us until we are facing each other, her soft pajama top pressing to my chest and the ridge of my cock nestled at the junction of her thighs.

"Feeling a little needy tonight, Sunshine?"

Rubbing her body against the length of mine, she replies, "Yes, Duke. Please, it's been long enough. I need you." That sentence falling from her lips is the sexiest thing I have ever heard in my life, I think.

Grabbing the hem of her shirt, I tug it over her head, revealing her gorgeous skin in the moonlight shining in through her window. Lowering my mouth to a peaked nipple, I pull it into my mouth, clamping my teeth gently around it, drawing a gasp from her. Caroline writhes against me as my cock strains against my boxers, begging to be a part of the action. Running my hand down the soft skin of her back, I cup her round ass, discovering to my delight that she's bottomless. Slipping my hand under the curve of her cheek, I run a fingertip across her slick opening, slipping it just inside of her.

Lifting myself, I turn her so she's under me, her knees bracketing my hips. Pushing my pelvis into her, I rub my cock against her.

"Please, Duke. Please," she whimpers desperately from beneath me, pulling me against her.

"Please what, sweetheart? Tell me what you want."

"I need you inside me, Duke."

Whatever blood was left to feed my brain flows into my cock, and I'm unable to form a coherent thought. The last time I had her, it was frantic and desperate, on a table, while I held my hand over her mouth. This time, I will give her the devotion she deserves. Bringing my mouth to hers, I plunge my tongue inside, resting my body against her. She is eager and pushes her pelvis up to me, but I put the weight of my hips on her to keep her in place.

"Baby, we've got all night, and last time I was inside you, it was rushed. This time, I intend to take my time. Settle down."

Her breath whooshes out of her in a gasp. "Okay. I just want you so badly. I need you inside me."

"You may actually be the death of me," I reply.

Her giggle causes our bodies to rub together, and my skin is on fire with need.

"Stay put," I tell her, leaning back on my haunches as I take in her glowing skin in the moonlight. "Fuck, you're so goddamned gorgeous, I can't think around you."

Placing my palm open against her heaving chest, I run my hand down her body, across her stomach, and grab her hips, just feeling her soft skin in my hands. Lifting a leg, I bring it to my mouth and kiss the top of her foot, before peppering kisses up her shin and nibbling on the inside of her knee. Putting her leg down, I repeat the motion on the other side. She vibrates with need below me, her breathing labored. Leaning forward, I lay a wet kiss to the scar on her ribs that matches one Cash now wears. Lifting my hips, I push my boxers down my legs and taking my cock in my hand, I give it a few strokes to try and relieve some of the pressure.

Running the head of it through the wet flesh between her thighs, we both hiss at the contact. "Fuck. I've missed this so much. I can't wait to be inside you," I whisper into the darkness.

"So, fuck me, Duke." She has no idea what those words do to me.

"Soon," I tell her, rubbing my cock against her swollen, wet pussy.

Lowering my body, I press my mouth to hers, pushing my tongue between her lips, tasting every part of her mouth that I can reach. Memorizing every inch of it, reveling in the taste of her, as I thrust my hips against her, pushing myself into the wetness, but not allowing myself to slip inside her just yet. Moving to her neck, I suck the blood to the surface, flicking my tongue against her, hoping I leave a hickey like a teenager. The thought makes me chuckle.

"What?" she asks.

"Just hoping you wake up tomorrow covered in my marks."

She lifts her head, giving me more access to her neck and I dive back in, eager. Moving down her body, I pull each nipple into my mouth, tugging gently before moving down her stomach where I bite and nibble the skin, before settling on my stomach between her thighs. Her perfect pussy right in front of my face, I press my face against the wet skin and suck her clit between my teeth, tugging gently. Lifting her knees to my shoulders to give me better access to her, I spear into her wet heat with my tongue, pulling a full moan from her as her back bows off the bed.

Continuing down, I run my tongue across the tight skin of her ass, to which she responds with a squeak that causes me to laugh against her. Holding her thighs pushed back, I lave at the sensitive skin as she writhes above me, her fingers going into my hair, tugging gently at my scalp. Moving my hand to her swollen clit, I rub gentle circles around it as my tongue makes matching circles around her tight opening. Her breathing gasps out in pants and moans that cause my hips to buck involuntarily against the mattress, my erection painful where it's trapped beneath me.

When her thighs begin to shake where they are wrapped around my shoulders, I move up and suck her into my mouth, pushing two fingers into her dripping wet pussy and it pulses around me. Suctioning my lips to her, I move my tongue in time with my fingers as they plunge into her, her breathing accelerating and her back bowing off the bed.

She comes in a rush of wetness against my face. Squeezing my fingers, she feels so tight and perfect. As she shudders and shakes beneath me, I sit up quickly and slide my straining cock into the wetness that still pulses with aftershocks of her orgasm, causing her to cry out at the intrusion.

Her body squeezes me so tightly I almost come then, embarrassing myself. I push into her until our bodies are glued together and there's no space between us. Capturing her mouth again, I swallow the moans as I begin moving inside her.

"Duke, fuck..." My name slips between her lips like a mantra spurring me on. She clamps a hand over her mouth which I promptly pull away.

"Why are you covering your mouth? I did that the first time; this time I will hear you."

"What about Cash?" she whispers to me in the darkness.

"Let him listen, he might learn something." A gasp escapes from her before she giggles, slapping my chest lightly as I continue to slide into her body, a slow, soft rhythm. "You feel so fucking perfect wrapped around me, baby. Like a dream come true."

We create a gentle pace, our bodies moving in perfect sync as I stare into her eyes, moving inside her, and pour every ounce of love and devotion I have in my body into her. I can feel the love radiating off her skin as we move together. Rolling onto my back, I pull her on top of me, and grabbing her hips, I watch her find her own pace above me.

She slides her body against mine, creating the friction she needs, and she starts to pulse against me. Reaching down, I rub circles against her, my other hand cupping her breast and pinching her nipple. Her movements become increasingly erratic as she pushes herself closer to the edge, her skin covered in a fine sheen of sweat.

"Come for me, gorgeous girl. I want to feel you squeeze my cock." Her moans increase in volume as she pushes herself closer to the edge, riding my cock and pressing into my fingers.

"Duke...Duke..." My name falls repeatedly from her lips as she sets a furious pace, pushing us both closer to the edge. The heavy wood of the bed frame hits the wall and Caroline's eyes widen slightly, causing me to chuckle.

"I'm going to come with you, okay baby? Come on my cock. Fuck, fuck." I feel tingles creeping up my spine as I'm pulled closer to the edge with her, as we both sit balanced on the edge. Grabbing her hips, I pull her tight to my pelvis, and as her moans and gasps reach a fever-pitch, I feel her pussy clamp tight on my cock.

Pulling her mouth to mine as she cries out through her orgasm, I piston my cock inside her, pouring myself into her. I hold her close as we both breathe through the aftershocks of our joint ecstasy. My heart feels like it might burst out of my chest, and I gasp to catch my breath. I want to marry this woman and spend the rest of my life with her wrapped around me, just like this.

Feeling her extricate herself from my now heavy limbs, I watch her climb from the bed and close the bathroom door behind herself. I'm asleep before she returns.

My eyes pop open as I hear the door crack and I take in the sun-filled room, realizing I slept here and it's morning. And Cash is standing in Caroline's doorway, a shit-eating grin on his face, where he leans heavily on the door frame, a crutch under his arm. I narrow my eyes at him, tilting my head in question.

He jerks his head back, beckoning me, before pulling the door quietly closed. Looking down, I see the ray of sunshine spread across my chest, a cute little snore escaping her every once in a while. I smile at her peaceful face before pressing a gentle kiss to her forehead and begin trying to free myself without waking her. Sliding out of bed, I grab my stuff and head into her bathroom, then slip out of her room, closing the door softly behind me.

"And how was your night?" Cash says with a knowing smile as I walk into the kitchen.

Giving him a narrowed glance, I walk to the coffee machine which now exclusively brews the coffee Lizzie has at the inn. "'Twas fine."

"She's pretty amazing, isn't she?"

"Cash, I'm not talking about this. Not now, not ever." I take a huge gulp of hot coffee, scalding my mouth.

"Okay, okay. But hear me out..."

Chapter 43
Sweet Caroline

Callie

A Monday morning a few weeks later dawns cool as the weather starts transitioning to winter. My first Montana winter and I'm looking forward to being trapped here with my men. I hear music start to play from downstairs, *Sweet Caroline* filling the whole house. I smile as I dig myself out from the pile of blankets and pillows.

Skipping down the stairs, I find Cash and Duke sitting on opposite ends of the couch, the music filling the space. Cash has finally gotten all his plaster casts off and is almost back to normal, except he isn't cleared for riding horses yet, and I think he's going a little stir crazy.

"What's up? You summoned?" I ask them.

"Come sit, Hurricane." Cash pats the couch next to him, between them.

Wandering over hesitantly, I watch them, trying to figure out what's going on. Sitting, I place my hands on my knees and wait. I'm not sure what's happening but I don't want to do anything weird. The music continues to play in the background.

"Hey, Sunshine. We were thinking maybe you would like to hang out with us, with both of us." I hear some extra meaning in Duke's words, but I can't figure it out. I look at him, studying his face and find him looking serene and satisfied. Swiveling my head, I see Cash wearing a look of anticipation.

"Wha—" I start before Cash grabs my face, sealing his mouth to mine before sliding his tongue between my lips. I lose all thought as I become absorbed in his kiss. I twist my body until I'm more facing his direction as he twines his fingers into the hair at my nape, tugging against the strands. I moan huskily into his mouth.

I feel Duke move behind me until his chest is touching my back before he starts laying wet kisses against my neck. I startle at this, unsure what's happening but far from complaining.

"Just relax, sweetheart. You look so fucking good with Cash's mouth on yours."

Wetness pools in my panties, and I pant at his words while Cash continues to kiss me. Reaching down, Duke grabs the hem of my t-shirt pulling it over my head, forcing me to break my kiss with Cash. Turning my head, I capture Duke's mouth, kissing him, tasting him.

Cash removes his shirt, only wearing a pair of lounge pants, his hard dick on display through the thin material. He reaches for me, tweaking my nipples before grabbing a handful of my hair and pulling my head back. Both men latch onto my neck, sucking roughly at my pulse points as Duke begins removing his clothes. First, he unbuttons his flannel, and I'm enchanted by the slow reveal of his skin. Then his belt buckle comes loose and he pulls the belt though the loops. There's something so hot about it, I pant and moan just watching him. Peeling his jeans down his legs, he stands before me in just his boxer briefs, the outline of his thick cock visible and my mouth waters in anticipation.

Sitting back in his spot on the couch, he grabs me, lying me back against Cash and pulling my leggings down my legs and off, leaving me in just a pair of lacy black panties. Reaching out, he presses through the fabric, onto my clit.

"So wet, so warm," he mutters, as Cash wraps his arms around me, rubbing and pinching my nipples, his erection digging into my back. My wet panties quickly follow my leggings until I'm completely naked and exposed, lying against Cash while Duke kneels between my knees.

"What do you think? You up for it?" Cash whispers in my ear.

Nodding my head, I lean heavier against him.

"Say it baby, say you want us both," Duke commands.

"Yes. Yes, I want you."

"Good girl," Cash breathes against my neck.

I watch as Duke adjusts himself, sliding down until his face is right in front of my pussy. He blows on my overheated skin, and I writhe against Cash as Duke swipes his tongue through me. Turning my head so he can press his lips to mine, Cash moves his tongue against mine, into my mouth, mimicking the motion going on between my thighs as I shake between them. Cash continues to tease my hard nipples as Duke slides two fingers into my dripping pussy, licking and sucking on my flesh, pushing me closer and closer to the edge.

"You going to come for us, Hurricane? Show us. Come all over him; I can't wait to see it." Cash's words turn me to liquid as my skin lights on fire against the expert tongue of Duke.

My walls start to quiver as he strokes harder inside me. I shake, my skin covered in goosebumps, Cash's mouth latched to my throat, nibbling and biting, while his hands rub every inch of skin he can touch. As I begin to tumble over the edge that they've been pushing me toward, Cash's hand wraps around my throat, squeezing my pulse point until I'm gasping and coming all over Duke's face.

I scream through my orgasm as my men rub and touch and kiss me everywhere. Pulling me up, Cash adjusts himself until he's sitting up and pulls his lounge pants down his legs, his thick cock standing straight up against his stomach.

"Come here, baby." He pulls me to him and deposits me on his lap, facing away from him, until his cock is nestled against my wet, sensitive skin. The movement makes me gasp. "I'm going to fuck you now, okay?"

"Yes, please Cash," I beg.

I can hear the satisfaction in his voice. "Good girl. That's my girl. So needy," he tells me as he lifts my hips and slides me down onto his cock, stretching me so perfectly until I'm completely full of him.

Reaching over, I drag Duke to me, kissing him and tasting myself on his lips. Grabbing his dick where it strains against his boxers, I try to free it. He chuckles at my efforts before pulling them off and giving me the access I want. His cock is long and thick and leaking at the tip, the shiny bead of pre-cum making me lick my lips.

"Do you want Duke to feed you, baby?" Cash asks me as he pushes his cock inside me, hard and fast. Leaning back so I can see him sliding into me, my back against his chest, I put my hands on his forearms and let him guide my hips. My skin is red and flushed.

"Yes, Duke, yes."

"You heard her, Duke. Give her your cock, she looks so hungry for it." Cash's filthy words cause me to flush harder, my pussy pulsating with need. "Oh, you liked that, my dirty girl. You like when I talk like that? I love seeing my cock sliding into your greedy cunt. Yes baby, take it all. Slide Duke's cock between your lips, Hurricane, let me see you swallow him while I fuck this wet pussy."

I almost come from his words alone as Duke stands up between our knees, so his dick is level with my face. Grabbing my chin, he opens my mouth and slides his thumb inside, rubbing my tongue before bringing the head of his cock to my lips. As he shoves it down my throat cutting off my air momentarily, I can feel Cash's piercing rubbing inside me, causing delicious friction that pushes me closer to the edge. I pant around Duke as he fills my whole mouth and throat.

With both men thrusting into me, I'm on the edge again, Cash rubbing hard circles against my clit while he fills me. Duke's head is thrown back as he pants through gritted teeth.

"Fuck, baby. You're fucking perfect," Duke tells me as he grips my chin, watching me struggle to breathe around him, tears running down my cheeks and spit running off my chin, while I bounce up and down on Cash's cock.

Cash pants as he lifts his hips to meet me thrust for thrust as he chants curse words and 'Callie' over and over, his movements more erratic by the second. Duke's thrusting into my mouth gets deeper until I choke, sucking hard as he withdrawals his head then pushes it all the way back in. We are all hurtling toward our orgasms and at this rate, we are all going to come together.

"Yes baby, almost there. You going to come for me?" Cash whispers as his hips slam into me.

"Fuck, sweetheart, yes, suck my cock, so good, so perfect," Duke puffs out through gritted teeth.

Grabbing Duke's cock and twisting my hand while I hollow my cheeks, I feel him start to swell in my mouth, simultaneously, Cash starts pounding harder, grunting as he fucks me harder and harder, rubbing my clit and pushing me closer and closer.

Duke utters, "Caroline," as he hisses out a breath, grabbing my head and shoving so far down my throat I can't breathe as he comes. His orgasm shatters me, and I pulse around Cash moving inside me as I scream out in pleasure, both Cash' and Duke's names on my lips before Cash follows behind us seconds later, filling me.

I collapse against Cash as he wraps his quivering arms around me, his chest heaving, his heart beating a rapid rhythm, thumping against me. Duke flops down next to me and peppers my shoulder and back with wet kisses. The three of us, entwined, feels like home. Perfect. I don't stop to consider what this means.

"I love you, Hurricane," Cash speaks into my hair.

"I love you, Cowboy," I reply, pulling his arms around my abdomen, feeling his heart thump against my back.

"I love you, Sunshine," Duke says with a kiss against the side of my breast.

"I love you, Grumpy," I say, grabbing his hand and lacing our fingers.

I'm finally home.

I Cross My Heart

Epilogue

Callie

Picking up my champagne flute, I take a gulp before placing it back on the makeup table.

"What do you think, Caroline?" the makeup artist asks me as she reveals the makeup look that perfectly captures everything I want to convey. My cheeks are flushed pink, and my lids are lightly dusted with shimmering gold. My lips are a dusty rose, and my dark lashes make my eyes look huge. The tan I sport from spending my afternoons riding my black mare, Tulip, around the ranch perfectly accentuates the colors she has applied to my face.

"It's perfect," I breathe.

Sadie kneels in front of me, holding out a boot and I push my foot in, grabbing the boot strap to pull them into place.

"I can't believe it's finally time," she says, looking up at me.

"I know. I never thought we would get here." Standing, I affix my stark white cowboy hat to my head, its long ribbon trailing down my back. Gazing in the mirror, I smooth the floor length white gown over my hips before fixing the little gold chain with the cowboy hat hanging between my breasts.

I take a deep breath. "Okay, let's do it," I say as I exit the room, my dress trailing behind me.

Walking down the long aisle as *I Cross My Heart* plays quietly, I look at the smiling faces of Duke and Cash waiting for me, one on either side. Sleepy stands as officiant to our unorthodox wedding, where the three of us will pledge ourselves to each other. Who I am legally married to doesn't matter. Being here on our ranch, surrounded by the people who know and love us, is indescribable.

The last two years with these men by my side have been the greatest days and weeks and months of my life.

"I, Duke Williams, take Caroline Pearce, to be my wedded wife. The time we have spent together has cultivated a love that is deep and abiding. I never could have imagined standing here, with my best friend, marrying the love of our lives, but I have learned that love can only multiply if it is fed and nurtured. I intend to love you wholly and completely for the rest of my life, nurturing your heart, and allowing your love to encompass both of us, as long as we live. You are my present and my future, and I pledge myself to you today. I love you."

Tears roll down my cheeks and drip from my lips.

"I, Caroline Pearce, take you, Duke Williams, as my wedded husband. My love for you grows daily like a carefully loved flower, growing larger and stronger every day into the most beautiful thing I have ever seen. We have been through so much together, the three of us, and you have stood by our sides when we were all afraid of losing everything. You are my choice every day and my heart has never been divided; it grew twice as large to love you."

I turn to face Cash.

"I, Ashley Colter, take you, Caroline Pearce, as my wedded wife. Hurricane, you blew into town when I was lost. I was drifting through a sea of confusion with no plan or consideration for the future. You lit up the world and made me want to change, want to be a better man, and earn you every day. I will be worthy of you now and for the rest of our lives. I look at the life we are creating, all of us together, and ask myself how I got so lucky to have everything I would have ever asked for, if I considered myself capable of asking. You are a tempest in my world, and I am so grateful you changed everything. I love you more every day and I will continue to love you until my heart can't anymore."

I'm damn near sobbing now as I hold both their hands, my own trembling.

"I, Caroline Pearce, take you, Ashley Colter, to be my wedded husband." My voice cracks as I'm overcome with the gravity of today. "You bring light and levity to my life in a way I never knew possible. The love you flood me with every time I look at you makes me believe in fate. It was fate that brought me here, to you, both of you, and I intend to prove it was the right choice because you are my choice every day and I am thankful for you."

Sleepy recites the rest of our ceremony before telling my men they may kiss their bride. Duke captures my mouth first in a searing but slow, deep kiss. Cash follows with a sweet kiss and a backward dip. The two displays are exactly what I would expect from the two men who devote themselves to me every day.

Turn the page to see our feature in the special edition issue of Bull-Riders Weekly.

. . .

SPECIAL EDITION

Sunday
June 6th

Bull-Riders Weekly

Sunday,
June 6th

Retired Former World Champion Bull Rider and Montana rancher Ashley Colter marries long-time girlfriend Caroline Williams in an intimate ceremony on his ranch.

On June 5th, Ashley Colter married girlfriend Caroline Williams in a small ceremony held at their Montana ranch, just outside Inspiration, Montana. Ashley struck a handsome figure in a cowboy tux, donning his signature black Stetson and a shiny new pair of black Lucchese's. His blushing bride wore a floor length white sheath-style silk wedding dress with an opening all the way down her back and a long train decorated with embroidered tulips, daisies, violets, dragonflies, and, an unconventional choice, the occasional rain cloud. She opted for a white western hat with a large trailing ribbon in lieu of a standard veil and wore custom white Tecovas on her feet.

Ms. Williams was unescorted down the aisle and neither bride nor groom had a wedding party except for Colter's childhood best friend, Duke, standing in as best man for both sides. The trio are often seen out and about and it seems they are quite close. The marriage was officiated by Colter's long-time trainer, Thomas "Sleepy" Jenkins.

Ashley Colter retired from the professional bull-riding circuit two years ago following a devastating fall which almost cost him his life. He has devoted his life since then to growing his ranching operation, expanding to an additional ten thousand acres and thousands more cattle.

The family includes dogs Snapper and Tank, Daisy, Colter's dun mare, and Tulip, Caroline's black mare.

We are told the former Ms. Williams intends to hyphenate her name and adopt the moniker 'Caroline Williams-Colter.' We wish the happy couple nothing but peace in their future together.

Acknowledgments

To all the people who helped make this happen, thank you. It's been so fun.

A certain rodeo association- Thank you for the thirst traps that got us to this book even if you said I can't use your brand name in the book.

Walton's Whiskey- Thank you for letting me use your brand in my book.

Amber- Thanks for listening, I love you so big.

Mr. Fox Kelly– I heard that you're going to read this since vampires aren't your thing but cowboys might be? Buckle in, it's a wild ride.

Son– Without you, how would I know what size weapon I needed?

Editor– Thank you Mallory, I just have a feeling that you got tired of correcting ok to okay. Also, I like grey better than gray.

My alpha readers– I appreciate you taking the time to read the rough (and I do mean ROUGH) version of this book. I hope you're proud of where we ended up.

Besties in the group chat- Thank you for being the sounding board for me. If there is one thing about me- if I shenan, I will shenanigan.

Special Thanks

Thank you Walton's Distillery for allowing me the use of your brand for Caroline's signature Walton's and ginger ale.

Because we all love a woman who drinks whiskey.

Find Walton's Here

www.Waltonsdistillery.com

About the Author

Fox Kelly is an emerging author of romance, paranormal and contemporary books.

Fox Kelly is a writer/mom/project manager/kid taxi driver from Ohio. Fox has been reading since childhood, and dreaming big dreams even longer. In her spare time (away from my grown-up job), Fox writes. And reads. And writes some more. And sometimes watches vampire television.

Fox's upcoming projects include a dark romance set in North Carolina and maybe a few motorcycle club books too, book 2 in the City of Blood duology, and a romantic suspense trilogy. Fox writes what comes into her brain so you get what you get.

Stay in touch with Fox Kelly by visiting foxkelly.com, subscribing to my newsletter, and following me on socials.

Also by Fox Kelly

City of Blood Duology

Blood Ties

Book 2 Coming August 2026

Unexpected Weather

www.ingramcontent.com/pod-product-compliance
Lightning Source LLC
Chambersburg PA
CBHW060519160726
47991CB00001B/96